When the Evil Waits

M J Lee has worked as a university researcher in history, a social worker with Vietnamese refugees, and as the creative director of an advertising agency. He has spent 25 years of his life working outside the north of England, in London, Hong Kong, Taipei, Singapore, Bangkok and Shanghai.

Also by M J Lee

DI Ridpath Crime Thriller

Where the Truth Lies
Where the Dead Fall
Where the Silence Calls
Where the Innocent Die
When the Past Kills
When the Evil Waits
When the Guilty Cry
When the Night Ends

MJ LEE

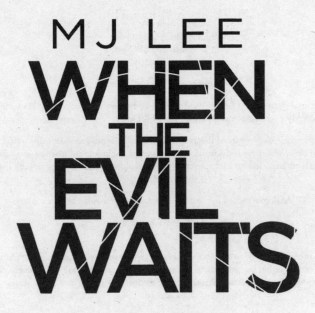

WHEN THE EVIL WAITS

CANELO CRIME

First published in the United Kingdom in 2021 by Canelo

This edition published in the United Kingdom in 2022 by

Canelo
Unit 9, 5th Floor
Cargo Works, 1–2 Hatfields
London, SE1 9PG
United Kingdom

Print ISBN 978 1 80032 256 1
Ebook ISBN 978 1 78863 746 6

Look for more great books at www.canelo.co

Printed and bound in Great Britain by Clays Ltd, Elcograf S.p.A.

2

Thursday, July 23

Chapter 1

They had first met in the early days of lockdown.

Walking their dogs in Chorlton Ees to get out of the stifling atmosphere in their homes, finding a few moments' rest in the peace and quiet of the trees and meadows bordering the Mersey.

It was their dogs who encountered each other first, with her male Jack Russell being more than a match for his rather docile Labrador.

She had apologised profusely in a very English way for the behaviour of her dog and he had accepted in an equally English manner; all diffidence and explaining it was actually his dog's fault.

It wasn't long before they were timing their visits to meet each other and chat each morning, without their respective spouses' knowledge, of course. And not long after that, they were discovering the quiet pathways of the Ees, holding hands like a couple, while their dogs explored the surrounding forest.

It was on one of these walks that they found the body of a child.

Or rather, the Labrador discovered it, followed by the Jack Russell; the frenzied barking of the latter forcing the couple to leave the comfort of each other's arms and discover why their dogs were so excited.

The woman, Shirley Burgess, led the way. 'What's the matter? Why such a racket?' she shouted as she brushed aside a branch blocking her way.

'Oh my God.' Her hand went to her mouth and she stood there, transfixed.

The naked boy – he wasn't more than seven years old – was lying on the ground with his arms stretched out at either side, his sightless eyes open and staring up at the sky, a kiss-curl of blond hair like a comma across his forehead. Around his neck, a snake of rope dug deep into the skin. By his side, his clothes were folded neatly as if coming straight from a laundry, the bright red of a United shirt lying on top.

'Where are you, Shirl?'

Her lockdown lover, Jon Morgan, was pushing aside the same branch. 'Jesus Christ.'

'Is it alive?' she asked, still not moving.

He took two steps and then leant forward, peering down. 'I think he's dead.'

The Labrador was wagging his tail and sniffing the lifeless head. 'Come away, Major.'

The dog obeyed, returning to his master to be put back on the lead.

The woman called her dog too and, for once, he responded. 'What are we going to do?'

The man checked over his shoulder. 'I think I should call the police.'

'I can't be found here with you. My husband, he…'

'Of course, you take your dog back and I'll ring them. We can't leave him lying here.' He stared down at the boy.

'You sure?' she asked.

He nodded his head. 'You go home. I'll wait here for the police.'

She turned and pushed her way through the undergrowth, dragging the reluctant dog behind her, moving as fast as she could to escape.

She didn't look back.

Jon Morgan waited until he could no longer hear her before he took out his mobile and rang 999.

'Emergency Services. How can I help you?'

'I think… I think I've found a dead body. It's a young boy and he's naked. You have to get here quickly.'

'Where are you, sir?'

'Chorlton Ees, not far from the school.'

'And are you alone?'

The man looked over his shoulder. 'Yes.'

'The police are on their way. Their ETA is seven minutes.'

'Should I go back to the main road?'

'Are you sure the boy is dead?'

Jon Morgan looked down at the pale, almost white skin. There was something missing from it. That spark of life, that animation that everybody had. This boy looked more like a mannequin in a store than a human being.

'He's dead,' he finally answered.

'Please don't touch anything, sir.'

'I won't.'

In the distance, he could hear the faint whine of a police siren.

Closer at hand, there was the screech of a hawk or an owl hunting for prey in the forest. Beside him, Major was gnawing at one of the Jack Russell's toys, trying to get at the bell inside.

There was no sound from the boy.

Chapter 2

Detective Chief Inspector Paul Turnbull arrived at the scene of the crime less than thirty minutes after the first call had been made by Jon Morgan.

The local coppers had done a good job; the first tapes were already going up and two plods had been posted on the lane leading to Chorlton Ees.

He quickly found the sergeant in charge, showing him his warrant card. 'Right, I'm taking charge. Has the medical examiner been called?'

'He's on his way, sir.'

'Who is it?'

'A Dr Schofield, sir.'

'Squeaky voice? Couldn't we get someone else?'

They were both walking down the lane to the Ees, DI Harry Makepeace, DS Emily Parkinson and one of his new hires, DC Sam Arkwright, trailing in their wake.

'He was the one on duty, sir,' the sergeant answered.

'Right, where's the body?'

The sergeant pointed off to the left, towards a clump of trees. 'Over there.'

'Nobody's touched it?'

'No, sir.'

Turnbull did a 360-degree turn, taking in the surroundings. 'Weird, you could almost be out in the country rather than the middle of Manchester. Who discovered the body?'

The sergeant checked his notes. 'A dog, sir, Major by name.'

'I'm not going to get much by interviewing a dog, am I, Sergeant?' said Turnbull with heavy sarcasm and a roll of the eyes. 'What's the name of his owner?'

The sergeant checked his notes again. 'It's a Mr Morgan, he's standing over there.' He pointed off to the right towards a middle-aged man on his own, a docile Labrador on a lead chewing a toy at his feet.

Turnbull grunted once. 'Sam, get on to the doctor and the CSI team, find out when they will arrive. Sergeant—?'

'It's Morrison, Sergeant Bob Morrison.'

'Sergeant, extend the perimeter out to the top of the lane and start signing new arrivals in. This is a crime scene and you need to implement all the usual protocols.'

'Yes, sir.'

'Harry, you're with me.' He strode off towards the body.

'What do you want me to do?'

Turnbull turned back as if noticing Emily Parkinson for the first time. 'Check out what's down there.' He pointed airily down a path leading through the Ees to the river.

Turnbull ploughed through, pushing aside the branches of the trees in his way, letting them fall back against Harry Makepeace. Within six yards, they could see the outline of a body, lying in a small glade behind the trees.

They forced aside the last few branches and stepped into the edge of the glade.

They could see the body more clearly now. It was naked with two arms stretched out at either side like Jesus on the cross. The eyes were open, staring sightlessly up to the sky, and a rope was still wound around the small boy's thin neck like a hemp collar.

Walking closer, they saw a neatly folded pile of clothes, the bright red of a United shirt lying on top with its red devil badge standing out clearly.

A horsefly landed on the white stomach for a moment, scratched its feelers and took two steps forward. Turnbull leant closer to the body and the fly took off, buzzing around heavily before being joined by another, both attracted to the dead body by the prospect of a possible feast.

'How long do you think he's been dead?' asked Harry Makepeace.

Turnbull was now standing over the body, staring down at its face with the carefully combed hair draped across the forehead.

Before he could answer, a high-pitched voice shouted, 'I'll thank you to move away.'

Chapter 3

A man dressed in a white Tyvek suit with green edging stepped into the glade followed by another person.

'Please move away, you are contaminating the crime scene.'

Turnbull reached for his warrant card. 'I am Detective Chief Inspector—'

'I don't care if you are Little Lord Fauntleroy, this is my crime scene until I have certified the victim is dead and the crime scene manager, Audrey,' the woman in the white suit raised her hand, 'has cleared it. You are improperly dressed and should know better.'

'I… I…'

Dr Schofield moved out of the way to let the detectives leave using the path they had created through the trees.

'Come on, Harry, we'll have a chat with the witness.'

'You can make yourself useful by making sure there is an inner cordon at least fifty yards away from here. I want to make sure we have no more contamination.'

Turnbull grunted and pushed his way back through the trees, finding the sergeant and ordering him to set up an inner cordon.

The discoverer of the body, Jon Morgan, had moved and was now standing back on the path with his dog. He was frantically smoking, his eyes flickering left and right.

'Mr Morgan?'

The man looked up.

'I'm DCI Turnbull, I believe you discovered the body?'

The man nodded once before saying, 'Actually, the dog discovered it. I heard him scrambling through the trees and making a whining sound. He doesn't normally do that so I left the path and saw the body lying there. At first, I thought he was asleep so I went to wake him but then I saw the rope around his neck...' He stopped talking and took a rapid tug at his cigarette.

'Let's just step back a moment, please, Mr Morgan. What time did you arrive here?'

'About 8.15. I always walk the dog at this time. Just a habit we've started since lockdown. Means we both get some exercise at the start of the day. Keeps me sane.' He glanced in the direction of the clump of trees. 'Or at least it did until today.'

'You came alone?'

A slight hesitation. 'Yes, I drove here alone. My wife prefers to sleep in, as do my kids. I take the same route every day, parking on the main road, walking down the lane and onto the path to the river.'

'And you discovered the body immediately?'

'Not immediately, I started walking about eight thirty.'

'Why did it take so long?' asked Harry Makepeace.

'Take so long?'

'Before you started walking. Usually my dog is so excited when he's in the back of the car and we get to the beginning of our walk.'

Jon Morgan's eyes darted left and right, before he finally held up his hand with the cigarettes clamped between the index and middle fingers. 'I had one of these. My wife hates me smoking in the house so I have to do it outside.'

'I know how you feel,' sighed Turnbull. 'So you started walking at about eight thirty and ten minutes later Major started snuffling and whining in the undergrowth over there. You couldn't see the body?'

'Not from here. But I wondered why he was making so much noise, it's not like him. So I went through the trees and saw it lying there.' Another frantic tug at the end of his cigarette, expelling the smoke almost immediately into the warm air.

'Did you see anybody else?'

Jon Morgan looked at him quizzically.

'When you were walking. Did you see any other people?'

The man shook his head.

'So there were no other dog walkers this morning?' asked Harry Makepeace.

'I don't remember any. Why? Is it important?'

'It's just to see if there were any other witnesses, Mr Morgan,' added Turnbull.

'I don't remember seeing anybody else.'

Emily Parkinson arrived back and hovered five yards away.

'Right, Mr Morgan, if you would go with DI Makepeace, we need to take a statement from you.'

'Is that necessary? My wife will be getting worried.'

'I'm afraid it is, Mr Morgan. Perhaps you could call your wife and let her know you'll be back late.'

'Come this way, Mr Morgan, we'll drive you to the station.' Harry Makepeace ushered him towards the lane.

'What about my car and the dog?'

'If you give me the keys, one of our constables will drive it back for you. As for the dog, bring him with you. We like Labradors at the station.'

Their voices trailed off as they walked away.

'Where does the path lead, Parkinson?'

'Down to the River Mersey, sir. It's a T-junction with another path along the river.'

'Right, the river will form the edge of our cordon. Can you get the sergeant to put one of his officers there to stop anybody coming from that direction?'

'Yes, sir. There's a bridge further along the river upstream.'

'There usually is.'

Emily Parkinson raised her eyebrows. 'Sorry, sir?'

'A bridge. There usually are bridges across rivers. But just block the path. There's no other way to get to our crime scene other than this path?'

'I don't think so, sir.'

'You don't think so or you know so?'

Emily Parkinson stayed silent.

'Check it out. I want to be sure this is the only way to get to our crime scene.'

'Yes, boss.'

As Emily walked away, Sam Arkwright came running up.

'What is it?' snarled Turnbull.

'A boy was reported missing on Tuesday, boss.'

'What's the description?'

Arkwright checked his notebook. 'David Carsley, aged seven, from Wythenshawe – last seen two days ago, on 21 July. Blond hair, tall for his age, thin build, wearing a United shirt and dark shorts.'

Turnbull glanced back towards the trees. 'I think we've found him.'

Two Weeks Later

On the First Day

Tuesday, August 4

Chapter 4

Ridpath stared in the mirror, noticed a large lump of shaving cream dangling off his earlobe, and wiped it away with a towel.

He splashed on some Bulgari aftershave, the one Polly had given him last Christmas, and walked back to the bedroom.

The suit was hanging behind the door where he had put it last night, freshly dry-cleaned and pressed. It looked strange hanging there, an empty suit.

Isn't that what they called business executives who were useless at their jobs? Empty suits. He wondered fleetingly if he had become one of those in the last six months.

He took a white shirt from the wardrobe, seeing Polly's work clothes hanging next to it. Her special clothes, the ones she saved for interviews or for when the Ofsted inspectors visited her school.

He pulled on the suit pants, adjusting the notch on his belt and tucking the extra-long strap into the trouser loop. He had lost weight recently, his features even more gaunt than usual.

Grabbing the jacket, he took one last look in the mirror and hurried into the living room of the service apartment. She was waiting for him in the kitchen, next to the coffee machine.

'All ready and set, Ridpath?'

He didn't answer her, instead pouring himself half a cup of coffee.

'Have a good day.'

He knew he shouldn't answer but he did. 'First day back, I don't know what's going to happen.'

'You'll be fine. You'll always be fine.'

He missed the little morning rituals they used to have. Brewing Polly's coffee. Shouting up to Eve to get dressed and go to school. Making his daughter breakfast and forcing her to eat, whether she wanted to or not. The chaos and anarchy around him as both of them prepared to go to school while he was as organised as ever.

He missed all that.

Eve was with her grandparents. It seemed like the right decision given the circumstances. She had moved in with them when he had moved out to the service apartment. At least, her grandparents could look after Eve, giving him time to look after himself.

'Don't forget your notebook.' Polly pointed to the kitchen table.

'I won't,' he answered, picking it up, 'you know me, I never do.'

He finished the coffee, took his keys from the hook, and picked up a fresh mask from the pile he kept on the table by the door.

'Have a good day,' she repeated.

'It's good to be going back to work, Poll.'

'I know.'

He turned back to look at her, sitting at the kitchen table, as fresh and young as the day he had met her all those years ago. 'You made me a better person.'

'I know that too. Women are constantly bringing men up to their standard. It's our job.'

He smiled. She hadn't changed, even in death.

He knew she wasn't real, wasn't really there. But he kept seeing her, and worse, hearing her voice.

Polly was dead.

There. He had admitted it.

She died from a massive internal haemorrhage on a trolley in A & E with doctors desperately trying to save her life.

He couldn't live at home any more, it was a crime scene, with hot and cold running CSIs all over the place, one murder and one suicide to investigate.

Two bodies. One of which was the woman he had loved and lived with for the last fourteen years.

Wasn't admitting your partner was gone and never coming back one of the final steps in the stages of grief? One of the many things he had learnt in the last six months since her death.

The problem was, he still saw her, still talked with her.

Every day.

It was something he kept hidden from the psychiatrist appointed by Greater Manchester Police to help him with his PTSD. Sometimes secrets had to be kept. He couldn't let just anybody wander inside his head.

He took one last look at her and said, 'See you later,' closing the door on the apartment, leaving her there all alone.

After six months off, it was time to go back to work.

Finally.

Chapter 5

'Ah, Ridpath, good to have you back.'

Mrs Challinor was seated at the head of the table, with everybody else arranged around the room, ensuring they were socially distant and wearing the inevitable masks. The weekly work-in-progress meeting had been put back a day due to the bank holiday.

Sophia was there, as was Jenny Oldfield, the office manager. David Smail, the part-time coroner from Derbyshire, was seated on Mrs Challinor's right, and a new woman he didn't know was on her left.

'Have you met Helen Moore? She's recently been appointed, her first day too. Carol has gone to the warmer climes of Weston-super-Mare to be the coroner for Somerset and Helen is her replacement.'

They both nodded to each other, avoiding the formal act of shaking hands.

Mrs Challinor continued speaking. 'Ridpath is our coroner's officer. He's been on sick leave for six months.' The rest of the sentence was left unspoken. Mrs Challinor didn't feel the need to say any more.

'Ridpath? That's a strange first name.'

'My Christian name is Thomas, but everybody calls me Ridpath.' He found his voice cracking, and had to adjust the pitch. It was so long since he'd been part of these meetings, so long since he'd interacted with other human beings – other than the police psychiatrist, of course, and many of those meetings had been on Zoom.

'Let's get started, shall we? We have a lot to get through. I'll go first.' Mrs Challinor held up an official-looking piece of paper. 'As you know, Greater Manchester was placed in another lockdown on 31 July.'

'What a shambles,' grumbled David Smail, 'announcing it on Twitter two hours before it was introduced, without telling the mayor or the people.'

'Nonetheless, we will need to be extra vigilant in applying the new measures.'

'What are they? There was no detail. Another cock-up.'

Margaret Challinor raised her hand slightly. David Smail took the hint and stopped speaking. 'The guidance seems unnecessarily complicated. Essentially, there should be no mixing of households...'

David Smail was about to speak again but she stopped him once more.

'...but I will seek to get clearer rules. The instructions from the chief coroner's advice given on 26 March remain in force; Medical Certificates of Cause of Death can still be signed by any doctor and we need to issue Form 100A, Sophia, for every death.'

'Of course, Coroner.'

'However, the chief coroner has made it clear that the coronial service in England and Wales should now routinely conduct hearings again. The coroner must be present in court, otherwise it is not a legally constituted tribunal, and the proceedings must be open to the public. We can still use remote video and audio for evidence but it is illegal to live-stream court proceedings.'

David Smail frowned. 'So we can take evidence, but we can't show the court in action? Even Parliament is live-streamed these days.'

'According to the 1925 Act, it is still illegal to film the proceedings of a court. One day the criminal justice system will be dragged kicking and screaming into the twenty-first century, David, but that day is still to arrive.'

'What about jury trials?' asked Helen Moore.

'The chief coroner would like jury inquests to recommence but suggests using smaller juries of eight or nine.'

'How do they socially distance in our jury room? It's impossible.'

'We'll have to work something out, Jenny. The chief coroner has left it to our discretion.'

'What about the Coroners' Court Support Service?' asked Sophia. 'Is it still suspended?'

It was Sophia Rahman, Ridpath's assistant, who asked the question. To Ridpath's eyes, she seemed to have matured immensely in the last six months. Gone was the callow girl, fresh from university, and instead a confident, able woman had taken her place. Even her clothes had changed. The casual but comfortable shirts and dresses replaced by a more formal black suit, echoing that of Mrs Challinor.

'The CCSS helpline is operative but I'll talk to the local resilience forum to find out when the full service will be up and running again. The chief coroner has insisted we catch up with any backlog of cases that may have built up. I am in discussions with our local authority regarding resources to enable us to do that. As ever, money is tight...'

'Is there no extra funding from the government?' asked Helen.

'Coroners' Courts still come under the local authority so the answer is negative, Helen. The chief coroner warns that we must not exhaust our staff or put them under undue pressure. He is wary of a second wave of Covid-19 occurring. Training, even residential training, remains compulsory. Now Ridpath has returned we will arrange for you to attend more courses, Sophia, particularly in coronial law.'

'Thank you, Mrs Challinor, I'm looking forward to them.'

'Any more questions?'

Everybody, including Ridpath, shook their heads.

'Right. I will continue to work with our local resilience forum to let you know if there are any more changes. As of now, the ruling applies as it did from the beginning of the pandemic.' She picked up the chief coroner's guidance and read it out loud. 'A death is typically considered to be unnatural if it has not resulted entirely from a naturally occurring disease running its natural course, where nothing else is implicated. Covid-19 is an acceptable natural cause of death and is still a notifiable disease under the Health Protection Regulations 2010.'

'Are there any occasions when a Covid-19 death is considered unnatural?' asked Helen Moore.

'As ever, the chief coroner has left it up to each individual coroner to decide. For example, it may be considered unnatural if the virus was contracted in the workplace setting by frontline NHS staff, public transport employees, care home workers, or emergency service personnel...'

'Including police officers?'

'Yes, Ridpath, including the police. However, the investigation should focus on the circumstances of the particular death. It should not, the chief coroner emphasises, be a forum for addressing concerns about high-level government policy. I will be seeking further guidance on this.'

'And what about meetings with a family?'

'My own thoughts are we should carry on, keeping social distance and wearing masks, of course. I would dread to think we would break the details of a loved one's death over Zoom.'

The coroner ran her fingers through her tight grey curls. Ridpath thought she looked tired, extremely tired.

'Try to do what you can remotely, but we must always remember our duty to those who have died and the bereaved. Some things have to be done in person. What do you think, Ridpath?'

Mrs Challinor was deliberately trying to involve him.

'I agree, Coroner. It's difficult enough losing a loved one...' The rest of his sentence trailed away to be followed by silence.

'Good, let's go through the work in progress, shall we? Jenny, can you start?'

Jenny Oldfield hadn't changed in Ridpath's absence. She was wearing a bright orange bubble skirt with matching make-up. 'Coroner, you have an inquest on the Sullivan case on Thursday.'

'The man who fell from the factory roof?'

'Yes, Coroner. I've reconfigured the courtroom so everyone keeps socially distant, there will be hand sanitiser available, we'll check temperatures on entry to the court, plus people will be asked to wear masks when they are not speaking.'

'Is that all necessary?' It was the new coroner, Helen Moore.

'Yes, is the short answer.'

Ridpath recognised the steel in Mrs Challinor's voice. She was making it absolutely clear who was in charge. He had missed her.

'If that's clear, we'll move on. Jenny?'

'Last week, we had 127 reported deaths in Manchester, only two of which were classified as Covid-related. That brings the total number of deaths from the virus in Greater Manchester to 2140 by the end of July. But cases are rising again, leading to the new rules.'

The stark numbers quietened everybody.

'I have put the reports on your desk, Mrs Challinor. There is one case I should highlight. The murder of David Carsley.'

'The boy found near the Mersey? The one in all the newspapers?' asked Helen.

'The family have been asking if the police will release the body for burial.'

'Can you follow up, Sophia?' asked Mrs Challinor. 'Check if the post-mortem has been completed.'

'I'd like to take that case.' Ridpath found himself speaking.

'Are you sure? We agreed you would only work in the office on your first two weeks back. This case will involve liaising with a family who have lost a child in frightening circumstances.' Mrs Challinor was looking at him over the top of her glasses, waiting for his answer.

'I'd still like to do it, Coroner.'

'Let's talk about it separately.' She looked at the other people around the table. 'Meanwhile, shall we continue with our work in progress?'

The rest of the cases were handled in the next thirty minutes. Inquests to be held, families to be contacted, details and data to be sent to London.

'Good, if we're all finished, I'd like to remind everyone, despite the effects of the pandemic, the job of the Coroner's Office does not change. We are here as an advocate for the dead to safeguard the living.'

She paused for a moment. 'Ridpath, could you stay behind? I'd like a few words.'

Chapter 6

When everybody had gone, there was silence between the two of them before Mrs Challinor took off her glasses and rubbed her eyes, brushing her curly grey hair away from her forehead and tucking it behind her ear. 'How are you feeling?'

'Fine,' he answered immediately.

'Good. It's great to have you back, we missed you. It's been strange here during the pandemic, but we've managed as best we can.'

'I missed being here, Coroner. How was Sophia in my absence?'

'Brilliant. She handled her workload extremely well despite Covid and all the rest of the crap we threw at her. She's become an indispensable member of our staff.'

'I knew she could do it.'

Again the silence. Mrs Challinor glanced at the pictures on her desk of her daughter and seven-year-old grandson before speaking again. 'How's Eve bearing up?'

'Well, I think. She's with her grandparents at the moment, but we talk most nights on FaceTime. She starts her new school next month.'

'That's good.' Another silence. 'I spoke with Claire Trent, she told me about your counselling and was good enough to share your Wellness Action Plan and the psychiatric assessment.'

'I've been cleared as fit to return to work, Mrs Challinor.'

'I know. The psychiatrist was most complimentary about your progress.' She picked up the folder in front of her. '"Thomas has come a long way since we started the EMDR treatment and is fully aware of the strategies he should implement to cope with his loss.'''

Ridpath laughed. 'She kept calling me Thomas. I tried to stop her but...'

'You may have fooled her, Ridpath, but I know you well. How are you really feeling?' Mrs Challinor was as direct as ever – nothing had changed with the coroner.

Ridpath thought for a moment. Should he tell her he still saw Polly every morning? That he still talked to her? That she was there with them right now, listening to the conversation?

'I'm fine, Margaret, honestly. I need to get back to work. I can't stand staying at home all day with nothing but Paul bloody Martin and re-runs of *Flog It!* for company. Work is what I'm good at.' He paused for a moment. 'You can get addicted to grief, wallow in it, but there comes a time when you can't do that any more, you have to return to the world.'

'I know, Ridpath, that's why I wanted you back. But I'm not going to be the cause of another breakdown.'

'You weren't the cause of the last one, Coroner. My wife was murdered in front of me and I could do nothing to stop it.'

Ridpath's voice rose at the end of the sentence. He calmed himself by focusing on his breathing and taking three deep breaths, a technique given to him by his EMDR therapist, and continued speaking. 'I know I'm not to blame. The person who did it, James Dalbey, is to blame. He arranged for Mrs Seagram to go to my house and shoot Polly. It was his final revenge.'

'Where is Dalbey now?'

'Still in a coma at Manchester Metropolitan Infirmary. Last I heard, the doctors were deciding whether to shut off the life support systems. They should have done it six months ago, saved the bed for somebody who was ill.'

Another long silence.

'And the myeloma?'

Ridpath had been diagnosed with multiple myeloma – bone cancer – three years ago. He had spent nine months off work

24

while he went through chemotherapy. Luckily, he had been pronounced free of the disease, but his boss at the Major Investigation Team, Charlie Whitworth, decided to second him to work with the coroner.

'Still in remission. The doctors were initially worried the additional stress of Polly's death might lead to a recurrence of the disease. Apparently, that didn't happen, but during the Individual Stress Risk Assessment they found I was suffering from PTSD.'

'So you went into therapy?'

Ridpath flashed back to his days immediately following Polly's death, hidden in a fog of alcohol and grief. 'Not immediately, because of the lockdown, but eventually I saw an EMDR psychiatrist suggested by Greater Manchester Police.'

'Are you sure you're ready to come back to work?'

'The psychiatrist thinks I am. Occupational Health have signed off too.' He pointed to the folder. 'You've got all the documentation in front of you, Mrs Challinor.'

She glanced down at the folder. 'These are just bits of paper, Ridpath.'

'It's all we have. Bits of paper, I mean.'

She frowned and then sat forward. 'You really want to take on the Carsley case?'

'If there's one thing I understand now better than before, it's grief. I've had six months of it.' He stopped speaking and his eyes glazed over as if staring off into the far distance. 'Grief seems to be slowly coming to terms with the idea that Polly isn't here any more. Long hours of numbness followed by sharp bursts of extreme pain. If I can help this family to cope, then I'll have done something useful.'

'That's why you want to handle the case?'

He nodded. 'One thing I learnt is the Seven Stages of Grief isn't just words. It's a process... a lonely process.'

The coroner angled her head, encouraging him to say more.

'Grief isn't a straight line, one thing leading to another. It's a series of realisations and obstacles, two steps forwards and one step back.' He stared straight ahead, remembering the last six months. 'Often one step forward and three steps back. But we can get to a good place, a safe place, with help.'

'And that's where you are now?'

'I think so. I believe so.'

The coroner nodded her head slowly. 'Alright, pick up the file from Jenny and check with Sophia on everything we've done so far on the case.'

He stood up to leave.

'But take it easy. It's still early days. Your Wellness Action Plan says you shouldn't work long hours and you still need to see your psychiatrist for monitoring twice a week.'

He stood in front of her. 'Easy is my middle name, Coroner. I'm meeting with her tomorrow.'

He turned to go.

At the door, the coroner spoke again. 'Ridpath, it's good to have you back.'

'It's good to be back, Coroner.'

Chapter 7

Ridpath picked up the Carsley file from Jenny Oldfield and returned to his desk to read it. He already knew a few details of the case from the newspapers. The investigation had even replaced Covid-19 as the hot topic in the newspapers for a few days, before inevitably the press moved on.

David Carsley had gone missing on 21 July, kidnapped from a park. A huge search and rescue operation to find the seven-year-old had been mounted, but despite all the efforts he remained missing. His body was found two days later in Chorlton Ees by a man walking his dog. The police had released two photofits of a woman they would like to interview who had been seen in the area where the body was deposited plus another photofit of a man seen in the park walking an Alsatian when the boy was abducted. Neither had so far come forward.

Immediately, the press had linked the case to that of Ian Brady and Myra Hindley, the Moors Murderers. One of their first victims had been kidnapped and murdered around the same date, fifty-seven years previously.

A search had even been arranged on Saddleworth Moor, despite it being over twenty miles from where David had gone missing.

Personally, Ridpath would never have released the photofits so early in the investigation. It merely brought out all the fantasists, conspiracy theorists and nutters to clog up the phone lines. And as for a link to the Moors Murders, it was one of those coincidences that happened to sell a lot of newspapers. Strange, that.

He shook his head and opened the file. There were obviously no details of the police investigation, except for the mobile numbers of the Senior Investigating Officer, DCI Paul Turnbull, and of the Family Liaison Officer, DS Emily Parkinson.

'Poor Emily, they have her looking after the family,' he muttered under his breath.

'What was that, Ridpath?' Sophia returned carrying two coffees. 'I brought you a latte.' She put it down on his desk.

'Nothing, just reading the Carsley file. But thanks for the coffee, exactly what I needed.'

'No worries, good to have you back.'

'Good to be back. Mrs Challinor tells me you did well in my absence.'

'That's kind of her. Anyway, anything to escape my mum. She was even worse during the lockdown.'

'Still trying to marry you off?'

'And then some.' She did an impression of her mother. '"You are twenty-three and you are still not married. What man would want a single old maid?" I always tell her one with brains, intelligence and a six-pack to die for. She then wanders off blaming the schools, my teachers and my father for putting ideas into my head.'

'Sounds awful.'

'Nah, it's worse. At least once a week I have to meet these nerds introduced by the matchmaker – socially distant, of course. If I see one more engineer with a row of pens in his top pocket and his mobile phone in a pouch on his belt, I'll scream.'

Ridpath checked his mobile. It was in the inside pocket of his jacket. 'But work's been OK?'

'Work has been my lifesaver.' A short pause. 'You know I've decided to do a Masters in Law?'

'I didn't. I thought you wanted to join the police.'

'I thought about it but realised I loved this job. Helping people, not helping put them away.' Then she covered her mouth with her hand as she realised what she had said. 'Sorry, no offence.'

Ridpath held up his hands. 'None taken. But good news, when do you start?'

'Mrs Challinor was a great help. It's only part-time over two years, but I start next month.'

'And at the end?'

'I can start to specialise as a coroner.'

'Brilliant. Good for you.' He tapped the Carsley file in his hand. 'What do you know about this?'

'Not a lot. The man's a single dad, with two sons... with one son now,' she corrected herself. 'I opened the file under instructions from Mrs Challinor late last week.'

Ridpath frowned and began reading. Other than the contact at the police, there was only a home address – 16 Apted Road, Wythenshawe; the name, age and date of birth of the deceased – David Carsley, aged seven, born 9 March 2013; and the details of the other son, Daniel Carsley, aged ten, born 6 November 2009.

'There's no mother listed? Why is that?'

Sophia looked over her coffee cup, shaking her head. 'No name was given to me. I was told he was a single dad.'

'Right. Mrs Challinor said the family had requested the release of the body. Who made the request?'

Sophia checked her notes. 'The father, late last Friday. Sorry, I haven't updated the contact report yet.'

'No worries. You do it now while I make the call.'

He picked up the phone, dialling the mobile number in the file. It was answered after two rings by a female voice. 'DS Emily Parkinson, how can I help you?'

'You're the FLO on the Carsley Case?'

'Yes,' she answered back suspiciously.

'It's Ridpath, calling from the Coroner's Office.'

The voice immediately brightened. 'Ridpath, you're back at work?'

'They couldn't keep me away. I'd like to speak to Mr Carsley, he's requested the return of his son's body for burial. How's he holding up?'

'OK… I think. I'll put him on. Good to hear your voice again.'

A few seconds later, a male voice spoke down the phone. It was quiet and subdued, speaking softly. 'Michael Carsley.'

'Mr Carsley, this is Ridpath from the Coroner's Office. We're so sorry to hear of the loss of your son.'

As soon as he spoke the words, Ridpath could hear their blandness. Why was sympathy so difficult to express to those in grief? We always relied on platitudes on such occasions, a form of words dictated by the circumstances.

Michael Carsley hadn't suffered a loss. His son had been murdered. But to say the truth out loud was taboo.

There was no response from the other end of the phone. All Ridpath could hear was breathing. He continued on. 'I wonder if I could come to see you this afternoon, to arrange some details?'

'I… I… I don't know,' the man mumbled. Was he still drugged after almost two weeks?

'I'm afraid it's necessary. The Coroner's Office is here to help during these trying times.'

'I… I…'

'Let me take some of the burden from you.' Ridpath didn't know why he said the last words.

'I suppose it would be OK. There's so much to do. I didn't realise there was so much to do.'

'Shall we say three o'clock?'

'I suppose so.'

'I'll see you then.' Ridpath put down the phone. The man sounded like he was floating at the bottom of a deep, deep sea.

Ridpath knew exactly how that felt.

Chapter 8

It was 2.50 when Ridpath parked the car round the corner from the house in Wythenshawe. He'd driven past a few minutes ago and seen a few socially distanced reporters still lounging around outside. The road in front of the house was cordoned off with a solitary police constable standing guard at the front gate.

He showed his warrant card to the man. 'DI Ridpath, seconded to the Coroner's Office. I have an appointment to see Mr Carsley.'

'I'll get the FLO, sir.'

Ridpath looked over at the reporters. 'Been trouble, has there?'

'Two reporters managed to get into the back garden last week taking pictures, pretending to be council workers. Arseholes. Could you wait here a minute?'

Ridpath stood at the gate as the PC strolled to the front door. He used the time to put on his mask. Mrs Challinor had insisted he understood the protocols for visiting clients before leaving the office.

He hated wearing it. Not because it was uncomfortable but because it made him feel anonymous, kept his face hidden behind some fabric. How was he supposed to create empathy with a client from behind a sky-blue piece of polypropylene?

The house was one of the old type, built immediately after the war when Wythenshawe was created as the biggest council estate in Europe, filled with new residents rehoused from the slums and tenements of Hulme. Most of the council houses had been sold off by Mrs Thatcher under the right-to-buy scheme, including this one.

You could always tell the difference from the ones still owned by the council by the colours and the shapes of the door. In this case, it was a snazzy art deco number, painted in a non-council-approved shade of bright crimson.

Emily Parkinson appeared at the door and shouted down to him. 'Come in, Ridpath.'

He walked up the path towards her.

'You're looking good,' she said as he approached.

'You sound surprised.'

Emily Parkinson had worked with Ridpath on the Dalbey case, helping him discover the murderer of the judge. They had come to respect each other despite a rocky start.

'When did you get back to work?'

Ridpath smiled. 'First day.'

'Today?' she looked incredulous. 'You don't make it easy on yourself, do you?'

'If I wanted an easy life...'

'I wouldn't have become a copper.' She finished the sentence for him.

'You the Family Liaison?' he said, stepping inside.

'Yeah, Turnbull gave me the short end of the straw.'

'How's Mr Carsley handling it?'

She made a moue with her mouth. 'As well as can be expected. He blames himself, of course.'

Ridpath paused a moment before answering. 'Don't we all?'

Emily Parkinson covered her momentary embarrassment by pointing back over her shoulder. 'He's waiting for you in the living room. The son is upstairs.'

'And the wife?'

'She did a runner a few months ago.'

'Leaving behind two kids?' Ridpath shook his head. 'How does a mother leave her kids?'

'Don't judge, Ridpath. Not yet. We all make decisions we're not proud of.'

She opened the living room door. A small, compact man was sitting on the couch in a tidy, if old-fashioned, living room. A television set was on in the corner with the sound turned down. The man was wearing a pair of fluffy rabbit slippers. He rose when Ridpath stepped into the room.

'Mr Carsley?' Ridpath immediately stuck out his hand and then withdrew it, remembering he wasn't supposed to shake hands any more. 'My name's Ridpath, from the Coroner's Office.' He gestured for the man to sit back down, taking a seat opposite him. 'I'm sorry for your loss, but please understand I'm here to help you in any way I can.'

The man only nodded. Was he still on drugs?

'I rang the mort—' Ridpath stopped himself from saying the word. '—the place where your son is being kept. They say he can be released. I simply have to get the Senior Investigating Officer of the police...'

'Mr Turnbull.' The voice was Scottish, a lowland accent.

'...to sign off and then we can return him to you.'

'What do I have to do?'

'Who is your undertaker?' To Ridpath's ears the words sounded blunt and cold but there was no reaction from Carsley.

'I don't have one.'

'It's Michael, isn't it?'

The man nodded slowly.

'Like I said, I'm here to help, Michael. I can arrange for an undertaker to come to see you.'

'I don't know if I can afford one. I got laid off four months ago. No work, they said.'

Ridpath noticed the man's hands were trembling. 'Don't worry, there is help with the costs if you need it.'

'That's why I was at home, you see.'

It was as if the man hadn't heard anything Ridpath had said.

33

He was staring at a picture on the mantlepiece. Michael Carsley with his two sons, David in a United shirt and Daniel in his City blue. 'The kids had been stuck inside for so long during the lockdown. That's why I told them to go out. Go and play in the park, I said.'

There was a long silence.

'Daniel came back an hour later looking for David, but he wasn't here. We checked in his bedroom and in the shed out back but he wasn't there either. Sometimes, he liked to go and sit in the shed all on his own. But he wasn't there.'

'So you started looking for him?'

'We went to the park first, shouting his name. He liked the horses, watching them. I was planning to let him ride one of them for his next birthday. I was going to save for it.'

Ridpath glanced across at Emily Parkinson. 'Let me contact the undertaker and handle the details of the funeral for you.'

'Can you do that? There's nobody else, see. It's why we moved to Manchester. We were doing OK until the bitch walked out.' The words were suddenly harsh and strident.

Ridpath took out his notebook. 'Do you have an address for your wife, Michael?'

'I gave it to the police.' The man spat the words out.

'I've got it, Ridpath.'

'I have to let her know all the details, Michael. She's part of your son's family.'

'She's not,' he said, shaking his head, 'not any more. Not since the day she walked out.' The man was becoming agitated. 'Not any more,' he repeated.

Emily glanced across at Ridpath and he took the hint, putting his notebook away and standing up. 'I'll organise everything and let you know. I'll also keep Emily informed.'

'Emily?' the man said.

'DS Parkinson.' He pointed at the policewoman.

She walked Ridpath to the front door. 'Is he OK?'

'That's why I'm still here. He's on twenty-four-hour watch. The doctor has seen him this morning again but he's finding it difficult to take it all in.'

'How's the investigation?'

She shrugged her shoulders. 'I don't know. Turnbull's running it and he's all over the place. Word is Claire Trent is not a happy bunny.'

Detective Superintendent Claire Trent was the head of the Major Investigation Team and Ridpath's direct superior at Greater Manchester Police.

'I'm seeing her tomorrow at the weekly meeting.'

'Be careful, she's biting the heads off frogs at the moment.'

They both heard a noise from the top of the stairs. A young boy was standing there in his pyjamas, holding a bright red car. 'I'm all alone,' he said.

Emily Parkinson laughed as she climbed up the stairs. 'Don't worry, Dan, Auntie Em is here. You want to play Xbox with me?'

She ushered the boy back into his bedroom, looking back down at Ridpath, her mouth pursed, shaking her head.

The detective let himself out. Something wasn't right in this house. All his copper's instincts were telling him, something wasn't right.

Chapter 9

That evening, back at the service apartment, Ridpath made himself a cheese and ham sandwich and sat down in front of the television.

He'd already called Padraig Daly, an undertaker he'd worked with before. 'It's the Carsley case, Padraig, so you'll have to be discreet.'

'The murdered child? Discretion it is, Inspector. I'll put my best man on it – who happens to be a woman.'

'I think it's probably better if it's a man, Padraig.' Ridpath wasn't sure why he said that, but Michael Carsley's reaction to any mention of his wife made him think it was a better option at the moment.

'No worries, I'll make the best man, a man.'

'And one other thing, Padraig, the family is broke.'

'I wondered why you were calling. I'll do him a special deal even if the government is picking up the tab.' There was a slight pause at the end of the phone. When the funeral director spoke again, his usual jocular tone had vanished and something quieter had emerged. 'Nobody should go through the pain of losing a child, Mr Ridpath. I'll make certain he's well taken care of.'

'Thank you, Padraig.'

Ridpath took a bite out of the limp sandwich, flicking across a few channels until he found something that wouldn't tax his brain. He'd found staring at the box a great comfort in the days after Polly's death. The noise, the chatter, the general brain-dead inanity of the programmes were exactly what he needed to stop the voices in his head.

'It's time to call her.'

He checked his watch. 'I'll do it in five minutes, after I've finished my sandwich.'

'You have to eat better. A cheese and ham sandwich isn't good enough.'

He could hear Polly's voice but he couldn't see her.

'OK, OK, I'll do it now.'

For an instant he remembered the first time he had met Eve after the lockdown restrictions had been eased. In many ways, he was glad of the lockdown. At least, it meant Eve hadn't seen him at his worst and his lowest.

She only saw him when he was ready to return.

It was 4 July. Independence Day for him.

He had gone to a cafe in Longford Park and waited. The grandparents finally brought her to see him at three p.m. For a moment, they stood there looking at each other, then she ran the six yards to him, wrapping her arms around his thin waist and squealing with the delight that only an eleven-year-old can squeal.

It had been three months and nine days since they had last touched. Three months and nine days in which he had plunged deep into the lows of drunkenness, depression, self-doubt and self-hate.

He'd always remember that first touch until the day he died. It was the beginning of his rehabilitation, of his return to what passed for normality.

It was almost as if Eve gave him a reason to come back to the world.

To come back to her.

To come back for her.

He brought out his laptop and FaceTimed his daughter. Her image popped up immediately as if she had been waiting for his call.

'Hi, Dad.'

'Hi, Eve, how are you?' He asked the same thing every time. He tried to work out a different question but the same one always popped into his head.

'Good, Paw Paw and Ah Kung took me to Trafford Centre today. I was so glad to get out of the house. We went to Yang Sing and they had chickens' feet. Yeuch! Paw Paw spat the little bones out on the saucer. Gross.'

'I like chickens' feet.'

'You always were weird, Dad. How was your first day back?'

'Good. The place hasn't changed. Mrs Challinor sends her love.'

'Say hi from me. She was great after mum…' The voice trailed off.

Ridpath quickly sought a question to fill the silence. 'How are your grandparents?'

Eve smiled. 'They're OK, but *soooo* traditional. You know Paw Paw wouldn't let me go outside into the garden yesterday after I had washed my hair. Said I would catch a cold. I tried to explain to her the common cold is a virus, not something you get from washing your hair, but she wasn't having it. My Chinese wasn't good enough anyway.'

'You have to be patient, Eve, there are a lot of Chinese traditions I never understood but it was easier just to accept.'

'Like?'

Ridpath thought for a moment. 'Like your mum not washing her hair for the first month after you were born. Apparently, you would be washing away good luck and the health of your child.'

'That's silly, Dad.'

'But you have to remember it comes from a culture where many children died in their first month of life. All these traditions and beliefs were there to protect the baby and its mother.'

Ridpath remembered something Polly had told them after they first met. 'I always love the Chinese character for "good". It's a combination of the characters for a "mother" and "child".'

'Still, it's so annoy-ing.' Eve had developed that teenage habit of lengthening and stressing words. 'Maisie says her mum is worse with the superstitious stuff and she's Irish.'

Ridpath's mother had been from the same stock. As Irish and as Catholic as they came. In his case, the religion gene seemed to be totally absent. He wondered why that was.

'Dad,' Eve interrupted his thoughts, 'when can I come back and live with you?'

So that was where this was all leading.

'We've talked about this, Eve, it's best for you to stay with your grandparents at the moment. I'm on my own here and it's a service apartment, and what with me going back to work and everything, I'm not sure I could look after you too.'

'I don't need much looking after, Dad, I'm pretty independent.'

'I know that…'

'And besides, I miss your mash. If I have to eat another bowl of rice, I'll…' Eve searched for a response, '…I'll die.'

There was a long moment of silence.

'Sorry, Dad, didn't mean that.'

It seemed like people, even his daughter, were treading on eggshells around him, avoiding using the word 'death'. Pretty bloody difficult when you worked in a Coroner's Office.

'It's all right, Eve. Your mum is dead and we have to come to terms with that.'

'You have to come to terms with it, Dad.'

She was right. It was his problem, not hers. Had he accepted Polly was dead? The police psychiatrist thought he had, but he'd always been good at dissembling. For most coppers, it came with the territory. And why did he still see and hear her?

'I know, dear. Give me time… please.'

'I want us to be together again, to be a family even if it's just you and me.'

'I'm working on it, Eve, I promise.'

A muffled voice behind his daughter speaking in Cantonese. 'I have to go now, Dad, time to eat more bloody rice.'

'Don't swear, Eve, it's not very nice. See you tomorrow night, same time?'

'Same time. I love you, Dad.'

'I love you too, Eve…'

Chapter 10

He waited for his mother to fall asleep before he placed the underpants with their delightful Chip and Dale characters into the special drawer beneath his bed. His fingers trailed over the other objects lying there.

A St Christopher's cross.

A sock from the boy in Liverpool.

A beanie from the runner who got away.

A tennis ball from the one he met beside the canal.

A shame about him. Such a waste. He'd read the newspaper reports about how he'd died accidentally. Only he knew the truth, of course. It had been so easy to hold his head under the water, watching his feet kick and struggle, fighting to hang onto life. Rolling the dead body into the dark water and walking away without looking back.

Too easy.

Each time his fingers touched an object they trembled slightly, memories of these beautiful times filling his body. Sweet memories.

He closed the drawer slowly, reluctantly.

A querulous voice from the other room.

She should be asleep already. 'Coming, Mother,' he shouted.

He mustn't indulge himself now, save the pleasure of his trophies for later.

Time for her medicine. She liked taking her medicine. It helped her to sleep.

He wondered what she dreamt about. The men she had brought home? Or the times she hadn't returned at all? Or the ones who thought he was part of the deal too?

He would have to begin increasing the dosage soon.

It would help put her to sleep forever.
And then he wouldn't have to wait any more.

Chapter 11

It all seemed to be happening in slow motion.

The bubbles rising to the top of the pan as the water reached boiling point.

The sound of muffled voices from the living room.

The rip of the packet of *har gau* as he opened it.

The ring of the doorbell echoing again and again and again.

Polly's voice as she ran to open the door – 'I'll get it' – sounding muddied and indistinct.

Leaning over the dim sum to look out of the kitchen window, feeling the heat of the steam rising from the pan onto his face.

A woman at the door.

An old woman at the door.

An old woman he knew.

The slow formation of questions in his mind. Were they expecting visitors that evening? What was she doing here? Was she supposed to come to his house? Had they arranged a meeting?

Mrs Seagram should have been at home mourning the death of her son, not standing outside his front door.

What did she want?

Hearing Polly's footsteps in the hall, the latch turning, the slight creak as the draft excluder he had installed last winter gave way and the door began to open.

And then it hit him with all the force of a pile driver.

He shouted. His voice echoing around his head again and again and again.

'Don't open…'

'Don't open…'

'Don't open…'

'Don't open…'

He tried running towards the hall, but his legs were held fast to the kitchen floor, as if running through a lake of glue.

Then the sound of two gunshots, one after another in quick succession.

And he woke up, sitting upright in the bed, his body and the sheets drenched with sweat. His breathing heavy, as if he had been chasing some nutter through the streets of Manchester for miles.

'You have to tell her, you know.'

Polly was sitting at the end of his bed.

'Tell who?'

'Don't use your copper's tricks on me, Ridpath. It's Polly, remember? Tell your psychiatrist. The one who wears the cheap clothes from Primark. Mrs Underpriced…'

'It's Underwood. Doctor Underwood.'

'Whatever. Tell her.'

It was the Polly from when they had first met twelve years ago, in her dad's Chinese restaurant. Her hair dyed green, the make-up showing traces of the goth phase she was going through.

'Not yet.'

'She has to know. You can't spend every night like this.'

'But if I tell her, she'll put me back on sick leave.'

'Perhaps you shouldn't be working.'

'With you gone, it's all I have.'

'You still have Eve and you still have me. Tell her.'

'I will… soon.'

'Tell her today.'

He didn't answer. There was no point, Polly always had the last word.

And besides, he knew she was right.

On the Second Day

Wednesday, August 5

Chapter 12

The following morning, Ridpath was up early. The day had a perfect clarity to it, with a few fibres of clouds drifting across the sky and the birds harmonising in the trees like an avian barbershop quartet.

He'd noticed fewer contrails in the skies above Manchester recently – fewer puffy, straight lines like chalk on a blue blackboard, a small black dot at the front. People weren't flying any more, the skies quiet and untroubled. Even the air seemed clearer, or was that his imagination?

He felt tired, the routine of shaving, washing his face and brushing his teeth taking far longer than normal. He put on his suit and was out only a little late to drive to Police HQ on Northampton Road.

He switched on the radio and listened to the news. It was a non-stop litany of screw-ups and mistakes; PPE nightmares, pensioners having to pay for their TV licences, chaos in care homes, and one quango even saying they should close pubs to open up schools, which was as likely to happen as a squadron of pigs taking off from Manchester Airport.

Nothing about the Carsley case. Most of the nationwide news reporters had moved on to bigger and better things, leaving only a few intrepid and persistent local stringers to carry on.

The only time he really listened was when they reported on the lenient sentencing of the killers of a young copper, Andrew Harper. 'Should throw away the key,' he muttered before switching off the news and putting on a Bowie CD.

The strident chords of 'Jean Genie' filled the car and he found himself singing along with the music. He'd recently found out that Mick Ronson had once been a parkie in Hull. Something to remember for the next pub quiz.

At HQ, he parked up and entered the building, going through the now expected rigmarole of hand sanitisation, temperature checking and social distancing.

Up to the fifth floor where the usual MIT detectives were assembling in the Situation Room. Well, not the usual crowd; there were fewer coppers than normal and they were all spread out around the room rather than being clumped together.

Ridpath waved to Emily Parkinson sitting in the far corner. She didn't wave back.

Chrissy Wright, the department's civilian researcher, popped up next to him. Her right leg was in a cast and a bandage on her right arm, but her Manchester City scarf was still around her neck. 'Welcome back, Ridpath, great to see you again.'

'What happened, Chrissy? Looks like you were in the wars?'

'Knocked over crossing the street. My head was in the investigation, not on what I was doing. First day back myself.'

DCI Paul Turnbull grunted as he passed Ridpath, clapping his hands loudly. 'Get to your seats. I don't want to waste too much time on this meeting, we've got a bloody killer to catch.'

The boss, Detective Superintendent Claire Trent, joined him at the front, carefully maintaining her social distance from Turnbull. Ridpath couldn't work out whether this was because of the virus or something else.

The DCI began the meeting. 'Right, we have a lot to get through and even more to do.'

Claire Trent coughed and Turnbull stopped speaking. 'I'd like to say a few words if I can, Paul.'

'Of course, boss.' He stepped back a pace, allowing Claire Trent to come forward.

'A couple of announcements. We are incredibly busy at the moment, with more investigations than we can deal with and some people off sick. Manchester was placed in lockdown on 31 July. The chief constable will be issuing instructions, as he did in March, on how we are to police this new situation. Despite the new regulations, we're not going to let the ball drop in any of our investigations. There will be no sloppiness in any of our work. Whether it's the killer of the child found on Chorlton Ees or the stabbing in Rochdale or the post office robberies, we will follow up on every lead, gathering evidence as we always do. We will have one focus: apprehending the men who perpetrated these crimes. Do you understand me?'

A chorused reply of 'Yes, boss' and 'Right, guvnor.'

'I would also like to welcome back two people to the MIT fold. First, I notice we have DI Thomas Ridpath who has been certified fit for duty again.'

All eyes were on him. Everyone knew what had happened to Polly.

'Welcome back, Ridpath. He will be returning to his old role of coroner's officer liaising with MIT. He will be reporting directly to me.'

A wary glance from Turnbull to his boss. It was obviously news to him.

Claire Trent continued on. 'Plus we have Chrissy back after her failed wrestling match with a two-ton truck. Good to see you again, Chrissy.'

The researcher pointed to her leg. 'If I hear any jokes from you lot about Hopalong Chrissy, you'll get a wallop from this.' She held up her walking stick.

Somebody from the back said quietly, 'Truck 1, Chrissy O.'

Laughter from the assembled coppers and civilian officers which Turnbull quickly killed by raising his hands. 'Settle down, people, let's get started. Harry, where are we on the post office robberies?'

DI Harry Makepeace stood up. He was one of the few surviving members of the old MIT under John Gorman and Charlie Whitworth. Somehow he had managed to keep going by being a diligent copper and just getting on with the work.

'We got a lead to a gang from Liverpool, boss. We're liaising with the Scousers to follow up. The last robbery was two weeks ago, but following their MO, we should be due another one soon.'

'Anything from your confidential informants?' asked Claire Trent.

'Not a squeak, guvnor, that's why we think they're not from our manor.'

'Right, keep going, Harry. If you need any help talking to Liverpool, let me know. I made quite a few friends in Merseyside when I was with Cheshire police,' said Turnbull.

Ridpath laughed to himself. Turnbull was still going on about his time in his previous force, as if the cases in a small county operation could ever compare to working in Manchester.

'Right, it's me up next on the Carsley case. We're following up leads and we have the criminal profiler coming in to deliver his ideas in person this afternoon. His final report is on your desk and we've booked your time, guvnor.'

Claire Trent hardly acknowledged the words, staring straight ahead.

'The photofits we released to the newspapers led to over 3000 leads, some of which are proving extremely useful at narrowing down our suspects. HOLMES 2 has given us a couple of links but nothing substantive. Plus we've shaken down the pervs on the Sex Offenders list within a fifty-mile radius, going through their alibis as we speak.'

Claire Trent nodded and spoke softly. 'The newspapers are all over this case. Luckily the nationals have backed off, finding another bone to gnaw on, but the local papers are still on it like a dog in heat.'

A male voice from the back. 'I thought it was a bitch in heat, guvnor.'

A few laughs but Claire Trent kept her jaw clenched. 'If you are referring to Molly Wright, then you are correct, John, she is all over this. But she's only doing her job. Somebody here, however, is not doing theirs.' She slowly scanned the assembled officers. 'Somebody has been feeding her information about the case. If I find out who it was, they won't be in MIT for long – they won't even be in the police any more. And if I had my way, they would be sharing a cell with a gang of spice dealers in Strangeways. Do I make myself clear?'

'Yes, boss.'

'Understand I am under pressure from everybody to clear this case up. The mayor, the police and crime commissioner, the chief constable and Ms Wright have all called me this morning and it's only…' she checked the time, '…nine twenty. But none of that matters. What is far more important is that a young boy has been murdered on our patch. His killer is still at large and could strike again. In fact, according to the initial report from the criminal profiler, he will definitely kill again.'

A silence descended on the room. Claire Trent let it lie there like a shroud until she finally broke the tension, saying, 'Anything from the Coroner's Office, Ridpath?'

'My first day back was yesterday, so I'm still getting up to speed, but everything seems to be working well, nothing to report. Mrs Challinor has been liaising with the police through the local resilience forum.'

'Recent Covid cases?'

'Only two deaths in the last week, guvnor, but cases are apparently rising, particularly in Blackburn, Rochdale and Oldham. Greater Manchester declared a major incident on Sunday.'

'At least the Coroner's Office are operating efficiently.'

Was that a sly dig at Turnbull? Before he could check the room's reaction, Claire Trent spoke again.

'Remember, people, to be extra careful these days. All department Covid safety protocols must be used. Is that clear?'

The assembled detectives nodded their collective heads.

She spoke directly to Ridpath. 'You are the family liaison with Michael Carsley for the coroner, aren't you?'

How did Claire Trent know? Had Emily Parkinson reported back or had she talked to Mrs Challinor?

'I am, guvnor,' he answered.

'What did you think? I heard you visited the house yesterday.'

All eyes turned on him. She was putting him on the spot in front of everybody and especially in front of Turnbull.

'I don't know, guvnor, it was a quick visit to introduce myself.'

'I asked you what you thought, Ridpath.'

She was pushing hard. He breathed out. 'I don't know, guvnor, but it didn't feel right…'

Turnbull snorted. 'There he goes with his feelings and hunches again.'

Claire Trent ignored him. 'What do you mean?'

'I'm sorry, guvnor, nothing concrete, I just felt they were hiding something. Not telling me everything they knew.'

'And where's your evidence for that assertion, Ridpath?' Turnbull was confronting him directly, a bright red vein standing out in stark relief on his bald head.

Ridpath shrugged his shoulders. 'No evidence, boss. I felt that there was something there, something hidden.'

Turnbull rolled his eyes towards the ceiling. 'In the meantime, the rest of us will keep gathering the evidence while you gather your "feelings".' He formed quotation marks in the air with his fingers.

A couple of the detectives on the left laughed. Ridpath didn't know them, they were new to the department. Obviously, Turnbull's hires, as they knew when to laugh at their boss's jokes.

Claire Trent brought the meeting to a close. 'Our most important case is catching the Chorlton Ees killer before he strikes again. Make it happen. Something must have given him away. A small slip-up that could lead us to him. Find those little mistakes and we find our killer. That's all. Stay safe, people.'

Ridpath got up and filed out of the meeting. He noticed Turnbull staring in his direction, a scowl plastered on his face.

It wasn't until he reached the car park that Harry Makepeace caught up with him.

'The boss wants to see you, Ridpath.'

'What does Turnbull want?'

'Not him. The real boss. Claire Trent.'

Chapter 13

Ridpath knocked on the door of her office and waited for the call to enter.

It came after a few seconds. He walked in to find Claire Trent closing a file on her desk and placing it carefully to her left.

'Is that me, guvnor?' He pointed at the file.

'It is. Your psychological and occupational health report. The psychiatrist has cleared you to return to work but still wants you to attend sessions with her. Why is that?'

'I don't know, you'll have to ask her.'

'I'll do that.' Claire Trent made a note in her diary and then pointed to the chair, 'Sit down.'

Ridpath wondered what all this was about. Was he due for a bollocking again? He'd only been back on the job for a day, what had he done wrong this time?

'What do you know about the Carsley case?'

'Not a lot. I met the father yesterday to begin the coroner's liaison with family. He's asked for the release of his child's body for burial.'

'We can't release it yet, Ridpath.'

'Why?'

'As SIO, Paul Turnbull has to agree we don't need it for our ongoing investigations.'

Ridpath expected Claire Trent to say more but she stayed silent. Eventually, he spoke. 'I'll let the father know, but I'll also get the undertaker to liaise with the mortuary so we're ready when he gives the go-ahead.'

'Fair enough.' Claire Trent bit down on the end of her pen. Ridpath could see other indentations where her teeth had done damage. 'What did you think of him?'

'The father?'

She nodded.

'Obviously upset and trying to come to terms with the loss of his son. He seemed out of it – he's going through a lot.'

'Do you think he could have done it?'

'A father murdering his own son? It never occurred to me.'

'Think about it now.'

'Why are you asking?'

'Because he has no alibi for the time of the boy's disappearance. He says he was in the house watching TV but when we asked him about the programmes, he didn't have a clue.'

'That's not unusual. Sometimes we stare at the screen, not knowing what's on.'

Claire Trent looked at him for a moment before speaking. 'Paul Turnbull wants to bring him in for questioning. I'll ask you again, do you think he could have done it?'

Ridpath went back to his interview with Michael Carsley, replaying the answers, seeing the man's shaking hands and hearing the tremor in his voice. 'No, I don't think he did. There is something there, something hidden, but I don't think he murdered his own son. I don't think he's the type.'

Claire Trent's right eyebrow rose. 'There's a type?'

'No. But he struck me as a father who had lost a son he loved, not a man who'd committed murder.' Ridpath put his hands up. 'I could be wrong, though, and he may be one of the world's best actors...'

'But you don't think you are?'

'No.'

Claire Trent let out a long sigh. 'I'm inclined to agree, but Paul is insisting he wants to question the man formally.'

'If you bring him in, the press will crucify him.'

'That's where you come in.'

Ridpath knew there was a reason why she wanted to see him.

Chapter 14

'I'd like you to look at the Carsley case.'

Ridpath sighed. 'I've just come to work, boss, I don't know if I'm up to it.'

Claire Trent stared at him. 'Let me rephrase that. I *need* you to look at the Carsley case. Start from the beginning, leave no stone unturned, question all our assumptions.'

'An alternative investigation?'

'A *parallel* investigation.' Claire Trent leant back in her chair. 'Listen, Ridpath, the press is hounding me, half of Manchester is hassling me, the chief constable is up my bum checking what I'm doing and I'm worried the investigation is heading down so many blind alleys it's going to get lost. Turnbull is a good copper but he's a classic SIO – follows the handbook to the letter and lacks your—'

'Panache?'

'—Don't push it. I was going to say enquiring mind. We need a fresh pair of eyes to look at what we've done and see where we went wrong.'

'And I'm the eyes?'

'And the warrant card.'

Ridpath thought for a moment. 'What about the coroner?' Ridpath saw the look on his boss's face and answered his own question. 'You've already cleared it with her, haven't you?'

Claire Trent nodded. 'She was concerned about your health but I reassured her you wouldn't be pushing too hard, merely looking over our investigation.'

'And she agreed?'

'She wants you to help clear the backlog of work in the Coroner's Office, and, as this is one of their most important cases at the moment, she has – reluctantly – agreed.' His boss sat forward again. 'If you want my five pennyworth, Ridpath, you're happiest when you're working, when you've got a problem to sink your teeth into. All this sitting at home moping isn't good for you.'

For Ridpath the penny finally dropped. 'You put pressure on my psychiatrist to sign me off as fit to work, didn't you?'

Claire Trent sat back again, smiling. 'She agreed with me that a return to work was in your best interests… and those of the department.'

'That's why she still wants to see me?'

'She felt she wanted to monitor your progress.'

Ridpath was silent for a moment before he said, 'I'll need some help.'

Another smile briefly appeared on Claire Trent's lips. 'Who do you want?'

'Emily Parkinson is wasted as the FLO at Carsley's house. She knows the case already.'

'You've got her. We need to pull her off that duty anyway.'

'And Chrissy to do some of the legwork.'

'Very funny, Ridpath. She's not that mobile any more.'

'I don't need her mobility, I need her mind and her facility with the Police computers.'

'OK, you've got them both.' A long pause. 'I'll need a report on my desk before Saturday.'

'But that's only three days away.'

She shrugged her shoulders. 'Three days is a long time in policing.'

He stood up. 'I'd better get started.'

She passed across a file.

'What's this?'

'The criminal profiler's report. Read it quickly. He's convinced the killer will strike again. And soon.'

He took the file and walked to the door.

'One more thing, Ridpath.'

He turned back slowly to face Claire Trent.

'Paul Turnbull is not to know. This is your investigation and you report directly to me. Understood?'

'How can I access the case files without him knowing?'

'Find a way.'

'He's supposed to be my boss.'

'I'm your boss and I'm his boss. You have your instructions, make it happen.'

She went back to her report and began writing in the margins.

For her, he was no longer there.

Chapter 15

Emily Parkinson was sitting at her desk, typing an entry into her computer.

Ridpath plonked himself down next to her. 'Do you have a minute, Emily?'

'Not at the moment, I have to finish last night's report as a FLO at the Carsleys. I'm due at the house in...' She checked her watch. 'Shit. Thirty minutes.'

'I think your time as a Family Liaison Officer is over.'

'No, it isn't. I'm on the 12–8 shift.'

Paul Turnbull joined them. 'Emily, you're off the Carsley job, the guvnor wants to reassign you elsewhere.' And then, as if noticing that Ridpath was there, 'Hello, Ridpath, I see you're back in MIT.' He chortled to himself. 'But not back in MIT, if you know what I mean.'

Ridpath knew exactly what he meant. He was back in the office, but not back as a member of the team. What Turnbull didn't know was that he had already decided not to return even before Polly was shot. Seeing Turnbull's gurning face in front of him simply confirmed the correctness of that decision. He decided to play it straight.

'Yes, sir. Started at the Coroner's Office yesterday, glad to be back at work.'

'I bet you are. Now, shove off and let DS Parkinson finish her stuff. Just because you're single now doesn't mean all the female officers are fair game.'

Ridpath gritted his teeth.

Emily Parkinson quickly covered the tension. 'Where am I being reassigned, boss?'

Turnbull shrugged his shoulders. 'Beats me, you'll need to ask Claire Trent. Why should I know what you're doing? I'm only the boss round here.'

'OK, I'll ask her.'

'Do that.'

A detective Ridpath didn't know was hovering nearby. Turnbull finally acknowledged his existence.

'The car's ready to take you to the Carsleys', boss.'

'OK, about bloody time.'

The detective hesitated.

'Well, what are you standing there for? Bring it round the front, Sam.'

'Yes, boss.' The detective hurried away.

Turnbull took a few steps towards his office, turning back as if he had forgotten something. 'A word of advice, Ridpath: keep your nose clean. And by clean I mean spotless. Otherwise, I'll make it my life's work to ensure you never step inside this office again. Crystal?'

'As the Rochdale Canal, Detective Chief Inspector Turnbull.' Ridpath made the rank sound like a swear word.

Turnbull smiled and walked slowly back to his office.

'He's got it in for you.'

'You don't say? Looks like I'm not wanted in MIT.'

Emily Parkinson glanced around the room. 'New blood coming in, Ridpath. Turnbull's creating his little fiefdom.' She stood up. 'Anyway, nice chatting. I need to find out what I'm supposed to be working on now.'

'Don't bother, give me five minutes and I'll tell you. Chrissy is joining us too.'

DS Emily Parkinson's eyes narrowed. 'What exactly are you up to, Ridpath?'

Chapter 16

'What?'

'I said, the guvnor has asked me to look into the Carsley case from the beginning. Go through all the evidence, check assumptions, see if there is anything we missed.'

They were back in the Situation Room. With Turnbull gone, it was as good a place as any to meet. On the walls, pictures of the victim, a playground, the place where the body was found and photofits of possible witnesses, along with the usual detritus of any investigation; scribbled notes, questions to be answered and actions to be taken.

'I heard you the first time. But what's that got to do with us?' She pointed to Chrissy sitting next to her, the right foot in the cast sticking out from beneath the desk.

'I asked for you two to be assigned to help me.'

'But that's Turnbull's case. He's going to go apeshit when he finds out.'

'He's not supposed to find out.'

'What? We're supposed to go back over a case without him knowing?'

'Those are the instructions from the guvnor. Are you in or out?'

Chrissy smiled broadly. 'I'm in. I think we got this case wrong from the beginning.'

'And you, Emily? If you don't want to be part of it, I'll understand and ask for somebody else.'

'Who else? Harry Makepeace? He'd tell Turnbull what you were doing within five minutes and the rest are his poodles.'

'Is that an in then?'

'It's a "there's not a lot I can do about it" in.'

'Good enough. Tell me about the case, starting from the beginning.'

Emily tapped her fingers on the desk. 'Look, whatever you think about Turnbull, he's run this investigation by the book. I was part of the team from the start. We were called in at 9.10 on 23 July. A child's body had been found at Chorlton Ees by a man walking his dog.'

'How quickly was it identified as David Carsley?'

'Almost immediately. We'd been looking for a boy for a couple of days since he was reported missing from Wythenshawe Park.'

'Who identified the body?'

'The father, Michael Carsley. We showed him a pair of shoes and a United shirt found close to it first. He recognised them immediately and then identified his son.'

'Poor man,' said Chrissy. 'Imagine being the one asked to look at your dead seven-year-old's corpse.'

'You were there when he made the ID?'

Emily nodded.

'What was his reaction?'

'Stunned and then disbelief. He wanted to go back in and check he hadn't made a mistake. We had to restrain him, stop him from returning to the mortuary.'

'There was a post-mortem?'

'Yeah, done by Schofield. As detailed as ever.'

'Could you download the report for me, Chrissy?'

'Is there a case number for this job?'

'I don't know but could you ask Claire Trent and set one up?'

'Will do.'

'What was the cause of death?'

'Strangulation. The rope was still around the child's neck.'

'No DNA?'

'According to Schofield, the body showed signs of being washed and cleaned before being deposited.'

'So no fingerprints either?'

Emily shook her head. 'The boy's underpants were missing, though. We searched the area thoroughly and didn't find them.'

'A trophy taker?'

'Possibly, or they may have been lost when the boy was transported.'

'Any witnesses or CCTV?'

'None around the area, unfortunately. There were reports after we posted the photofit pictures of a woman seen walking away from the area around the time the body was discovered. She hasn't come forward.'

'A woman? That's a pretty detailed description,' said Ridpath sarcastically. 'Covers about half the population of Manchester.'

'Yeah, we've also checked all the traffic footage from both the Wythenshawe park area and Chorlton Ees, running a comparison to see if any car had been in both areas at the time of the kidnap of David Carsley and the disposal of his body.'

'And?'

'Nothing. Not a sausage.'

'It means the killer used two different cars, that's all,' said Chrissy.

'Or we haven't compared the right footage at the right time,' added Ridpath.

'Four of the cameras were down. Budget cuts, according to the Highway Authority. They hadn't got round to repairing them yet.'

'How long were they not working?'

'At least a month before the abduction of the boy.'

'Shit.'

'My words exactly, Ridpath.'

He thought for a moment, his eyes darting left and right as he considered the possibilities. 'Where did we get the photofit?' he eventually asked.

Chrissy answered. 'David's brother Daniel was with him in the park.'

'They were together?'

'No. Daniel was playing basketball with his school friends while David was playing on the swings. Daniel said he stopped playing and ran over to David when he saw a man talking to his brother.'

'What time was this?'

'One twenty roughly. Daniel ran over and spoke to the man, telling him to leave his brother alone.'

'What happened after Daniel spoke to the man?'

'Apparently, he hurried away after Daniel said he would call the police.'

'Good lad,' said Chrissy.

'And the man's not come forward?'

They both shook their heads. Emily carried on speaking. 'After the man left, Daniel ran back to his friends and they continued their game.'

'When did he notice David was missing?'

'About ten minutes later. He looked up from his game and he couldn't see his brother anywhere.'

'What did he do?'

'He panicked, I think, because he was supposed to be looking after David. He ran straight home to check whether David had got bored and gone home without him...'

'A seven-year-old walking home on his own?'

'Listen, he's a young kid. Anyway, he wasn't there so he screwed up the courage and told his dad.'

'What time was this?'

'About two o'clock. The dad went back to the park with him and they spent an hour looking for the boy, shouting his name and checking everywhere, but couldn't see him.'

'When did he call 999?'

'He didn't. One of the horsey brigade called it in a few minutes before three p.m. The local plod hesitated, they were short-staffed. Then there was another call a couple of hours later, so they finally got their act together and began searching too. It was escalated when the boy was still missing as the sun went down.'

'So they had been searching for six hours and found nothing?'

'That's right. The search was called off that night, and a proper search of the park with dogs, beaters and members of the public was organised at eight the following morning.'

'But the boy wasn't found?'

'No. The body turned up a day later and a couple of miles away at Chorlton Ees. We interviewed Daniel that afternoon. He sat with the artists and they produced the photofit of the man.'

'So the next step was to organise a door-to-door canvas of the area around Wythenshawe Park where the boy had disappeared.'

'Exactly. We were checking anybody and everybody who had been in the park between one and two p.m. on the day of David's disappearance.'

'Did anybody report the man?'

'No, but we got a description of somebody similar hanging around the local school. Year 1 and Year 6 had already returned.'

'We checked all the local pervs?'

'Every single one. Plus we've canvassed the area twice more since then, with coppers hanging around in a marked tent in the park asking if people saw anything.'

Ridpath thought for a moment. 'So from the park, we've only got this to work with?' He pointed to the photofit on a whiteboard. It was a pretty good likeness of a man, not as generic as these sometimes were.

'Dark hair, spectacles, aged twenty-five to thirty, slightly under six feet in height. No scars, no tattoos, wearing a dark green bomber jacket and jeans. The kid's description was good.'

'But nobody's come forward?'

'Not a whisper.'

'If he's out there, he may have changed his appearance,' added Chrissy, 'dyed his hair, used contacts, ditched the clothes.'

Ridpath stared at the photofit. Was this the man who had kidnapped David Carsley? The mere fact he hadn't come forward was significant. There was so much information about the case in the papers, people couldn't miss it. If they were in the park that day, they would have identified themselves.

'Right, that's the abduction. What about the disposal area?'

'Chorlton Ees, a lot of dog walkers use the spot. He was found at 8.40 a.m. on 23 July.'

'So the boy was missing for over a day. Where was he?'

'We don't know,' answered Emily. 'According to Schofield, he hadn't been in the open for long, a couple of hours at most.'

'Time of death?'

'The pathologist was cagey as usual, but Paul Turnbull eventually pinned him down to from two a.m. to six a.m. on the day he was found.'

'It means he was kept somewhere before he was murdered. I need to talk to Schofield.'

'You want me to arrange that, Ridpath?' asked Chrissy.

'No, I'll get Sophia to do it. She has a special "arrangement" with our pathologist.' He formed quotation marks with his fingers. 'Or at least she did have last time we talked.' Ridpath realised he hadn't asked Sophia about her life other than the ongoing problem with her mother. Not that he had any right to know, but he should have at least asked her about what was happening and how she was. In truth, he realised he had become a little self-obsessed in the last six months.

He changed the subject, pointing to another picture that could have been any woman. 'So how did we get this photofit? This woman hasn't come forward either?'

'A witness saw her leaving the area around the time of the discovery of the body, but she hasn't responded to any of our notices.'

'Strange. And the dog walker who discovered the body?'

'Jon Morgan.'

'We checked him out?'

'Of course. Normal bloke, lives nearby, walks his dog regularly, married with two kids. A regular Joe, according to the neighbours.'

'So basically after nearly two weeks, we have nothing.'

'That's about the size of it.'

'Whose brilliant idea was it to release the photofits to the press and TV?'

'Take a guess?'

'But didn't Turnbull realise he was going to be swamped with calls?'

'Over 3000,' said Chrissy, 'and we're still getting them. There was one woman today who was talking about MPs, satanic death rites involving young children and a pizza place on Chester Road. I've referred her to the Trafford social workers.'

'So from over 3000 calls, didn't we get anything?'

Emily posted to another whiteboard. 'We've responded to every single one of them, checking them all out. Other than the two people in the photofits, there are only three other sightings we haven't been able to explain. One: a man was seen walking an Alsatian in Wythenshawe park thirty minutes before the disappearance of the boy. He hadn't come forward either. Two: a white car was seen in the area of the park with a young man and a boy sitting in the front. The boy wasn't wearing his seatbelt; that's why the witness noticed it.'

'Any description?'

'Nothing clear. A white car, no numberplate and a man and a boy.'

'Could be anybody. Go on...'

'Number three: a dark van was seen reversing down the lane into Chorlton Ees at 5 a.m. on the morning of the discovery of the body. I say "seen", it was more like heard. The witness was getting up and the noise of the engine made her go to the window to check. She just caught a glimpse of a dark van.'

'That's it?'

Emily cocked her head. 'That's it.'

'No wonder Claire Trent is scared. After two weeks, there's nothing else?'

'Nothing.'

'What about HOLMES 2? Anything?'

HOLMES 2 was the Home Office Large Major Enquiry System, used to coordinate the investigation of major incidents such as serial murders and high-value frauds.

'Turnbull has been using it to consolidate all the information from members of public, enquiry officers and the house-to-house enquiries.'

'Has it given us links to any other crimes?'

'Not a lot,' answered Chrissy. 'There was the stabbing to death of a young boy in Liverpool six weeks ago, where the body was also dumped in a park. The Scousers have already got a suspect, plus the MO is completely different. There's no DNA evidence linking the crimes.'

'It's a bit of a coincidence that we have two child murders in the space of six weeks in two cities less than thirty miles apart?'

'But the deaths are so different, Ridpath. After talking with Merseyside, Turnbull ruled out any connection between the two crimes,' said Emily Parkinson.

Ridpath scratched his ear, staring at the boards and pictures on the walls around him.

'We're stuffed. No wonder Turnbull wants to interview Carsley again. According to Claire Trent, he thinks the father may have been involved in his son's murder.'

'What?' Emily's mouth dropped open and then her features twisted in something that resembled both scorn and disbelief. 'That's a crazy idea.'

'You don't think he could have done it?'

'Not a cat in hell's chance. Listen, I've spent two weeks with the man, I'd know if he topped his own son. Nobody, I don't care how good an actor they are, can keep up the pretence for that long.'

Ridpath breathed out. 'Well, if that's true, we not only have to solve this case. We may also have to clear an innocent man.'

Chapter 17

At the end of the meeting, they decided on a plan of action.

Ridpath would bring himself up to speed on the case. 'I'll also visit the man who discovered the body.'

'Jon Morgan.'

'Him.'

'You want his number?'

'No thanks. I think an unannounced visit would be better. No point in spooking him unnecessarily.'

Emily would check the 3000 phone calls to see if anything had been missed, while Chrissy would trawl through the police database looking for similar crimes or MOs going back ten years. She was also going to check the Sexual Offenders Register to see if anybody had moved into the area and somehow been forgotten.

Ridpath went to the Coroner's Office without bothering to have lunch – the idea of eating never occurred to him. Sophia was sitting at her desk, nibbling a samosa.

'Are you still in touch with Jonathan Schofield?'

She raised her eyebrow. 'What's that supposed to mean?'

'Nothing meant. I wanted to talk to him about the post-mortem of the Carsley boy.'

'Why don't you just ring him?'

'I... I...' Ridpath stammered.

'But if you are asking are we a couple? The answer is no. We had a few dates but it sort of fizzled out. Clear enough for you?'

'What I meant was...'

'If it's an office enquiry, shouldn't you be using official channels, not me?'

Ridpath held his hands up. This was obviously a touchy subject. 'You're right. Sorry, Sophia, I didn't mean to pry into your private life.'

'Everybody seems to be doing it at the moment, why not you?' Then a sigh. 'Sorry, Ridpath, but I've had my female cousin who's getting married next week, her mum, my mum, and even the bloody caterer asking if I am going to be bringing somebody to the wedding? And that's only today. I'll ring him if you want.'

'No worries, you're right, better make it official, I'll do it.'

He made the call himself as he should have done in the beginning. Schofield was as busy as ever but could see him early tomorrow morning.

As he finished, he heard Mrs Challinor calling him from her office. 'Are you back, Ridpath?'

He walked in.

'Claire Trent spoke to you?'

'She did.'

'If you don't want to investigate the case, let me know and I'll have a word with her. I'm worried you're taking on too much too quickly.'

At that moment, Ridpath realised he hadn't thought of Polly once that morning. He hadn't even seen her. Perhaps Claire Trent was right. What he needed to do was get back into work and stop moping around.

'No, it's fine, Mrs Challinor, if I felt I couldn't handle it, I would have said no.'

'OK, but let me know immediately if it gets too much for you. I'll have none of this macho male rubbish, keeping it all in and hiding emotions. That sort of thinking should have gone out with the Flintstones, but unfortunately, it's still with us.'

'I'm fine, Coroner. I'll let you know immediately if I feel I can't cope with it.'

'And I made it clear to Claire that if I feel your work as a coroner's officer suffers, I will pull you off the case. Understand?'

'Completely, Coroner.'

'When is your next session with Dr Underwood?'

Did Mrs Challinor know everything about him?

'This afternoon, after I interview the man who discovered the young boy's body. The EMDR therapy is useful and I don't mind seeing her.'

'You are open and tell her everything?'

Ridpath crossed his fingers behind his back, a strategy his mother had taught him when he told a white lie. Even though that was thirty years ago, he still did it. 'I tell her everything that occurs to me.'

He hoped Mrs Challinor didn't call him out on all the weasel words in his last sentence. She seemed to be about to before thinking better of it.

'I've had a terse note from the SIO on the Carsley case…'

'Paul Turnbull.'

'That's the man. It reads, "The pathologist has completed his investigations, you can release the body of David Carsley to the family."'

'That's it?'

'That's it. A personable fellow, is he?'

'Life and soul of the party.'

'Has the pathologist signed off too?'

'I'm seeing Dr Schofield tomorrow morning. I'll get him to do it then.'

'Does Mr Carsley have an undertaker?'

'I've arranged for Padraig Daly to see him.'

'Good, stay on top of this one, Ridpath. This man has been through enough without this office adding to his woes.'

'Will do, Coroner. Anything else?'

She shook her head.

He turned to leave.

'But do call me if it all gets too much, Ridpath, I'll always be here for you.'

'Thank you, Coroner, I'm sure I can handle it.'

As he closed the door, he wondered if he should have told her about Polly.

Was it strange that she still talked to him or was this perfectly normal?

Chapter 18

Molly Wright had a problem.

She was sitting in the cafe nursing her Americano – although it was lunchtime she couldn't face food. Coffee was her drink of choice, her fuel which kept her going all through the day and long into the night. Sometimes, she drank ten cups a day. She knew this probably wasn't great for her body, and time as the health reporter for the *Mirror* had more than confirmed this. But she couldn't stop drinking now. Her addiction was complete, even down to the inability to sleep at night. Just another one of the curses faced by reporters.

At the moment, though, it wasn't her health that was a worry, but her future.

The Carsley story was fading fast.

She'd done her best to keep it in the public eye, even paying a photographer to climb over the back fence to get pictures of the man and his son. The police had spotted him sharpish, and he'd been taken off and put in the cells for a few hours to cool down.

She still had to pay him, even though he hadn't taken any pictures. It was one more expense in an investigation that was starting to cost more than it made. As a stringer, she wasn't on expenses any more, only making money when she could sell a story.

At the beginning, it had been lucrative. She'd congratulated herself on making the link to the Moors Murderers. The tabloids had lapped it up, paying for a team to go up to

Saddleworth Moor with a couple of spades and a gardening fork. The pictures even made it into the broadsheets.

Her fingers hovered over the keys of her MacBook Air. She was compiling a list of possible interviews to keep the story going and the nationals interested.

Unfortunately, Michael Carsley was no Kate McCann. For a start, he wasn't middle class, photogenic or articulate. In fact, he was exactly the opposite – poor, fat and quiet to the point of being comatose. The police had been successful at keeping him bottled up in his home. Even her source in MIT gave her little new intel these days.

She typed MICHAEL CARSLEY? in block letters anyway.

What about the wife? The one who had run out on her kids. There must be a reason why she left, mustn't there?

Molly searched for the standard tropes the newspapers used on such occasions. Battered housewife? Independent woman? Victim of a system that didn't care?

She shook her head. It had all been done before. She had to find something different to get the nationals interested – that was where the money was. Something with a news element?

She typed IRENE CARSLEY NEWS? in her list.

Anything else?

She'd already approached David's teachers, there was nothing left to mine there except more banalities.

Lovely boy.

A real charmer.

Worked hard.

Popular with all his classmates.

It all sounded like the stuff they'd write in a school report. The only one missing was 'Must do better' and that probably applied to her rather than the boy.

Next she wrote POLICE in capitals. She couldn't interview her source, that would give the game away. Better stay clear of him.

What about the SIO? She'd met Turnbull at the police briefings and took an instant dislike to him. She typed in his name anyway. PAUL TURNBULL.

Maybe an attack piece along the lines of 'Two weeks and still no suspect'. She added the idea next to his name. A definite possibility but maybe not yet. She'd save that for when there was nothing left.

What about the head of MIT, Claire Trent? One of the rising stars of GMP, perhaps she would give an interview. A woman talking to another woman about the loss of a child. Something emotional, making the investigation personal, even for a seasoned detective.

The *Guardian* or the *Independent* might take a punt on a trope like that. Not for the front page but for the inside or a supplement. Almost an opinion piece. What it's like to be a woman in a man's world as the subtext. She thought it funny that even for the more liberal papers she had to write in tropes, something instantly recognisable that she could pitch to a tired editor.

She typed in CLAIRE TRENT? adding the name to her list on the screen.

Not much left, unless they found or charged the killer. She'd give this case another week and then move onto something else.

For all reporters, there was the law of diminishing returns. When a story was no longer news only something big could revive it.

Unfortunately, the death of David Carsley was no longer news.

The world had moved on, as it always did.

Chapter 19

Ridpath pressed the bell and stepped back from the porch. The house was one of the classic semi-Ds, thousands of which had been built as the sprawl of Manchester had extended its brick-covered tentacles into the garden suburbs in the 1930s.

In those days, they had been the apotheosis of the middle-class dream; a front and back garden, three bedrooms, inside toilet, electricity and 2.4 kids. After decades of deprivation, decline and division, they were an oasis of security and safety in an insecure world. Later in the 1960s, they bred the young who rebelled against the stolid and stable hypocrisy that oozed from every window. Now, they were the home of the barely-managing, those who fought every month to pay the mortgage, the water rates and the credit card bills while still trying to enjoy life.

A woman answered the door. She was pretty in a school teacherly way.

'Mrs Morgan?'

'Yeessss,' she said tentatively.

'My name is Ridpath, I'm a detective inspector with GMP.' He showed her his card. 'Is your husband at home?'

'He's just got back. You want to talk to him again? He's not going to be happy.' She shouted over her shoulder, 'Jon, it's the police for you.'

'Not again,' the voice came from the back room. Two seconds later a head popped around the door. 'I only spoke to your lot yesterday. They said it would be the last time.'

'Just a few things we need to clear up. It won't take long. Can I come in?' Ridpath displayed his largest, most charming smile. It produced a grimace from Jon Morgan and a grunted, 'You'd better come through here.'

'A cup of tea, Inspector?' asked the wife.

'That would be lovely.'

'And I think I have some digestives left over from the last time your lot came round.'

'Perfect.'

Jon Morgan showed him into the front room. It was obviously the one they kept for visitors as it had that rarely used smell. A child's ball lay forgotten in the corner.

As Ridpath stood there, a big lolloping Labrador pushed the door open and bounded in, all dangling tongue and wagging tail. The dog immediately rushed up to sniff Ridpath's leg.

'I presume this was the dog you were walking in Chorlton Ees?'

Jon Morgan tried to pull the dog away by grabbing his collar. 'Yeah, sorry, he's a bit of a handful.'

The dog was reluctantly ushered out of the room and the door closed. A few plaintive whines and scratches followed before Mrs Morgan called him away.

Ridpath sat on the chair with Jon Morgan facing him, pulling out his files as Morgan started talking.

'I wish I'd never found the body now. Such a palaver and my face plastered all over the papers. One of my customers even asked me about it.'

Ridpath took out his pen and notebook. 'What do you do, Mr Morgan?'

'I'm a sales manager for an IT company, I cover the North West.'

'So your region is…?'

'Manchester, Liverpool, Cheshire, Lancashire, all the way down to Shrewsbury and up to Carlisle.'

'A big area. You must do a lot of driving.'

'Used to, not anymore.'

'In lockdown, you worked from home?'

He rolled his eyes. 'What a pain that was! The kids were off school too. Trying to get anything done was a nightmare.'

Ridpath listened; the house was pretty quiet for one with kids.

Jon Morgan watched him and smiled. 'They're away with Margery's parents in the country. You obviously have kids yourself...'

'Only the one, but she makes enough noise to wake the dead.' Ridpath coughed and quickly moved on. 'Can you tell me again what happened on 23 July?'

'I've told the story so many times. I can see you have my witness statement.'

Ridpath held up the photocopy. 'We're going over everything to see if we missed something – a detail, an incident that people might remember now.'

'So you haven't found the killer yet?'

Ridpath ignored the question and its implied rebuke. 'You left the house at eight a.m.?'

'Yeah, around then, and I drove to Chorlton Ees.'

'You walked the dog there every morning?'

'During lockdown it became a habit, getting me out of the house even if it was only for a short while. We walked the dogs, letting them off the leash.'

'You said "we"?'

Jon Morgan seemed confused. 'Did I? I meant I walked the dog.'

There was a knock at the door, and Mrs Morgan came in with a tray of tea things and a plate of digestive biscuits, placing them on the coffee table.

'Thank you, that's great.'

'Shall I be mother?' She picked up the teapot and poured the tea, straining it through a small metal strainer. It was a rich, dark colour. 'I always use loose tea, I can't stand teabags, can you, Inspector?'

Ridpath only ever used teabags. He wouldn't know where to start with loose tea.

'Milk and sugar?'

'Milk but no sugar, please.'

'Sweet enough, are you?' She added the milk and stood up.

Ridpath didn't answer her. He continued the interview with her husband. 'You said you were walking the dog?'

'I let him off the lead. He went off as usual into the undergrowth as I stayed on the path. I must have been walking for about ten minutes when he began to whine.'

'He?'

'The dog, Major.'

All through this speech, Jon Morgan had been glancing at his wife, seeking her approval.

'He doesn't whine normally,' added Mrs Morgan, 'unlike my husband.' She paused, waiting for Ridpath to register the joke before continuing. 'He's a good dog, a quiet dog. I can fetch him if you like?'

As if hearing his name, the Labrador bounded into the room again, sniffing Ridpath's leg.

The detective scratched the dog's head between the ears. 'He's a lovely lad, but I don't think he's going to add anything to Mr Morgan's statement.' He paused, waiting for a laugh but received nothing but silence. 'So you followed the dog into the undergrowth…'

'And that's when I saw the body and called the police.'

Mrs Morgan knelt down and put her arm around her husband. 'How awful for you, dear. He's been having nightmares about it, terrible nightmares.'

The husband now had a hangdog look that reminded Ridpath of a bloodhound. He wasn't going to get anything useful here.

He closed his notebook and put his pen back in his inside pocket. 'Thank you for your time, Mr Morgan, I think I have enough.' Ridpath stood up.

'You haven't finished your tea, Inspector.'

'Thank you, Mrs Morgan, but I've drunk so much today, I could float the Titanic.' He suddenly remembered one question. 'Oh, before I forget, did you see anybody else that morning?'

Jon Morgan shook his head emphatically. 'No, didn't see anybody.'

His wife frowned. 'But that's not what you told me when you came home that day. You said you'd seen the woman with her stupid Jack Russell. The dog that Major stole a toy from? Remember?'

Her husband shook his head again and laughed. 'I think you've got the wrong day, Margery.'

She pursed her lips. 'I don't think so. I remember it clearly. Major came home with another dog's toy that day.'

'He must have found it in the bushes?'

'But you said he took it off a woman's dog. What was the name you said – a Mrs Burgess? I remember you had her number on your phone so you could contact her to give it back.'

Jon Morgan reddened visibly.

'Do you have Mrs Burgess's number, Mr Morgan? It would help us to eliminate her from our enquiries?'

'Is that necessary, Inspector? My dog only took a toy from her Jack Russell.'

'It would help, sir. Perhaps she had walked her dog on the day the body was discovered, as your wife remembers?'

'It was definitely another day,' Jon Morgan said firmly.

Ridpath persisted. 'If I could have her number, perhaps she saw something?'

Reluctantly, Jon Morgan handed over his phone. Ridpath copied the number into his notebook.

'One last question, Mr Morgan, is there anything else you remember about that day? Anything unusual that has occurred to you?'

Morgan glanced at his wife and shook his head slowly.

Ridpath stood up. 'Thank you for your time. If you do remember anything, here's my card.'

'If I do, Inspector, I will call you.'

Ridpath rubbed the Labrador's ears. 'You shouldn't steal other dog's toys. It's a criminal offence.' He looked up at Jon Morgan. 'Almost as bad as giving the police false information.'

Ridpath made his goodbyes, closing the front door behind him. On the path, he stopped to check the house. Jon Morgan and his wife were arguing in the living room. He was pretty sure he knew what the argument was about.

Jon Morgan was lying.

Not about discovering the body or being involved in the killing, but about who was with him at the time.

He'd give the man until tomorrow morning to come clean. He had no desire to wreck two marriages – they were perfectly capable of doing that on their own. In the meantime, though, he would stir the pot.

He opened his car door and sat behind the steering wheel. Taking out his mobile, he rang the number for Mrs Burgess that Morgan had given him. As he expected, the call went straight to voicemail.

'Hello, you've reached Shirley Burgess. After the beep, well, you know the drill.'

Ridpath waited for the irritating noise to end. 'Hello, Mrs Burgess, this is Detective Inspector Ridpath of Greater Manchester Police. I'd like to discuss your presence on the morning of 23 July 2020 in Chorlton Ees. Please ring me back on this number.'

He switched off the call and held out his phone over the passenger seat, letting it fall.

'Boom,' he said, mimicking the dropping of a bomb.

He started the car engine, working out in his head how he was going to drive into the city centre.

Time to face his psychiatrist again for the twice-weekly struggle to avoid revealing himself.

The only person he allowed inside his head was him.

And Polly, of course. She was always there.

Chapter 20

'Good afternoon, Thomas, how are you feeling?'

Dr Underwood was sat in her usual upright chair, her legs crossed and a writing pad on her knee. Today, she was wearing a Primark two-piece suit that looked far too warm for the weather and her hair was tied in a rather severe bun. With her square glasses, she looked like Miss Jean Brodie in her prime.

The office was on the third floor of a nondescript building in Central Manchester which she shared with about ten other practitioners of various forms of therapy, from Reiki to Massage to Bereavement Counselling.

She specialised in EMDR – Eye Movement Desensitisation and Reprocessing. A psychotherapy that supposedly enabled people suffering from PTSD to deal with the symptoms and emotional distress of a disturbing experience. The Occupational Health Unit of Greater Manchester Police employed Dr Underwood in a consultant's role, particularly for its officers suffering from severe PTSD.

Sometimes, it was witnessing the horrific aftermath of a car crash. Or being involved in a murder or fire investigation. At other times, there was no single cause, but the gradual build-up of dealing with daily traumas that was the life of a copper.

Eventually, these traumas revealed themselves in the classic symptoms of PTSD: intrusive memories and flashbacks, hopelessness about the future, feeling detached, emotional numbness, anxiety, and for Ridpath, a total inability to sleep followed by a feeling he was getting up every morning to fight the same demons that had exhausted him the day before.

Shortly after Polly's death, he had been referred by his GP to a mental health practitioner, receiving a full psychological report and a diagnosis of PTSD. Following the bureaucracy of GMP, he completed an Individual Stress Risk Assessment questionnaire, and was finally referred to Dr Underwood as part of his Wellness Action Plan.

But then lockdown began and his treatment was postponed and then postponed again until finally, in late April, it had begun on Zoom.

It felt strange at first, talking to a stranger about Polly over a computer link. But Dr Underwood soon set him at ease.

In June, after the lockdown restrictions had eased, they met for the first time in her office.

Despite being the one undergoing therapy, Ridpath couldn't stop being a detective. He looked for clues to her personality but found very few. A porcelain elephant on her desk was perhaps a souvenir from a trip to Thailand. A pen marked with the name of a hotel in Glasgow suggested she may have been to a conference in that city. There was little else to help him; no pictures, no personal items. Nothing that indicated a life outside this office.

When he had gently probed her to discover more, she had quickly shut him down, returning to his life and his relationship with himself.

It was here that their battle began, with Ridpath desperate to reveal as little about himself as possible yet aware that he needed Dr Underwood's approval in order to return to work.

'I'm feeling fine, glad to be back at work.'

'How's it going, work, I mean?'

'Good, I'm busy, there's lots to catch up on.'

'Do you feel you were missed?'

Ridpath thought back to his conversations with the coroner and Claire Trent. 'I think so. Don't get me wrong, nobody is indispensable, the world carried on without me, but I think people are glad that I'm back.'

'No struggles or difficulties at work?'

'No, just the usual problems with workload. Everybody seems to be aware of what I went through and are making allowances.'

'Does that worry you?'

'No, I'm quite grateful.' Ridpath crossed his fingers. He actually hated it when people made allowances. He only wanted to be treated like any other copper.

Dr Underwood seemed satisfied with his answer, making a note in the little pink book she kept on her lap.

'Good,' she drew out the word, 'now as I have explained before, disturbing experiences, such as the death of your wife, can overwhelm an individual's ability to process the event, preventing the information processing system from making the internal connections needed to resolve the issue…'

Ridpath often felt she talked about him as if he were a computer rather than a human being, something to be examined and reprogrammed rather than truly understood. For some strange reason, he actually enjoyed her approach. It felt less personal, because the last thing he wanted, with a therapist appointed by his employers, was to reveal his true feelings. She didn't have to know he still talked to Polly.

'…instead the memories become stored in the brain. What you saw, what you felt, the rawness of the experience in its original unprocessed form, these memories rise to the surface and are labelled as Post Traumatic Stress Disorder. When memories like this in the present refuse to go away, it is because they are often linked to memories in the past.'

Ridpath gripped his chair. She was going to ask him about his childhood again. All he really wanted was the coping strategies she gave him, ways of handling anxiety and stress. He didn't need to dig up his father again, not his slow death from cancer or his mother's reaction to it. He just wanted to cope with the present.

With Polly.

With the fact she was dead.

With the knowledge he caused it.

'...this is one of the symptoms of PTSD; the past seems always present. Particularly, the feelings and emotions of a particular event appear heightened, almost visceral, leading to anxiety and tension. EMDR gives us the ability to control those memories and strategies for coping if they re-occur. Shall we begin today's session?'

'I thought we had.'

She blushed. 'You're right, of course, but I'd like you to dig deeper and search for your touchstone memories, if you can? Are you ready?'

Ridpath nodded.

'Now, you remember the safe place technique you learnt?'

Ridpath immediately went back to the top of the hill in the Peak District, the wind flowing through his hair, the sun shining, him looking down at the valley below. His breathing slowed and a gentle warmth flowed over his body.

'Good, now you can return to this safe place any time you want both during and after our session. Shall we begin?'

Ridpath nodded again.

'I'd like you to close your eyes and imagine the incident. What image or memory represents the worst part of what happened?'

Immediately Ridpath flashed to Polly lying on the ground, blood oozing from her wounds.

'When you hold the memory in your mind, what comes up for you?'

'Helplessness.'

'And where do you feel it?'

'Across my chest like a heavy weight, I'm unable to breathe.'

'Focus on those feelings and let your mind wander back to childhood and notice the earliest memory that comes up eliciting the same feelings. Anything?'

Involuntarily, Ridpath went back. Approaching his father's bed. The man he knew and loved lying there, unable to breathe, his eyes red, bloodshot, staring at him. Reaching out his small hand and touching the paper-thin skin on the back of his father's arm. His father weakly signing for him to come close, closer. 'Help me,' his father had whispered in his ear.

Ridpath could do nothing even though he'd tried.

Back in the clinic, the same person, now grown up, shook his head. 'Nothing. I don't remember anything from my childhood, the only memory is of Polly's death.'

'Not to worry, with some people the memories are harder to access.' Dr Underwood sounded vaguely disappointed. 'Now, I'd like you to go to your safe space again. And this time I'd like you to add a butterfly hug. Bring your arms onto their opposite shoulders and tap four or five times slowly, remembering your safe space. How does this feel?'

'Good, my breathing slows and I feel calm and relaxed.'

'Now, repeat this technique often, and the simple tapping of your shoulder will induce the same feelings of calm. It's a useful coping strategy, particularly in situations when you can't close your eyes. How do you feel?'

'Good, relaxed.'

'Great. We still have some work to do to elicit your touchstone memories but I think we've done enough for today.' She pulled out her diary. 'How does this time on Monday suit you for the next session?'

'I'm fine with that. How many more sessions do we have to do? I'm back at work now.'

'I'd like to do at least three more, and that was my agreement with GMP – we continue to monitor you for the first month of your return.'

She stood up and escorted him to the door. 'See you on Monday, Thomas, and keep building on what we do here. Remember to use the coping strategies every day.'

'Thank you, Dr Underwood.'

Ridpath stepped out of the office into the blaring traffic of a Manchester rush hour. He did find the sessions useful but he wasn't going to let the therapist get into his head.

That was the one space he kept for himself.

Chapter 21

Back home that evening, Ridpath was sat in front of the silent TV, eating another cheese and ham sandwich and devouring the case reports Chrissy had given him, making notes as he went along.

Emily was right. Turnbull had run the case by the book. He had done everything in the correct sequence and at the right time. He had been slow but systematic, following the SIO handbook for a murder investigation to the letter.

The only errors Ridpath could see were releasing the photofits to the press and perhaps not pushing Jon Morgan harder. But those were easy mistakes to make in the maelstrom of a murder investigation.

He finished off the sandwich and drank the tea. Suddenly, the desire for the sweet, bitter taste of a glass of whisky came over him. He glanced at the shelf, but the bottle wasn't sitting in its usual place.

In the weeks after Polly's death, he had hit the booze badly, looking at old videos and photos of himself and Polly, wallowing in his grief. He couldn't remember how much he had drunk, but from the evidence of the empty bottles, he'd made a serious dent in the Scottish whisky industry's stocks.

Then one night Polly appeared next to him.

'It doesn't help, you know.'

'What doesn't help?'

'Drinking.'

He glanced down at a near-empty bottle of Laphroaig. 'But it does. It makes me feel… comfortably numb,' he slurred. 'It fills the emptiness. You know, there were nights when I used to wake and just listen to you snoring gently beside me.'

'Snoring? Just what I want to be remembered for.'

'But it was warm and lovely your snoring, a comfort when I couldn't sleep.'

'And now you drink.'

He held up the glass of whisky as if to make a toast. 'Now I drink.'

'Your daughter, what does it do for Eve?'

He stared at the golden liquid glistening like honey in the crystal glass. 'Not a lot.'

'That's why you need to stop drinking. Stop it now.'

'But I was to blame for your death, if I hadn't...'

'You did your job, Ridpath. His mother was manipulated and mad, so she decided to take it out on you when her son died.'

'That's the point, though, she didn't take it out on me, but on you.'

'That's not your fault. You didn't kill me, the mad woman did and then she killed herself. All this guilt you are feeling, who does it help?'

Ridpath swirled the whisky around in his glass. 'Me,' he finally whispered.

'No it doesn't,' she responded immediately, 'it helps nobody, least of all you. I'm dead and the sooner you come to terms with that, the better.'

'Don't sugar-coat it, will you?'

'I'm dead, we have no time for dishonesty. Stop the drinking and stop it now. Your daughter needs a father, not a drunk.'

He sat and listened to her, the whisky fogging his brain. And then he stood up, took the remaining bottle from the cabinet and poured it down the sink, inhaling the sweet intensity and bitter notes of the spirit as it vanished into the drain.

He hadn't touched a drop since, not even on the three-month anniversary of Polly's death, when a cheque had come through the post from the insurance company.

Her life insurance. A few pounds for a beautiful woman, his wife.

Getting rid of the alcohol hadn't helped diminish his sense of guilt, though. Whatever Polly said, he was as responsible for the death of his wife as the woman who had pulled the trigger.

He had deprived her parents of a daughter.

He had deprived Eve of a mother.

He had deprived her of her life.

Him. Detective Inspector Thomas Ridpath.

Nobody else.

The television suddenly flashed brightly. In its silent world, some movie star was on a red carpet, cameras exploding with light all around her.

As he watched the woman parade in her finery, his phone rang. Picking it up, he didn't recognise the number. 'DI Ridpath.'

A male voice at the other end of the line. 'Inspector Ridpath? It's Jon Morgan here.'

In the background of the call, Ridpath could hear the sounds of people speaking and the clinking of glasses.

'Hello, Mr Morgan, how can I help you?'

'Sorry for ringing so late, it's… it's, erm…'

'What is *it*, Mr Morgan?'

'I have a confession to make. I wasn't alone when I discovered the body.'

'Mrs Burgess was with you.'

'How did you know?' The voice was surprised.

'Why didn't you tell us before?'

'My wife… she wouldn't understand…'

'She wouldn't understand you were having an affair?'

'It wasn't an affair, we were just good friends, Mrs Burgess and I, just good friends, you understand?'

Ridpath smiled to himself. 'So she was there when you found the body?'

A long pause. 'Correct.'

'Why didn't you both report it?'

'We... I... thought it would be easier if I did it... alone.'

'How long did you wait?'

'How long?'

'Before you rang 999?'

'I rang almost immediately. I waited for her to walk out of sight with her dog.'

So Shirley Burgess was the woman at the scene. Well, that was one part of the mystery solved. 'You'll both have to come in to give statements.'

'Do we have to?'

'I'm afraid it's necessary. You signed a false statement and Mrs Burgess didn't make a report despite multiple attempts by the police to find her. I suggest you ring DCI Turnbull to arrange a time to come in.'

'Not you?'

Ridpath thought quickly. 'No, it would be better to talk to the Senior Investigating Officer. It would also be better if the statement was seen to be voluntary, i.e. you came forward because you felt guilty, not because you were discovered.'

'It would be better?'

'Definitely. If you do that, I won't mention my interview this afternoon with anybody. I'll keep it quiet.'

'What about my wife?'

'If you make the statement voluntarily, she's less likely to find out, isn't she?'

Another pause. 'I'll ring him first thing tomorrow.'

'You do that, and thank you for coming forward, Mr Morgan.'

'You know, it's a relief to admit it. You don't know how much it's preyed on my mind.'

'It always does, when honest people are dishonest.'

The phone went silent and Ridpath stared at the empty screen. At least the mysterious woman was known now. He hoped Turnbull went easy on Jon Morgan, but he doubted he would. Jon Morgan wouldn't be charged with wasting police time, though. Not in the middle of a murder investigation. Even Turnbull wasn't stupid enough to do that.

He glanced down and picked up the criminal profiler's report from where he had put it on the floor. Was there anything in it except the usual psychobabble?

He opened the folder and began reading.

Chapter 22

Lying in bed, staring up at the ceiling, he realised where it all began.

His mother was responsible, of course. Who else? He never knew his father, neither did she, apparently.

They were living in Great Clowes Street at the time. In the big house. He didn't know why they lived there. It was far too big for only the two of them.

Too old, too draughty and too damp. But mother seemed to like it there. She liked the cold.

He had asked her one day. 'Where's my father?'

She'd looked up from the television. 'Don't ask such stupid questions. You don't have a father.'

'Everybody has a father.'

'You don't.'

He'd stayed silent. He couldn't have been more than seven years old at the time. For some reason, the idea of being born without a father had troubled him even then.

Later, the teacher at school had asked him where his father was and what he did for a living. He had repeated the answer from his mother.

Not a good move. The other kids taunted him mercilessly. Even the teacher joined in, laughing about 'our virgin birth, verging on the ridiculous'. He didn't know what it meant then and neither did the other kids, but they laughed anyway.

For the rest of his school life, he was pointed at, laughed at. Ridicule that descended into bullying; his money and pencils stolen. Abuse that continued at the next school and the next and the one after that.

Always alone, shunned.

He only tried once again asking his mother, 'Who is my father?'

His mother was completing one of her quizzes in the magazine. This one was all about the correct clothes to wear at a dinner party. Mother didn't like to be disturbed when she was doing her quizzes.

'I've told you already, you don't have a father.'

She went back to her quiz. He shouldn't have persisted but for some reason he did.

'But the teacher said everybody has a father, who is mine?'

She threw the magazine across the room, striding over to grab his hair and wrench him to his feet.

'I'll show you who your father is!'

She dragged him across the room to the door of the cellar.

He remembered screaming, 'No, Mum, please, no, Mum.'

She opened the door and pushed him down the stone steps. 'You'll find your father down there.'

He was cold and hungry in the cellar, but he never found his father.

Instead, he found his friends.

Real friends.

Friends who hurt people, especially the teacher in his class and the other boys.

He liked it when they hurt the boys.

Chapter 23

He looked up from the case notes and checked the time.

Eleven thirty.

Immediately, a wave of guilt washed over him as he realised he hadn't FaceTimed Eve that evening. Had she been waiting next to her computer for his call? He got up and checked his laptop. A message was waiting for him.

> Hi Dad, I called you but there was no answer. Where are you? Call me when you get this message. Lots of love. Eve.

Should he call her now?

He shook his head. She would be sleeping – her grandmother insisted she went to bed at nine p.m. every night. He would have to call tomorrow morning.

Stupid. Stupid. Stupid.

Why hadn't Polly reminded him?

He looked around, expecting to see her shaking her head in the corner, waiting to tell him off. But she wasn't there.

And then he realised, where was she? She hadn't spoken to him since he started the case. He hoped she wasn't angry with him for working late again.

Gathering up his notes, he put them in order, ready to brief Emily and Chrissy tomorrow. As he did, the photos of the crime scenes slipped out from the case file. He picked them up and looked at them again.

A wide shot of the location in Chorlton Ees.

A body stretched out on the ground.

A close-up of David Carsley's face, the noose around his neck just visible.

For a moment, an image of his own daughter flashed into his mind, replacing that of David Carsley in the photograph.

He closed his eyes tightly. There were some kinds of evil men in this world who had to be caught and sentenced. A child-killer was one of those.

In that moment, he vowed he would put this bastard away, whatever happened. Eve and thousands of other children deserved that from him.

He placed the photographs back carefully in the case file and picked up his own notes. On top was the page with the five main questions he needed to answer.

Who was the man Daniel Carsley had seen in the playground?

Who was the woman at Chorlton Ees?

Did the white car/dark van have anything to do with the kidnapping?

What happened in the day between David's disappearance and the discovery of his body?

Was a couple or a single man involved?

Who had kidnapped and murdered David Carsley?

That was six questions, but he was too tired to care. He had written a series of action steps to be discussed with his two conspirators tomorrow morning. From there, they would plan their investigation. At least now he was up to speed.

He reached for his pen and scored through the second question. At least one issue had been removed, but so many others still remained. 'There, now it's five,' he said out loud.

Would the killer strike again? According to the criminal profiler, it was more than likely.

One last time, he checked through all the questions and sighed. They were not so different from the ones he had seen written up on the whiteboard in the Situation Room at Police HQ.

He had less than three days left to report back to Claire Trent.

How was he going to make a difference? How was he going to stop this man?

On the Third Day

Thursday, August 6

Chapter 24

The following morning, Ridpath was up early. For once, he had slept well and couldn't remember any of his dreams, nor had he awoken in the middle of the night with the sweats.

After a quick breakfast, he drove into the centre of Manchester, parking close to the mortuary. As he stood outside, looking up at the nondescript building, the desperate craving for a cigarette flooded his body.

He dismissed it immediately and pushed his way through the entrance doors. In the lobby, the usual smell lingered in every corner, a mixture of carbolic soap, disinfectant and cleanliness.

Dr Schofield was already waiting for him, kitted out in his protective gear: face mask, surgical overalls, bloodied apron and cap.

'Ah, Ridpath, great, you're on time. I've just finished a job.' He held up his blue plastic gloves stained with dark blood and assorted gore. 'Give me a second and I'll clean up. My assistant has already moved the body from the fridge for us.'

The voice was high-pitched, almost squeaky, a consequence of the doctor suffering from hypogonadism. He had explained everything when they had first met two years ago – it was an explanation he was used to making.

Ridpath stood in the hallway, staring at the white tiled walls and desperately trying not to breathe in. He wished he had that cigarette now – at least his lungs would be full of comforting tobacco smoke rather than the disinfected air of the mortuary.

He was also glad Dr Schofield had not said how happy he was to have him back at work. In fact, it was almost as if the doctor was unaware he had ever been away.

Dr Schofield returned dressed in exactly the same way but his apron was now clean and he was wearing a fresh pair of blue gloves. 'You're not suited up yet?'

'Was I supposed to?'

'You know the rules.' He glanced at the clock. 'I've a pathology class for the interns at eight thirty, they've missed so much of their coursework because of the lockdown. We'd better get a move on.'

Ridpath followed him into the changing room and quickly donned protective overalls and a cap while Schofield went on into the mortuary itself. It wasn't dissimilar to the gear used at a murder scene by the CSI team. Ridpath finished it off by tucking his hair under his cap and going through the same door as the pathologist.

At the far end, Dr Schofield was standing in front of a stainless steel table. On it lay a tiny body covered up to the shoulders by a white sheet.

David Carsley.

'Come on in, Ridpath. I've dug out my notes for this client. I presume you've already read them.'

'Last night.'

'Any questions?'

'I'd like you to take me through the major points of the post-mortem.'

'I didn't know you were on the case. I thought the SIO was DCI Turnbull?'

'He is. I've been asked to review the investigation.'

'Checking if there were any mistakes, including mine.'

Ridpath didn't answer.

'Well, no matter, you won't find any in my work.' He turned to face the boy, placing his notes on a small table next to the body. 'I remember this case. Who could forget working on the body of a child?'

'You were the medical examiner?'

'Yes, called out at 9.15 a.m. on 23 July to a place near the Mersey. I certified the boy was dead at 10.05 a.m., and he was transported back to the mortuary an hour later after having been released by the crime scene manager. I took an internal temperature at the scene and another when it arrived here.'

'When did you start the post-mortem?'

'Almost immediately. As you can imagine, there was a certain amount of pressure to reach some quick conclusions, which I ignored. It was important to get it right, not to get it quickly.' He chuckled audibly. 'Turnbull was being his bullying self over the time of death. It gave me great pleasure to remove him from my examination room.'

'I bet he didn't take too kindly to being asked to leave.'

Another chuckle. 'He didn't. Threatened to have me removed from the police list of approved examiners. As if such threats could ever influence me.'

Ridpath was always amazed at the single-minded focus of Dr Schofield. The only thing that mattered as far as he was concerned were his clients lying on the table in front of him.

The doctor whispered a few words that Ridpath didn't catch and then slowly folded down the white sheet to reveal the young boy's body.

Ridpath caught his breath. On such a small, frail, thin body, the Y-section looked more horrific than usual. He looked away for a second before forcing himself to look back as Dr Schofield began speaking.

'You're looking at the body of a perfectly healthy seven-year-old boy. Or at least, he was perfectly healthy until somebody put a noose around his neck and strangled him.'

'I don't understand. I thought a noose was used in a hanging?'

'There is some evidence to suggest he was hung before he was strangled.' The doctor produced a long metal pointer. 'See here, the bruising around the neck and jawline close to the ear?'

Ridpath leant forward to look. There was a marked discolouration of the skin. 'I see it...'

'Classic evidence of a hanging. I also looked at both pedicles of the axis vertebra, the ones closest to the head, which show signs of compression. The mechanism of an injury by hanging is forcible hyperextension of the head, usually with distraction of the neck. The weight of the body has sufficient force to cause the fracture. Survival from this fracture is relatively common, as the fracture itself tends to expand the spinal canal at the C2 level. It is not unusual for patients to walk in for treatment and have such a fracture discovered on X-rays. Only if the force of the injury is severe enough that the vertebral body of C2 is dislocated from C3 does the spinal cord become crushed. This was not the case with this child.'

'Could the fracture happen during strangulation?'

'Possibly, but I don't think so. The classic signs of strangulation are also there. There's an abrasion to the front of the neck, there, and evidence of regional venous obstruction in the neck, petechiae in the skin, conjunctival hemorrhages, and a deep internal rupture of the organs of the head and neck. This child also bled from the ears; the veins are obstructed at the level of the stranglehold, but the arteries are still open, allowing the distal capillaries and venules to overfill with blood, and rupture.'

He stepped back from David Carsley's body and looked at it dispassionately. 'If I were to hazard a guess, which as you are well aware I hate to do, I would say this child was hung and then killed by a chokehold or *shime waza*. As practised, illegally I might add, by many police officers seeking to quickly quieten prisoners.'

'So let me get this right. You're saying this boy was both hung and strangled?'

'Didn't you read my report? I thought I made that clear.'

'Yes, Doctor, but I'm trying to understand. Why would a killer do both?'

'I would have thought that is a job for the police to discover?'

'Of course, but...'

'If I were to hazard a guess again – the hanging didn't kill the child so the murderer finished him off with a chokehold.'

'I see...'

'Shall we move on? We have so little time.'

Ridpath nodded.

'I made three other major observations. Here,' he pointed to the boy's mouth, 'there is bruising and a cut on the right upper lip as well as the musculus nasalis. These injuries are usually produced by a punch or slap to the face.'

'And the injuries were not old?'

'Definitely not – recent. They were perimortem.'

Ridpath raised his eyebrows, uncertain what this meant.

The doctor explained. 'Around the time of death. I found some grass seeds lodged in the hair and evidence of insect activity on the feet but nothing anywhere else. I checked the skin and a strong soap had been used to clean it, including the area around the mouth and nose.'

'So you concluded the body had been washed and cleaned to remove any DNA evidence before it was deposited at Chorlton Ees?'

'Correct. Normally, I would expect to see blood from such a cut on the face or lodged in the nostril but there was none. Nor was there any evidence of clothing fibres anywhere on the body.'

'Interesting. It suggests somebody who knows about forensic evidence.'

'Everybody knows the basics of forensics these days, you don't have to be a professional. I call it the CSI effect.'

'It hasn't helped our work.'

'No, but it was inevitable. Fortunately, our killer was unable to remove the toxicological evidence as easily.'

'Your report said there was evidence of triazolam in the bloodstream.'

'Quite a heavy dose. This boy had been heavily sedated before he was murdered. There was also the remnants of a meal – spaghetti and a tomato sauce – in the stomach. The food remains showed evidence of another drug, temazepam. Again, in a significant dose.'

'Our killer laced the food? When did he eat?'

'Our estimate is between eight to twelve hours before death.'

Ridpath nodded, trying to work out a timeline of the abduction in his head.

Schofield carried on. 'And now we come to the most distressing part of the post-mortem. Distressing for me even though I have performed over 1500 previous post-mortems.' The doctor took a deep breath. 'The boy was sexually assaulted multiple times both pre- and post-mortem.'

He reached forward to turn David Carsley onto his front.

Ridpath noticed the boy's hands for the first time, slightly curled inwards with the nails bitten down to the quick. 'I don't need to see, Doctor.'

Schofield stopped and stepped back. 'There is multiple evidence of anal penetration over a period of time.'

Ridpath didn't understand. 'Even before he was kidnapped?'

Schofield shook his head. 'No, I don't think so. There is anal tearing but it occurred sometime in the twenty-four hours after his abduction. Some of the tears had already begun the process of healing before death.'

Ridpath was desperately thinking of a question but couldn't formulate the words. What sort of animal would do this to a young child?

Finally, he decided he had heard enough. 'Can you tell me the time of death?'

'Not accurately. It had been a cold morning even though it was summer. Typical Manchester. The closest I can give you is the same as I told DCI Turnbull. Between four and eight hours before the discovery of the body.'

'So between two a.m. and six a.m.?'

'Correct, but it could have been another hour either way. Time of death is not an exact science. It's the closest I ever come to guesswork and that's why I hate doing it.'

'Thank you, Doctor. Anything else?'

'That covers the main points of my post-mortem.' He snapped his fingers as if remembering something. 'Not in my report but something I noticed later: the boy has bruising on the top of his arm.'

'Done by the killer?'

'Maybe during the abduction. It is much earlier than any other injury on the body.'

Ridpath made a note in his book. 'Finally, Doctor, if you have completed your examination of the child, could I release him back to the family for burial?'

Schofield stared down at the small body in front of him. 'I don't see why not. I'll send the release form to Sophia after my class. How is she, by the way?'

'Fine, I think. To be honest, we haven't seen each other much since my return.'

The doctor nodded as if understanding how work sometimes got in the way of human relationships. 'One last thing, Ridpath, and I don't normally say this. But the man who killed this child, and it was a man, needs to be caught and stopped. You have to catch him before he does it again.'

'You think he will?'

The doctor nodded. 'I'm sure of it.'

Chapter 25

Ridpath left the mortuary desperate to remove the stench of the cleanliness from his nostrils. He was tempted to cadge a cigarette from one of the passers-by, but didn't, walking briskly to let the diesel-tinged air of Manchester clear his lungs.

The image of the boy dwarfed by the stainless steel table stayed with him. The way the fingers curled as if trying to hang on to life.

He shook his head, driving the image from it, alternately tapping his fingers on his shoulders and thinking of his safe place.

He strode down Oxford Road, past the Students' Union and turned left before the museum. He hadn't been in this area for years, not since a school trip had taken him to see the Egyptian mummies. He should bring Eve here one day – she might enjoy all the beetles pinned and stuffed in row upon row of identical wooden cabinets.

They had arranged to meet in Christie's Bistro. Emily came here often but neither Ridpath nor Chrissy knew it even existed. As soon as he stepped through the doors, he understood why. The cafe was set in the middle of an old library, with paintings of famous luminaries, soaring plasterwork ceilings and pristine whitewashed walls, all in a gothic building created in a far less utilitarian age.

Emily was already sat at a table waiting for him. 'I ordered you a latte, Ridpath. I hope that's what you wanted.'

Actually what he wanted was a total nose and lung transplant to get rid of the smell of the mortuary. What he said as he sat down opposite her was, 'Great, exactly what I need.'

'Chrissy messaged. She's going to be late, trying to find somewhere close to park.'

'I know the problem.'

'Should get a bike, it's easier. Just lock it against railings.'

He saw a helmet on the seat next to her and realised she wasn't joking. 'You bike in every day?'

'When I'm working in HQ. Keeps me fit… sort of.'

Ridpath sipped his latte and brought out his notes from last night. 'How did you get on with the responses to the photofit appeal?'

'Still going through them. I've done about half but 3000 is not something you read in a day. Most were followed up and checked. A couple of things cropped up.' She checked her notebook. 'A man, Mr Peter Davies, rang through saying he was in the park that day walking his Alsatian. He gave a number but didn't want to leave an address. Either it was false or the operator took it down incorrectly, but he couldn't be contacted. He's sort of dropped through the net for follow-up.'

'Could be worth checking out. The Alsatian cropped up before.'

'OK, I'll try but Davies is such a common name, might be hard to find him. There's one other thing I've found interesting. One of the new boys was supposed to check it, but he seems to have been busy on something else. A woman walking in Chorlton Ees in the mornings before David Carsley was discovered reported a couple walking together with dogs. I checked the description against that of the man who found the body and it matches.'

'Jon Morgan?'

'That's him.'

'I interviewed him yesterday. He didn't discover the body alone. He was with another woman.'

Emily raised an eyebrow.

'Hence the reluctance to come forward. He's going to ring Turnbull and make a fresh statement this morning.'

'Turnbull will go apeshit.'

'But at least it clears up the mystery woman.' He looked across at Emily. 'You never bought into this Myra Hindley and Ian Brady story, did you?'

She frowned. 'That's newspaper bullshit, but you asked me to look for anomalies and that was one. But it looks like it isn't any more.'

As she finished speaking, Chrissy Wright bustled through the door, using her walking stick to open it, spotted them and waved. 'Hiya, sorry I'm late, not the quickest on my feet at the moment.'

'A coffee, Chrissy?'

'No thanks, never touch the stuff. If I have coffee in the morning, I'm wired for the rest of the day. Not a pretty sight. Like a hamster on speed.'

Emily took the time to explain what she had discovered as Chrissy settled herself down. 'Sounds interesting, you want me to find Mr Davies?'

'Can you?'

'Should be possible. Despite the surname being common, if he was walking his dog in Wythenshawe Park my bet is he lives close to there. I'll start with the area around the park, ringing anybody with the surname Davies, widening the search till I find him. Any other details from the contact report?'

Emily checked her notes. 'A male aged thirty-two, that's all.'

'Perfect. Narrows it down considerably. You can find anybody these days, if you know where to look.'

'Remind me never to get on your wrong side, Chrissy,' said Ridpath.

'I thought you already knew that. Anyway, I went through the HOLMES 2 result again, checked the police database for crimes against children in the last ten years and went over the Sexual Offenders Register, cross-checking it with recent contact reports.'

'And?'

Chrissy frowned. 'It's a nightmare. In the last five years there has been a 75 per cent increase in the number of child sex offences in Lancashire, Merseyside and Cheshire.'

'What about Greater Manchester?'

'We didn't report any figures for the period. The only data I have is for 761 online child sexual abuse offences in 2019–20.'

'Jesus, so many...'

'Why didn't we report any figures?'

Chrissy shrugged her shoulders. 'Perhaps because we were investigating the closure of Operation Augusta?'

Emily coughed. 'I have a friend who worked on that investigation. For some obscure reason, in 2005 senior police prematurely shut down Operation Augusta, an investigation into sexual abuse in children's homes. The report into why this happened was finally published in January 2020, nearly fifteen years later. It wasn't pretty reading. Many of the same men involved in Augusta were charged in the Rochdale grooming scandal in 2013. God only knows how many children could have been spared years of anguish if we had investigated properly earlier.'

'I tried to find the figures for child sexual exploitation for the UK. The only place I found anything was the NSPCC. According to them, last year there were, on average, more than two hundred child sex offences every day. In all, there were 73,518 recorded offences including online grooming, rape, and sexual assault against children in the UK in 2019–20. And those are just the ones that are reported. The tip of the iceberg, I think. Most crimes are not reported either because the family is ashamed or the child themselves keeps it quiet.'

'Jesus,' said Emily.

'I didn't realise it was so many,' added Ridpath.

'According to the latest figures, there were 62,435 people on the Sexual Offenders Register, but it's not up to date, people move and the police have problems keeping track of new addresses. The changes to the probation service by that idiot Grayling didn't help. There were 3,411 of them living in Greater Manchester.'

'So you're saying?'

'All the literature tells us that killers progress. They start young, torturing animals, bullying other children. Most come from broken homes or abusive backgrounds. They move on from minor offences, becoming more and more aggressive as their psychopathy takes hold.'

'So it could be one of the people in the Sexual Offenders Register?' asked Ridpath.

Emily answered him directly. 'But Turnbull checked everyone. It was the first place he looked.'

Ridpath thought of what the doctor had told him that morning. 'We still need to follow up. Can you go over Turnbull's checks, Chrissy?'

'OK, will do. But our perp might not be on the Register.'

'What do you mean?'

'Well, it could be someone who was let off with a caution, given a fine or who simply was never caught. Since the Saville case and the Rochdale grooming scandals, there has been far more awareness of child abuse, but there are still legacy cases we haven't got to. Look at Manchester City, for example: they had a child molester working as one of their youth coaches in the 1990s. He was only discovered when he was caught in Florida.'

'Shit.'

'Or our man has broken the law and was on the Register, but has moved to the area recently and not notified the authorities of a change of address. It's against the law, but who's going to follow up? Not the probation service, and we have enough on our plate dealing with day-to-day crime.'

'I'm beginning to see the problems that Turnbull faced.'

'And he had a team of thirty detectives to do the work. There's only three of us, Ridpath.'

'We can't think like that, Chrissy. We have a job to do…'

'And just three days left to do it,' added Emily.

'Two days, actually. We have to report back on Saturday to Claire Trent.'

Emily rolled her eyes.

'What about HOLMES 2, Chrissy?'

'I rechecked the report. The Liverpool case was the closest to ours in terms of an attack on children. A young boy. Alan McCarthy, abducted on his way to the shops, his body found four hours later about a mile from where he was kidnapped. But the MO was different; he was stabbed and wasn't sexually molested. Plus the Scousers have a suspect who's confessed. A man called Lawrence Scully. He has a history of sexual offences against children. And get this, he's demanding chemical castration.'

'What?' asked Emily. 'I thought we don't do that any more.'

'We don't, but he's still asking for it.'

'Could he have done both crimes?' asked Ridpath.

Chrissy shook her head. 'He has a cast-iron alibi for the dates in question.'

'No alibi is "cast iron".'

'This one is. He was in jail.'

'What for?' Emily cocked her head. 'Offences against children?'

'Got it in one.'

'Jesus.'

'And there's more…'

'Tell me,' said Ridpath, pinching the bridge of his nose.

Chrissy continued. 'Scully was found with a knife in his possession. The knife was plastered with…'

'…Alan McCarthy's DNA.' Ridpath sat back and exhaled. This case was becoming too complicated and he only had two more days left before he had to report to Claire Trent.

In that instant, David Carsley's hands flashed into Ridpath's mind, the nails bitten and the fingers slightly curled like claws.

Perhaps he should have stayed on medical leave.

Chapter 26

Molly Wright was starting to feel exasperated. This story was going nowhere.

She'd contacted her source in MIT and he could tell her nothing except that a new cop had come back from sick leave and may be working on the case.

'May be? Haven't you got anything for me better than a "may be"?'

'He keeps his cards close to his chest, does DI Ridpath. Turnbull hates his guts but somehow Claire Trent has a soft spot for him. The gossip on the street is the two of them may have had a bit of a fling in the past.'

'"A bit of a fling"? Which century are you living in? Are they fucking each other?'

'I don't know. Ridpath recently lost his wife so…'

'I remember the case. Wasn't she shot by some old loony who took her own life?'

'Yeah, that's Ridpath.'

Molly Wright thought for a moment. Was there an angle here? Cop whose wife dies shags boss? Or brave cop back at work to solve child killing case? Perhaps both? She filed it in her brain as a possibility for later.

'Anything else going on with the case?'

'Not a lot. They seem to be running out of ideas. Turnbull has a bee in his bonnet about the father. Keeps trying to get intel from Scotland.'

'What intel?'

'I dunno. He doesn't let me anywhere near it.'

'Find out.'

'I don't know if I can, I'm not—'

'Stop whining and find out. There's a pony in it for you if you get it to me quickly. Enough to keep you in bets for a couple of days at least. But with your luck…'

'I'm on a losing streak at the moment. It'll change soon.'

'That's what they all say. If you want the money, you'd better get your arse in gear.'

She ended the call before he could ask for any dosh for this phone call. She believed you should always keep your informants lean and mean. In this case, leaner and meaner.

The story was starting to cost her money. She didn't know how long she could continue to feed this particular dragon. The Ridpath stuff and the search for intel in Scotland sounded interesting, but it might be a long time before either of them bore fruit.

She checked the weather outside her window. It was one of those days that couldn't make its mind up whether it was the middle of summer or the middle of winter; a grey, remorseful sky, a racy wind and occasional bursts of sunshine lighting up the dreary red brick of the houses opposite.

She dragged herself out of bed and into the toilet, past the empty bottles of Rioja strewn around the floor. Her bladder was fit to bursting.

Maybe she should give it all up and retire to Spain to write the great British novel. At least the plonk would be cheaper and the weather better.

Maybe she should go further south. To Morocco, perhaps, indulge in a downy boy or three.

Maybe.

Maybe.

Maybe.

Was she catching a dose of the maybes from her source?

Maybe.

Chapter 27

'Right, it's a big job, so we need to work smart. Last night I went through the case files and the documents Chrissy downloaded for me. This morning, I met Dr Schofield at the mortuary and he took me through the post-mortem results again.'

'How was that?' asked Emily.

Ridpath ran his fingers through his hair. 'Not great. David Carsley was sexually assaulted and strangled. Schofield thinks the killer will strike again.'

'The same conclusion as our criminal profiler?'

Ridpath nodded. 'We have to stop him.' He opened his notebook, checking his action points from last night. 'From the documents, there was no evidence at the crime scene or DNA on the body, so it means we are left with the witnesses. And because we were swamped by all the calls from the photofit, I think the investigation became inundated with too much information. I want us to go back to basics.'

'I agree,' said Emily.

'We have two crime scenes: the place where David Carsley was kidnapped and the place where the body was found. The closest witness to the kidnapping was Daniel, the boy's brother. He noticed a man talking to David before he disappeared.'

'And we have the photofit,' added Chrissy.

'Right. I want to talk with him again. There may have been something Turnbull missed in his initial questioning.'

Emily sat quietly for a moment before speaking. 'I was with Daniel when he gave the description to the artists. He seemed pretty confident of the man he saw.'

'And since then? How was he in the house when you were there?'

'Quiet, reserved, missing his brother. He didn't like to be alone.' She paused for a moment. 'I think he was blaming himself for his brother's disappearance. You know his dad asked him to look after his brother before they went out to play in the park.'

'What a horrible responsibility for a ten-year-old,' said Chrissy quietly.

Ridpath breathed out. 'I'd like to question him again, see what he says. I can visit the house this afternoon.'

Chrissy was chewing the end of her pen. 'It strikes me...'

'Go on...'

'It strikes me that nobody has really interviewed the other children.'

'What other children?'

'The ones Daniel was playing basketball with in the park.' She took out Daniel's statement. 'See, he says he was playing the game while David was in the playground. He could have been playing basketball on his own but I doubt it. And besides, why not with his little brother?'

'Good point. We need to check out if there were other boys with him. I also want to go and see the park – we can go to the house afterwards and have a chat with Daniel.'

'He's pretty fragile, Ridpath, he's been through a lot.'

'It will be a chat, Emily, not an interrogation.'

'I'll come with you. He knows me and might be more open if I'm with you.'

'Good idea.' Ridpath tapped the second point on his list. 'Chrissy, I want you to check up on the father. Where he used to work, what he's like, his history. Why did they move down from Scotland?'

'It's all in the file, Ridpath, Turnbull already did the work.'

'Go over it again, find out if he missed something. Or if there's anything that's not in the file. I keep wondering why

Turnbull was so keen on interviewing the father last night.' He stopped, remembering something Dr Schofield had said. 'Check up if there have been any complaints by the neighbours or to the local nick. The pathologist said there was bruising on David's upper arm which wasn't recent…'

'You don't think…'

'I don't think anything, Chrissy, but we need to check it out.'

'OK, will do.'

He moved down to the third point. 'This leads me to the mother. I want to go and see her. Find out why she left the family and what she's doing now. It's not common to leave two young kids with the father. Did you meet her, Emily?'

The detective sergeant shook her head. 'Turnbull and one of the new guys handled the interview.'

Chrissy handed over the address. 'You want me to call and arrange a time?'

'Nah, I'll call and arrange to meet her this evening. The fifth area we need to look at is the place where the body was found.'

'Chorlton Ees.'

'Right.' Ridpath scratched his head. 'Why there? Why dump the body there? What's so special about that area?'

'It's out of the way. Not that many people around except a few dog walkers, and lots of cover to hide a body.'

'And yet the body was displayed.' Ridpath opened the case file. '"Arms spread out facing upwards. Like Jesus on a cross." Why go to all the trouble of displaying the body if you don't want it to be found?'

'But the discovery was by accident. The man's dog found it.'

'And now we know he wasn't alone when he discovered it.'

'What's going on in your head, Ridpath?'

'I don't know. I'm looking for anomalies. The body was displayed but hidden. Why? It may be nothing, but we need to check it out.'

'Anything else, Ridpath?'

'Two other things, Emily. Can you check any other CCTV cameras in the area of Wythenshawe Park or Chorlton Ees? Not traffic footage, but any house with security cameras, or a shop or a bank. Anything which might show us something different.'

'It's a big area. You want me to check everything?'

'Start with Wythenshawe Park and the surrounding streets.'

'Wouldn't the local canvas have picked up any CCTV?'

'It should have done, but I don't see any mention of checking for cameras other than those on the roads and the ones in the park.'

'The boy was kidnapped from the park. Why check anywhere else?'

'But we don't know that, Emily. He vanished from the park but we don't know if he was kidnapped from there.'

Emily made a moue with her mouth. 'I'll have a walk around later. See what I can find.'

'Good. Finally, Chrissy, can you get me the name of the SIO on the case in Merseyside? I want to have a chat with him. See if his perp's alibi is as airtight as we think it is. Won't be the first time, we've had crossed wires with Merseyside.'

'And won't be the last,' said Chrissy. 'I'll message you later, Ridpath.'

'Right, are we all clear?'

They both nodded before Emily said, 'You know Turnbull's going to hear about you sniffing around his case, don't you?'

The image of David Carsley's cold body lying on the even colder steel table flashed into Ridpath's mind. 'That's the least of my worries, Emily.' He stood up. 'Let's get going to Wythenshawe. I'll wait for your messages, Chrissy.'

'What about my bike?' said Emily. 'Somebody's bound to nick it if we leave it here.'

Ridpath smiled. 'Nick a copper's bike? They wouldn't dare.'

'They'd nick a Jumbo Jet if it was parked round here,' laughed Chrissy.

'No worries, we'll sling it in the boot of the Vauxhall. If I can fit three burly coppers in there, it can fit a bike.'

Emily didn't ask what three coppers were doing in Ridpath's boot, and he didn't tell her.

Chapter 28

There had been five minutes of silence between them as Ridpath drove from Central Manchester out to Wythenshawe.

The car smelt slightly of oil from Emily's bike jammed into the back seat. They had tried to fit it in the boot but it was too large.

It was Emily who spoke first. 'You know, Turnbull has run this investigation by the book. I've been working on it from the start – I don't think we made any mistakes.'

'Great, it means I'll have nothing to report when I speak to Claire Trent on Saturday.' He signalled left, glancing across at her as he did. 'I'm not out to get Turnbull, I just want to solve the case.'

She laughed. 'He's out to get you.'

'That bad, huh.'

'Worse. I think he blames you for upsetting his first invest-igation as the DCI in charge of the Major Investigation Team. He feels you undermined him and, as long as you're in MIT, you are a challenge to his authority.' She pursed her lips. 'He's not a man used to being challenged.'

'We caught the killer, I thought that's all that mattered.'

'Sometimes, Ridpath, I think you're so naive. How have you survived all these years?'

'By doing my job.'

Silence descended in the car again. Ridpath spoke next. 'How was life in my absence?'

'You mean how was MIT?'

He nodded, staring straight ahead at the road.

'The usual. The grinding boredom of preparing cases for CPS, followed by moments of exhilaration, and then the heartbreak of disappointment as yet another villain gets off through a technicality, or the trickery of a clever barrister. In other words, life as usual in the police. How was...' She hesitated for a moment.

'Go on, if you don't ask now, forever hold your peace and all that.'

She took the plunge. 'How were you?'

He began breathing in and out slowly as he had been taught by Dr Underwood, concentrating on the positive aspects of his breath. 'Not so good at first, after Polly died, I mean. It took me a while to accept she was gone.'

'I thought the force provided bereavement counselling?'

'They do, but you still have to work it out for yourself. The feelings. The guilt.' He paused for a moment, his fingers tapping furiously on the steering wheel. 'And then the doctors diagnosed me with PTSD.'

'As a result of her death?'

He nodded. 'Well, I was in a service apartment, drinking too much and sleeping too little. Eve was at her grandparents' and the treatment hadn't started because of lockdown.'

'Not a great time...'

He laughed ruefully. 'The understatement of the year. Gradually, though, time works and the treatment kicks in, and you use the coping strategies to handle the anxiety.'

'But you're back to normal now?'

'To quote my therapist, "define normal?"'

She laughed again. 'You seem like you're back to your old self.'

'I don't know if I'll ever be my "old self" again – perhaps he died with Polly.' Before Emily Parkinson could ask another question, he jammed on the brakes and pulled up the handbrake. 'We're here.'

They were in a car park in the middle of Wythenshawe Park. Ridpath stepped out of the car, immediately taking in his surroundings.

It was funny to think that here in the middle of one of the largest council estates in Europe was this little bit of the English countryside. Trees waved in the breeze, clouds scudded across the blue sky, a few children were shouting to each other but he couldn't hear their words. A horticultural centre from the old Tatton Estate was on one side – he could just see the tops of the glass greenhouses. On the other was a riding centre and a community farm.

'The playground is this way,' said Emily.

He followed her as she strode off to the right. The car park was open and easy to look around with no surrounding buildings. Had the killer parked here before picking up David Carsley?

There were no CCTV cameras. Why was that? He thought all car parks had them these days.

As if reading his mind, Emily answered, 'No CCTV. We checked with the council, they haven't got round to installing it yet. The cutbacks...'

Her voice trailed off. Cutbacks seemed to be the excuse for everything these days, but he wondered, if this park had been located in a more upmarket area, would the same restrictions apply?

'The park was created from the old Tatton estate when they built the council houses. The old Hall is over there.'

'Wasn't there a fire a few years ago?' He remembered the house from a school trip many years ago when he had been bright-eyed and bushy-tailed. It was an old Tudor mansion, with oddly shaped rooms and beautiful wooden floors. Stepping into one upstairs room was like stepping back into the past.

'Yeah, it was set on fire by somebody off his face. I think they're still repairing the damage. It was due to open this year but hasn't yet.' She threw her arms out. 'The whole park is about 270 acres.'

'Big.'

'I think I walked over every inch of it when we searched the place.'

'You didn't find anything?'

'Lots of stuff, but nothing related to David Carsley.'

They were walking along a path. On their right, Ridpath could see the playground through the trees. The equipment had obviously seen better days. There were swings, a slide and a few other smaller pieces for young kids, but it was all old and careworn, nothing modern at all.

'So David was playing here alone on the day he was abducted?'

'Right.'

Ridpath circled 360 degrees. There were picnic tables on one side and trees surrounded the site. 'Nobody was sitting at those tables?'

'Apparently not. You have to remember it was lunchtime, around one thirty.'

He wondered if the fact it was lunchtime was important but asked, 'And Daniel Carsley, where was he?'

'He was on the basketball court with his friends.' Emily pointed through the trees. 'Over there.'

Ridpath could make out a wire fence and some hoop stands through the trees. 'How could Daniel Carsley see his brother?'

'That's the same question Turnbull asked. The boy said he couldn't see when he was playing, but stopped to have a look for his brother, noticing the man talking to him.'

Ridpath strode out of the playground area towards the basketball court. Even though it wasn't far away, the trees surrounding the location blocked most of the view.

'The only place you can see the playground is from the left-hand corner of the basketball court. Daniel said he looked for his brother, couldn't see him, so he ran back to check.'

'Hmm,' was all that Ridpath answered.

'Look, I know, but we asked him three times and each time his story was consistent. Plus the description of the man was so detailed and it matched a similar description given by another witness of a man hanging round the tennis courts thirty minutes earlier.'

'Right, I've seen enough here. Let's go and see Michael Carsley.'

They walked out of the basketball court, across a field towards the Altrincham Road exit. A man sitting on a mower, his ears covered in large orange noise protectors, was heading towards them. Both Ridpath and Emily Parkinson had to jog to get out of his path.

As he ran in front of the mower, Ridpath flagged it down.

The man slowed and brought the machine to a halt. Ridpath flashed his warrant card, indicating the man should take off his noise protectors.

'Do you mow this park often?'

'What?'

'Do you mow Wythenshawe Park often?'

'About twice a month, we cut a lot of fields.'

'You work for the council?'

'Nah, we're contract, mate.' He pointed to another mower in a distant field. 'Do all over the North West, me and him.'

'Did you mow any of these fields on 21 July, the day of David Carsley's disappearance?'

'The young lad who went missing?'

Ridpath nodded.

'Nah, the police already asked us. We were here the day before, though.'

'Did you see anything unusual? A man hanging around, perhaps?'

'Nah, like I told the police, I just cut the grass. Bloody stuff never stops growing this time of year.'

'Right, thanks for your time.'

As Ridpath and Emily Parkinson walked away, they could hear the engine starting up again and that familiar earthy smell of freshly cut grass assaulted their nostrils.

Emily sneezed. 'Hay fever,' she mumbled.

'What's that?' Ridpath pointed to a group of garishly painted vans parked close to Altrincham Road.

'It's the local fun fair. They've been parking their trucks here for years.'

'In a park?'

'Where else? And before you ask, we interviewed them. There were a couple of lads working on the trucks but they saw nothing.'

'Kids always have an attraction to fairgrounds.'

'That's what Turnbull said. So we checked them out and interviewed them separately. Their stories were identical.'

'So we've got this big, open park, a seven-year-old boy goes missing and nobody saw anything?'

'That about sums it up.'

'Something doesn't smell right, Emily.'

'It's probably the grass,' she said, pointing to the long line of hay across the field. 'Lots of dogs here.'

Chapter 29

Michael Carsley was sitting in exactly the same place as the last time Ridpath had seen him. It was as if he hadn't moved in twenty-four hours. The television was blaring and the curtains were drawn, with only a thin sliver of the summer's day fighting its way into the room.

'Good afternoon, Mr Carsley, can I turn this off?'

Ridpath switched off the TV.

Carsley didn't move his head.

'I'd like to have a chat with you about the day your son went missing?'

'I've already told the police everything I know.' His head didn't move from the now darkened television.

'I am aware you've already given a statement; I wanted to go over some of the details with you.'

Carsley didn't say anything. It was as if Ridpath wasn't there.

'What happened on the morning of your son's disappearance?'

For the first time, the man's head swivelled slowly round to acknowledge Ridpath's presence. Then he looked across to Emily Parkinson.

'Why is he asking me questions? I thought he worked for the coroner?'

'He does. Detective Inspective Ridpath is seconded to the coroner from Greater Manchester Police.'

Carsley frowned. 'Another boaby.'

'What?'

'Boaby. Polis. Policeman.'

Ridpath tried again. 'Mr Carsley, could you answer my question? What happened the morning your son disappeared?'

'It's like I've told you lot again and again.' The voice was a monotone, repeating a story he had told many times before. 'That morning David and Daniel were watching the box, cartoons or something. David had got up first and Daniel later.'

'Where were you?'

'In bed, I was loused, hadn't slept well.'

'What happened next?'

'I heard fighting. They were arguing over the remote. So I got out of bed, went downstairs and gave them both a clip round the ear. They soon stopped fighting, I can tell you. Then I went into the kitchen to make myself a cuppa and have a fag.'

'What time was this?'

'Around eleven o'clock. I made the kids something to eat…'

'What was it?'

'Beans on toast.' He paused for a moment as if remembering something, his eyes staring at nothing. 'David loved his beans on toast.' Then he focused again, turning back to Ridpath. 'Afterwards, Daniel asked if he could go to the park. I said yes as long as he took his brother. They'd been cooped up for so long during lockdown, it was time for them to go out and get some fresh air.'

'So they went to the park?'

'Daniel wasn't too happy taking his little brother along, but he did.'

'Did they go to the park often?' asked Emily.

'Not that often. But I thought it was a bonnie day and they couldn't stay inside all the time, could they? The park is only five minutes away…'

'Across a busy road?'

'Yeah, but Daniel was used to it. He knew how to cross the road safely.'

'What happened next?'

'Well, about an hour later, Daniel came back to see if his brother was at home. I lost the plot with him, he was supposed to look after his wee brother. So I got dressed and we went out to look for him in the park.'

'You searched for about an hour and then reported it to the police?'

'There was a mounted copper in the park, I had a word with him and he reported it in.'

'But you carried on searching?'

There was a long pause. Finally, he said 'Aye,' his voice breaking.

'When the children went to the park, what did you do, Mr Carsley?'

He shrugged his shoulders. 'I sat here watching TV and smoking, like I do every day.'

'What was on?'

'On?'

'The box? Which programmes did you watch?'

He exploded. 'I told the other copper. I don't know what I watched. The box was on but I dinnae remember anything, I was sat here, staring at it.'

'OK, Michael, calm down, DI Ridpath is only asking a few questions.'

'I've had that other bastard here all day yesterday, asking the same bloody questions. What did I watch? When did I watch it? My son's been murdered and all you lot care about is what TV I watched!'

'We're just trying to help you, Michael.'

'You can help me by finding my son's killer. Because, I tell you this, if I find him first I'm going to swing for the bastard. I'll strangle him myself. I don't care if I get put inside for doing it. I'll kill the bastard.'

'What about Daniel if you're inside, Mr Carsley?' Ridpath said softly. 'What would happen to him?'

Michael Carsley seemed to stop for a moment, surprised by the question.

Ridpath followed up. 'I'd like to have a chat with Daniel, if he's around. With your permission, of course.'

Chapter 30

Michael Carsley leant forward, moving for the first time since Ridpath had come into the house, and bellowed through the open door. 'Get your arse down here, Dan.'

A few seconds later a young boy appeared in the doorway. 'What you want, Dad? I'm on my Xbox.'

'This boaby wants to talk to you.' He pointed at Ridpath.

'I've already talked with them a thousand times already.'

'Well, sit yourself down and do it a thousand and one times.'

The boy's shoulders slumped and he lurched into the room, sitting on a chair near the fire.

'Hi Daniel, my name's Ridpath, I'd like to ask you a few questions.'

Michael Carsley stared at the black screen of the television, as if taking no interest in the interview of his son.

'I've already told the police everything I know.'

'Ridpath works for the coroner, Daniel, he's here to help,' said Emily Parkinson, moving to sit next to the young boy.

'DS Parkinson is right, Daniel. I work with Mrs Challinor, the coroner.' Once the detective had settled in next to Daniel Carsley, Ridpath began asking his questions. 'Now what shall I call you? Do you prefer Daniel or Dan?'

'My mum always calls me Daniel, but everybody else says Dan.'

'I know what you mean, my mum always called me Thomas, but I preferred to use my last name. So Dan it is.' He opened his notebook. 'What time did you go to the park?'

The boy shrugged his shoulders. 'I dunno, around one o'clock I guess.'

'What was on TV when you left?'

The boy's eyes drifted upwards and to the right as he thought about the question. 'The news, I think. You know that awful music they play before it starts.'

'On the BBC?'

'I think so.'

'Great. It starts at exactly one p.m. every day so that gives us a pretty accurate time. So, you left the house with your little brother...?'

At the mention of David Carsley, Daniel's head dropped. 'Yeah.'

'What happened next?'

'We walked to the park together.'

'You crossed the main road?'

'Yeah, it's easy, you only have to wait for the green man at the crossing.'

'Good, well done, so what happened then?'

'We went to the playground and played on the swings. Then my mates came with a basketball.'

'What were their names, Daniel?' interrupted Emily Parkinson.

The boy looked quizzical. 'Who?'

'Your mates. The boys you played basketball with?'

'Just friends from school.'

'I guessed that, but what were their names?'

Daniel thought for a moment. 'There was Andy Greene, the Cassidy twins, Alan and Stuart, Mike Murphy, and Fred Simpson, but he didn't stay long.'

'So you went off to play with them?'

'Yeah.'

'Didn't your brother go?'

'He didn't like to play, he was too small.'

'So you went over to play basketball?'

'But I kept checking to see if my brother was OK.'

'How did you do that? The area around the playground has a lot of trees and bushes.'

'I could see him when I was taking shots at the bottom of the court.'

'And you saw him talking to a man?'

'Yeah.'

'What did you do?'

'I ran back to the playground. Dad always tells us not to talk to strangers.'

For the first time, Michael Carsley appeared to notice his son was being interviewed, turning his head away from the television.

'That's good advice. What happened when you approached the man?'

'I told him to leave Dave alone.'

'What did he say?'

'He said he was just chatting. So I said I would call the police if he didn't leave David alone and showed him my mobile phone.'

'You had a mobile phone?' Nobody had mentioned this to Ridpath previously.

'Yeah, Dad gave me one for my birthday.'

'And what did the man do?'

'He scarpered pretty sharpish once he saw the phone.'

'So you then went back to play with your friends?'

'Yeah, I asked Dave to come with me, but he wouldn't.'

'Why not?'

The boy shrugged his shoulder. 'I dunno, don't think he liked my friends.'

'So that was the last time you saw your brother?'

Daniel Carsley frowned, nodded and looked down again.

'When did you realise he was missing?'

'I didn't.'

It was Ridpath's turn to frown.

'I mean, I didn't realise he was missing, I only knew he wasn't there at the playground.'

'When was this?'

'About ten minutes after I spoke to the man. I looked across from the basketball court and couldn't see Dave.'

'So what did you do then?'

'I ran to the playground, but he wasn't there. I shouted his name, again and again and again. Then, me and my friends started looking for him...'

'I thought you ran home to check if he was there first.'

'No, we looked for him, but not for long, then I ran home, but he wasn't there.'

'What time was that?'

'Dunno, can't remember. My dad thinks it was around two o'clock.'

'So you told your dad?'

'Yeah, and we all went out looking for him. I thought he was lost, see.'

'If you thought he was lost, why did you run home?'

'Because he'd done it before. Gone home without telling me.'

'So it wasn't the first time you'd gone to the park with your brother?'

'Nah.'

Ridpath closed his notebook. 'Thanks Dan, that's useful. I've got to go somewhere else now, but I'll come back maybe tomorrow and we can chat again.'

'I'm finished? Can I go back upstairs?'

'Sure, we'll chat soon.'

The boy stood up, almost rushing to get out the door.

'One more thing, Dan.'

The boy stopped and turned back slowly.

'Do you still have your phone?'

'It's upstairs.'

'Can I borrow it? I'll give it back as soon as I can.'

'But I need it to text my friends.'

'Give him the phone, Dan,' growled Michael Carsley without looking away from the flickering television.

Daniel stared at his father, then left the room, stomping upstairs. He returned a minute later with his mobile phone, one of the cheaper Samsungs.

'You'll give it me back?'

'Of course. Emily will make sure I do, won't you, Em?' Ridpath took out an evidence bag and held it open for the boy to put the mobile inside. He then sealed the bag, writing the time and date on it and signing his name.

'Can I go back upstairs, Dad?'

'Yeah,' answered Michael Carsley.

Ridpath stood up. 'I need to go, Mr Carsley, thanks for your time. Did the undertaker call you?'

'Mr Daly? Yeah, he did. Said he'd organise everything.'

'Good, I'll liaise with him and let you know what's going on.'

'When are we going to bury David?'

'I don't know the date yet, but let me get back to the office and I'll let you know.' He looked at the mantlepiece with its photo of the man and his sons in their football shirts. 'Could I take the picture?'

'It's all I have of him.'

'I understand.' Ridpath picked it up and stared at it closely. There was a warmth, a happiness here. 'I know what it's like to grieve over someone you love.'

'Do you? Well, I don't want your understanding, right? Find my wee lad's killer. That's all I want from you.'

'We will, Mr Carsley, I promise.' He put the picture into his jacket pocket. 'I'll see myself out.'

Michael Carsley nodded once and then turned his head back to stare at the television.

As Ridpath was going out of the house, he heard the click of the remote and the sound of voices.

In the darkened room, the television was the only source of light.

Chapter 31

As they walked past the few press still standing opposite the house, a woman approached them.

'Hiya, Emily, got any news for a poor reporter?'

'You know I'm not allowed to speak with you, Molly.'

She eyed Ridpath up and down. 'And who's this tall, strapping young man? Your bit of stuff?'

'This is DI Ridpath… a colleague,' Emily added.

They both carried on walking with Molly Wright trotting along after them.

'Ridpath? The name rings a bell. Wasn't your wife killed? You were a coroner's officer, weren't you?'

'I still am,' mumbled Ridpath, increasing his speed to get away from the woman.

'Have they released the child's body yet? Are you here to arrange the funeral?'

Ridpath stopped dead and turned to talk to her. 'No comment. Don't you have anything better to do than feast on the unhappiness of others?'

'Oh, he is a feisty one. I'm doing my job, DI Ridpath. I wish you lot would do yours. Two weeks since the body was discovered and still the police have nothing?'

He turned and walked away. She followed after him, trying to catch up.

'Any comment, DI Ridpath? Why have GMP not arrested somebody? I've heard you have 3000 replies to your photofit appeal? Care to comment?'

Ridpath carried on walking around the corner with Emily trying to keep up with him. Eventually, the woman gave up and dropped back to rejoin her photographer.

'You shouldn't let her get to you.'

'She's a leech who doesn't care who gets hurt as long as she gets her story. I remember them after Polly died. Parasites...'

'She's dangerous, that one. I'd watch out for her.'

They approached where they had parked the car. 'She's not worth the time of day. The investigation is all that matters.'

For a second, Ridpath went to his safe place. Standing on top of Mam Tor, staring down into Castleton in the Peak District, the wind blowing through his hair and the sun shining on his face. Within seconds, he was feeling calm, collected and focused. 'What did you think of Daniel?' he asked, back on the job.

Emily thought for a moment before answering. 'A good kid, trying to handle a shitty situation. I'm sure he blames himself for his brother's kidnapping. Even worse, I think the father blames him.'

'That's why he's hiding upstairs all the time?'

'I think so. When I was the FLO, it was hard to get him to come out of his room, even to eat.'

'I had the same feeling, but...'

'What is it, Ridpath?'

'Some of his statement didn't ring true.'

'Like?'

'Meeting his friends by accident and they just happened to have a basketball?'

'You think he arranged to meet them?'

'Possibly, I don't know. The encounter with the man didn't feel right either. Almost as if it was scripted.'

'He's told it so many times now, he must know the words off by heart.'

'No, not scripted in that sense, but more expected. As if it was what I wanted him to say...'

'Rather than him saying it. A police training video?'

'Or the sort of safety films they show at schools.' He shook his head, trying to work out what he was trying to say. 'Something didn't feel right about it...'

'I wouldn't talk about feelings, not while Turnbull is in charge. He's only after facts, more facts and even more facts.'

'Facts don't tell the whole story, Emily. We choose the ones we like to confirm our assumptions.'

'What about evidence, Ridpath? Isn't it our job to collect evidence to prove someone's guilt or innocence?'

'True. But sometimes we know somebody is guilty but can't prove it. Or we have the evidence of guilt but can't convince the CPS that it will stand up in a court of law. Or, and this is the worst, we can prove guilt, the CPS wants to go forward, but some clever lawyer gets the guilty off on a technicality. A policeman's lot is not a happy one.'

'Where's that from?'

Years of doing pub quizzes gave him the answer. '*The Pirates of Penzance.*'

She looked at him quizzically.

'Gilbert and Sullivan.'

'Oh, I know him. Didn't he sing "Claire" or something like that?'

Ridpath rolled his eyes. 'I give up, Emily, you're a lost cause. But, before I forget...' He took the bag with the mobile phone out of his pocket. 'Can you get the techies to download the data on this?'

'Which bits of the data?'

'All the text messages and the specific location data for the day of David's disappearance.'

She eyed him suspiciously. 'What are you up to, Ridpath?'

He held out his arms. 'Me? Nothing. But I bet Turnbull didn't look at it.'

'I don't think he did. There was no point. We had the time when David disappeared.'

'But the location data will give us an exact time he went to the park and a time when he returned.'

'Is that important?'

'It might be, I don't know yet.'

'OK, I'll ask one of them to do it.'

'Today, if you can. I'd like to give it him back tomorrow.'

'But that means going back to HQ. I was planning to check out the local area for CCTV now.'

'You can do it later. Your bike will be handy for getting round the streets.'

'I know.'

'I can give you a lift back if you want?'

'The last of the gentlemen, that's you, Ridpath.'

'You're only just discovering the truth, Emily? And I thought you were a smart detective.'

Chapter 32

After dropping Emily Parkinson off at Police HQ, Ridpath drove back out to the Coroner's Court in Stockfield.

The place was quiet. Mrs Challinor was chairing an inquest and the new coroner, Helen Moore, was nowhere to be found. Only Sophia was in the office.

'I didn't think I'd see you today,' she said.

'Thought I'd check in. See if anything was happening.'

'Mrs Challinor will be back shortly. Her inquest should be finished for lunch.'

'Did Dr Schofield get in touch?'

She eyed him suspiciously.

'I only want to know if he released David Carsley's body?'

'Yes, the form is here somewhere.' She searched her desk. 'Here it is. Signed and sealed.'

'Great, can you see that Padraig Daly gets a copy and arranges a time to pick up the body from the morgue? Michael Carsley is in no shape to arrange a funeral, we'll have to do it for him. Can I leave the details with you?'

'No problem.'

As Sophia was speaking, Mrs Challinor came into the office, talking to David Smail. 'If that smarmy barrister interrupts me again when I'm questioning a witness, I'll…'

Ridpath never found out what she was going to do to the solicitor.

'…Ridpath, you're in. We weren't expecting to see you today.'

'It seems nobody was. Can we have a chat?'

'Come into my office.'

He followed her and watched as she arranged the inquest's files neatly on her desk, before sitting down heavily in her chair. 'Been one of those days, Ridpath. Witnesses not turning up, others turning up but not answering questions. And a junior legal counsel confusing a coroner's court with a court of law. How has your day been?'

'Interesting, Mrs Challinor.'

'Is that good or bad?'

'I met with the pathologist this morning.'

'And?'

'The details of the case are disturbing. He thinks we may have a child serial killer operating in Manchester. And so does the criminal profiler.'

She stared at him, her blue eyes, surrounded by the nest of grey curls and alabaster skin, boring into him. 'Do you agree, Ridpath?'

'Yes.'

'What does Claire Trent think?'

'I don't know yet, I haven't briefed her, but...'

'The mere fact she has asked you to look into the investigation tells me she's worried.'

'Exactly, Coroner.'

'What have you discovered?'

'Not a lot. The investigation seems to have been thorough, if a little pedestrian. Charlie Whitworth would have been scouring the streets, not stopping until he found the killer.'

'Policing has changed since DCI Whitworth's day, Ridpath. You of all people should know that. What are your next steps?'

He checked the clock. 'I'm going to interview the wife this evening, find out why she left.'

'Women leave the marital home for many reasons, Ridpath.' Her eyes then seemed to lose focus for a second. 'Mainly, because they start to hate the man they thought was the love of their life.'

'But to leave without her kids?'

'Don't judge, Ridpath.' She then paused for a moment, brushing an imaginary piece of lint from her blotter. 'Let me tell you about myself. When my children were six and four, I left my husband. The man I thought was the kindest, gentlest human being on earth turned out to be a controlling, jealous monster.'

'But you took your children with you?'

She shook her head. 'Not for a year. I had nowhere to go. The house was in his name, everything was in his name. The saving grace was that he loved the children. I set my own house up, starting almost from scratch, and finally, eighteen months later, petitioned for custody of my children. It took another year for them to come back to me. Two and a half years of hell.' She tucked one of the long grey curls behind her ear. 'Children change so much and so quickly at that age.' She glanced across at the picture on her desk of her daughter and her grandchild. 'In many ways, we are still trying to make up for the time we lost.' She sighed. 'My daughter and I had a difficult time together. I blame myself, I should have listened more, understood more, but I didn't. We're still working on our relationship to this day, even though she now has children of her own.'

This was the most open Mrs Challinor had ever been with him about her personal life. 'I'm sorry to hear that,' was all he could mumble in response.

'I tell you this, because you shouldn't judge her. You don't know what she went through and is still going through. I was an educated, professional woman with a good job, great salary and a brand new home and yet it still took me two and a half years to come to terms with what happened and get my children back.'

'I understand, Mrs Challinor.'

'And then to have one of your children abducted and murdered.' She shook her head slowly. 'I don't know what I would have done if it had happened to me.'

Chapter 33

Detective Sergeant Emily Parkinson rode her bike from Police HQ back to Wythenshawe, cursing Ridpath all the way.

She'd seen her friend in the digital department and asked him to do a quick job for her on the data on the mobile phone. He had ummed and ahhed for a minute or two as he always did, before agreeing after being bribed with a promise of a free latte and danish tomorrow morning.

She'd also asked him about the latest scanners and camera detection apps, looking for a way to short-cut her search.

'There are some detectors on the market to pick up spy cameras and microphones, but they don't find everything, and they are best used in a small room. Out on the street, they're pretty useless. I'm afraid you'll have to go old school.'

'Shanks's pony?'

'We used to call it the number 11 bus when I was a kid.'

'Looks like it's back to the beat. Thanks for your help – and I can pick up the phone tomorrow morning?'

'Sure, I may even have downloaded the data by then.' He smiled, to show he was teasing her. A techie type of teasing.

She was going to have to do this the hard way; by eye. Luckily the weather was good and it shouldn't get dark until nearly eight o'clock. But she wasn't walking around the area. At least with the bike, she could cover more ground.

She'd done the long pedal down Princess Road, cars rushing past her, and had finally reached Wythenshawe about forty minutes later, slightly tired but ready to get going.

Ridpath's plan was to try to find CCTV that may have been missed. She felt it was a bit of a stretch. The first thing any investigative team did these days was check for CCTV.

If there was one thing that had changed modern policing in the last ten years, it was the widespread use of security cameras. She'd been on a course which explained that London had a CCTV camera for every 67 people living in the city. Manchester didn't have that many, but there were still a lot of cameras out there.

Turnbull and his team would have picked up the obvious ones, on the lampposts and watching traffic. She had to look for the ones they might have missed. They could be on houses, in banks or shops, even in cars if they were parked in the same place every day.

She brought out her Manchester A–Z. On the map, Princess Parkway, the main road to the airport, was virtually a motorway. It formed a barrier on the west side of Wythenshawe Park. She was sure MIT would have discovered any CCTV on the road or its slipways.

That left the north, east and south sides of the park. Each one had quite a clearly defined housing estate on each side. Her plan was simple; to ride around looking for CCTV, crossing off each road as she completed it. She would then cross-reference the CCTV she saw with the CCTV on the list examined by Turnbull's team and note the differences.

If there were any.

It was going to be painstaking, detailed work, but it was the sort of investigation Emily liked. The nitty-gritty of digging deep and doing a job well.

Emily checked her watch. Four p.m. on the dot. But where to get started?

She checked the map again and decided to begin in the south, where the Carsleys' house was. She had to start somewhere and this was as good a place as any.

Tucking her suit trousers into her socks – mustn't get oil on them – she adjusted her helmet and began to pedal.

She was going to kill Ridpath when she'd finished this.

Chapter 34

Molly Wright had retired to the pub at five o'clock. There was nothing happening at the Carsley house and there was no point keeping a photographer on overtime on the off-chance that Carsley or his son would make an appearance.

It was one of those pubs that had the atmosphere deliberately designed out of it by some interior decorator with a penchant for red velour curtains, fake horse brasses and ugly brown carpets. Even the Stella had more gas in it than usual and actually lived up to its advertising promise of being French and 'reassuringly expensive'.

What a load of bollocks.

It was probably made in Warrington or some other benighted expanse of warehouses, business parks, motorways and megastores. A dormitory town whose sole purpose was to allow its citizens to sleep through their meaningless lives.

She had written reams of stuff praising places like that. The Milton Keynes of this world, garden cities where nothing grew except mould and wife-swapping.

She swallowed the last of her Stella and thought about ordering a bottle of wine but all they had was some cheap Chilean plonk which was better used as paint stripper.

She forced herself to think about the story.

Meeting the Family Liaison Officer, Emily Parkinson, and Ridpath on the street had been a welcome, if short, interruption in the endless boredom of standing outside the Carsley house.

It looked like her source had been correct. Ridpath was somehow involved in the investigation into David Carsley's death. But how?

She hated men like him. So full of themselves and their own self-importance. Men who obviously enjoyed their jobs and looked down on her like a cockroach that had somehow survived a nuclear attack.

All she was doing was providing a necessary service for the punters who liked a bit of a racy read in their morning *Sun* with the cornflakes. She could also do the highbrow stuff as well for *The Times* or *Guardian*. Slightly less risqué reads for the readers of Staines and Ongar with bigger words, longer sentences and at least an attempt at punctuation.

She had been good once.

Extremely good.

Believing in her vocation to educate mankind and reveal the hidden truths of society… The sort of journalism made famous by Harold Evans, *World in Action* and *Panorama*. That was what she grew up on, what she had tried to be when she started.

But they don't tell you in journalism school about the endless grind of it all. Or the fear of working for psychopaths who also called themselves editors. Or the necessity of toeing the party line on every little peccadillo of the bloody owners.

Her mind was wandering today.

Focus, Molly.

Where are you going with this story?

Was it time to give it up?

She looked at her notes from the other night. The word POLICE printed in block letters. Should she interview Ridpath? Give him his fifteen minutes of fame?

Nah, he'd never say yes, his sort never do. Too prissy, too perfect, too police.

But his boss might. Claire Trent. Talk to the engine driver not her cleaning rag.

She might be up for a one-on-one. The sort of in-depth shallow interview the *Guardian* specialised in.

What was the PR girl's name – Sarah whatsherface?

She scrolled through her contacts and found the woman.

'Hi Sarah, it's Molly Wright, I have an absolutely fab idea I'd love to run past you if you have a second.'

Sometimes, it was like taking candy from babies.

Chapter 35

Irene Carsley's flat was number 3 in a large old semi-detached house in Chorlton, not far from where the body of her son had been discovered.

Once, back in Victorian times, this place would have housed the family of a rich merchant or manager of a cotton mill, lavishly decorated and cared for by servants, housekeepers and gardeners.

These days it housed eight flats with paper-thin walls and 'cosy' kitchens.

The area had been transformed into flats for students in the Sixties, each large house subdivided and then subdivided again. The local estate agent described them as 'bijou properties'. It was estate-agent speak for small, cramped and jerry-built.

Ridpath stood in front of a long panel of illuminated doorbells, looking for number 3. He pressed it and almost immediately the security alarm buzzed and a thin reedy voice asked, 'Who is it?' in a broad Scottish accent.

'Hello, Mrs Carsley, it's Ridpath from the Coroner's Office, I rang you earlier.'

Without another word, the security alarm buzzed again and Ridpath heard the click of a lock being released. He pushed open the door and was greeted by a dark, dingy hall with stairs leading upwards. On the right, a pile of letters, circulars and discarded junk mail lay on a stained table. There was a strong smell of frying onions and sizzling spices, as if he had stepped into the kitchens of a restaurant on the Curry Mile.

On his right, the number on the door had a broad '1' painted next to a modern timed light switch. He pushed the button and a single light bulb illuminated the stairs. He climbed upwards, getting to the first landing before the bulb went off and he was in darkness again.

He took out his phone and brought up the flashlight. Using this, he found himself standing next to number 3, knocking loudly on the door.

It was opened by a small thin woman with mousy hair in a fringe that almost covered her eyes. 'Mr Ridpath?'

He showed her his ID. 'Actually, it's Detective Inspector Ridpath.'

'You a copper? I thought you said you were from the Coroner's Office?'

'I am employed by Greater Manchester Police but seconded to work at the Coroner's Office.'

She grunted and undid the security chain, walking away from the door, leaving it open.

Ridpath took that as an invitation to enter.

He pushed open the door and walked into the small, windowless bedsit. On the floor next to the bed, an open suitcase was being used as a wardrobe. Opposite, a two-ring hob sat on a wooden table with a gas bottle on the floor. A sink was doubling as a washbasin and a place for drying clothes. He couldn't see where the toilet was.

She sat on the bed.

He remained standing – there weren't any chairs.

'It's Mrs Irene Carsley, is that correct?'

'No.'

'Sorry?'

'It's Irene McMurdo. I've reverted to my maiden name. I prefer to use that.'

'OK. Can I call you Irene?'

'can call me whatever you want.'

Ridpath could see the woman was trying to put on a brave front, but the fact her hands were shaking gave away the shallowness of the pretence.

'As I said, I'm seconded to the Coroner's Office…'

'You've come about David?' she interrupted.

'I'm sorry for your loss.'

She brushed back the lanky ring of hair from her eyes. For the first time, Ridpath could see the pain in them as they darted from left to right, red-rimmed and swollen.

'Who could do that to him? He was such a bonny, wee bairn. Always happy, never cried.'

'That's what we will find out, Mrs— I mean Ms McMurdo.'

'David wouldn't hurt a thistle. He was such a good little boy.' Her voice began to break.

Sitting there alone on the bed, Ridpath could sense her loneliness, the terrible isolation, but at this moment, he had a job to do. 'When was the last time you saw David?'

The eyes stopped moving for a second as she thought. 'About a week ago. I used to send them a text and meet them in the park. I couldn't go back to the house, he would have killed me.'

'Who would have killed you?'

'Michael, who else? That's why I left. I couldnae stand it any more.'

Ridpath would circle back to that later. For now, he wanted to stay focused. 'You didn't text that day?'

She shook her head. 'I was at work, I couldn't go that day.'

He took out his notebook. 'Where do you work?'

'At Greggs.' She laughed as if remembering something. 'Daniel and David always joked that I smelt like a sausage roll.' The voice trailed away and she stared into the distance.

'Daniel, what's he like?'

'Loves his sports, does Daniel. Not one for his learning but loves his football and his basketball. He plays that a lot, tall for his age.' Then she looked at him directly for the first time. 'I

had to leave them both, though. I couldnae take it any longer.'
She repeated the last line like a mantra.

'Mr Carsley?'

She nodded. 'We were rowing all the time.'

'What about?'

'Money. Always money. He was on a zero-hours contract at the warehouse so we never knew whether he would be working or not. And then he was laid off right at the beginning of the lockdown. In early April, I packed my case and I left...' She began to weep silently, '...leaving the boys behind. I'll never see them again.' She lifted her head to stare at him again. 'Why didn't he take me instead of David?'

Survivor guilt, Ridpath understood it so well. You were left behind all alone when they died, like standing on a platform when a train pulls out of the station, knowing you will never see somebody ever again.

'Have you been to see a counsellor, Irene?'

She shook her head. 'I've seen my GP, he gave me some tablets. Can't afford counsellors. And anyway, how are they going to help me? It's my fault all this happened. If I'd been there...' Once again, her voice trailed.

'They can help you understand and cope with this difficult time. Here's my card, if you give me your phone number, I'll message you some free contacts who will be able to give you advice and counselling.'

She took the card but didn't reach for her phone. Instead she seemed to be staring off into the distance again.

Ridpath followed her eyes. A picture of the two brothers was on the table next to the sink. There was nothing else there.

Ridpath had to do his job. 'On the day that David disappeared, Irene, where were you?'

'That's what the other copper asked.'

'Who?'

'ull, he said his name was, accused me of kidnapping
'dren. Can you imagine? He said I'd kidnapped

'Sometimes, we have to ask questions, it's just part of the job.'

'But to accuse me of kidnapping and killing my own son?'

Ridpath couldn't justify Turnbull's questions so he didn't try. 'You haven't told me yet, where were you at about 1.30 p.m. on 21 July?'

'Where I always am at that time. At work in Greggs.'

'Can anybody confirm that?'

'Well, there's my manager and Doris who I work with, plus a couple of hundred customers I served. It's our busiest time and there's a construction site next door. Is that enough for you? It was for the other polis.'

'Sorry, we have to ask.' He closed his notebook. 'Thank you for your time, Ms McMurdo. Would you like me to get the undertaker to contact you regarding David's funeral?'

She suddenly became extremely frightened, her bottom lip trembling as she spoke. 'I couldn't go, he'd be there.'

'Don't worry, we could make arrangements to ensure you were protected.'

'You don't understand, he'd see me.'

'Who'd see you?'

'Michael.'

'But we'd make sure you were protected. I promise he wouldn't be able to touch you.'

'You don't understand…'

'What don't I understand?'

'He's evil, evil.'

Chapter 36

A little over three hours later and Emily was done.

By the time she cycled back to Police HQ, her hands were stiff, her legs were knackered and her bike had developed a slow puncture. She would have to leave it there for the night and grab a cab home.

Nobody was going to nick her bike at Manchester's Police HQ, were they? She'd better lock it up securely, just in case.

At least now, the roads around Wythenshawe Park on her Manchester A–Z were neatly coloured in purple with the positions of possible CCTV locations marked on the map in red. Luckily the area was mainly residential, with only a few shopping areas or restaurants. And being a former council estate, it still wasn't too wealthy, so CCTV on houses wasn't so common. Still, she now had a list of fourteen cameras on retail shops and a school, plus six cameras placed on the outside walls of houses. She would concentrate on the shops where she had seen CCTV, before checking the houses.

Back on the MIT floor, Chrissy was still at her desk, as were a few of the other detectives. Turnbull wasn't there, though.

'Hiya, Chrissy, still here?'

The police research officer leant forward and whispered, 'Still doing Ridpath's stuff. Why are you here?'

'The same. What's the file number for the list of CCTV cameras checked in the investigation?'

'I'll dig it out and send it to you.'

Emily Parkinson returned to her desk, taking off her jacket and cracking her knuckles. The building air con was off and the room had that stale smell of unwashed policeman.

She switched on her computer and logged on. Chrissy had already sent her the file number, so she searched for it on the server, pulling it up.

Turnbull's team had been diligent. They had used the house-to-house teams to log any CCTV but had only reviewed the main cameras on the roads and some of the cameras on the shops.

She checked the list against her log of cameras and found they'd missed an ATM in a convenience store, a camera in a chippy and one of the school's cameras, and they hadn't picked up any of the house cameras. Perhaps they were briefed to ignore those.

She heard a cough as a shadow arched over her.

It was Turnbull. What was he doing here this late?

She clicked off the page she was looking at and closed the A–Z as he walked round to her side of the desk.

'Still here, Emily? Claire Trent has you working late.'

'Nearly finished, boss. It's real no-brainer stuff. Tedious.'

She crossed her fingers, hoping he wouldn't look at her screen.

'Nothing is tedious if it helps solve a crime. What are you working on?'

He leant in to check her screen. As he did, she could smell his eau de cologne – it was a heavy, woody smell, like the air after bonfire night.

Luckily, her screen now displayed a long list of map coordinates and numbers.

'She's got me logging CCTV locations, boss. She's been asked to provide an up-to-date assessment for the ACC.'

He stretched his neck, turning his head as he did so. 'You're right, it is tedious. You'd better be off home, though, it's been a long day.'

'Just going, boss,' she said, logging off her computer.

'You need to let me know what you're working on in future, Emily. I checked the log sheets and there's nothing down.'

'Sorry, boss, forgot to do the time sheet.'

'Don't forget to do them, they're important. They allow us to see which detectives are busy and which ones are no longer needed in the organisation. They are telling me we're overstaffed at the moment.'

'Who's they, boss?'

He pointed up towards the ceiling. 'Always looking for savings, aren't they. So do let me know what you're doing, won't you?'

'Of course,' she said brightly.

He turned and sauntered back to the office.

The man was a total arse, thought Emily, but an arse who held her future in his hands. 'I hope Ridpath knows what he's doing,' she said out loud.

Chapter 37

After interviewing Irene McMurdo, Ridpath returned home to his empty house. Polly was nowhere to be seen. Or heard. Or felt.

He made himself a sandwich and sat down to FaceTime Eve.

'Hiya, Dad,' she whispered.

'Sorry I missed you last night, I was working.'

'I guessed,' she whispered again.

'Can you speak up? I can hardly hear you.'

'I don't want Paw Paw to hear. She thinks I'm asleep.'

Ridpath checked the clock. Where had the time gone?

He had walked the streets after the interview, going over the case again and again in his mind, her final words echoing in his head. *'He's evil, evil.'*

'I'll call you tomorrow.'

'No, no… Dad, let's talk now, she won't mind.' A pause while she checked her bedroom door. 'I got your message last night. Sounds like you're busy.'

'I am. This case, it's full of problems.'

'I know you can't tell me, but I hope you find him, the man who did it. I spoke with my friends and they're all scared.'

'Tell them to be careful at the moment. Don't talk to strangers and definitely don't accept lifts from strangers. And always stick together, don't go off on your own.'

'You sound worried, Dad.'

Ridpath thought of the criminal profiler's report. 'Just be careful, OK?'

'Will do, I'll tell my friends. Have you thought about what we talked about?'

Ridpath tried to remember. 'Yes,' he answered noncommittally.

'And?'

'And I need more time to think.'

'Dad, I need to move back home soon. Granny is driving me crazy. She wouldn't let me go out tonight to meet my friends. All she says is "Bad men, bad men", over and over again. I can't take it any more.'

'You can come home soon, dear, as soon as I finish this case.'

'You promise?'

Ridpath closed his eyes. Could he promise his daughter? Or would he let her down again? 'I promise,' he finally said.

A deep, commanding voice from the screen. Eve raised her head and spoke Cantonese. 'Ho lah, ho lah. Ngo jiu fan gau lah.'

He always loved it that his daughter could switch languages so easily.

'I have to go to sleep now, Dad, orders from the Granny Dragon.'

'OK, sleep tight, sweet pea.'

'Remember your promise, Dad. When the case is over, I can move to live with you.'

'I remember, Eve. Sleep well and take care.'

The screen faded to black.

Ridpath was left alone in the apartment. On the wall above the television a clock ticked loudly, counting down the hours. Outside the window, Manchester was quiet as the last rays of summer sank beneath the rooftops.

Ridpath rubbed his eyes. He knew he couldn't break his promise to her again.

Not again.

Chapter 38

He wanted to go hunting again.

He needed to go hunting again.

They were talking to him, the voices from the cellar.

It was time to hurt the boys again.

He hummed his little ditty as he prepared his mother's cocoa, adding the diazepam to sweeten it.

One day soon, she could sleep forever.

Sleeping Beauty or Sleeping Ugly?

He knew which he would pick.

On the Fourth Day

Friday, August 7

Chapter 39

They met at the Coroner's Court the following morning.

Chrissy was late as usual, but still wearing her City scarf, while Emily Parkinson had used her own car to drive to Stockfield. Her aching legs couldn't pedal another yard.

'Right, Emily, why don't you start?'

'I biked around the area near the park looking for CCTV and found quite a lot. I then cross-referenced the locations with those already checked by Turnbull's team...'

'And?'

'There are a few his team didn't find. I'll visit them after this meeting.'

'Great. We need some CCTV, Em.'

'The techies are working on Daniel's phone to give us location timings. They should get back to me soon.'

'Even better, well done.'

'You owe me a new pair of calves, Ridpath.'

'Sorry, but it had to be done. Did you check the interviews with the fairground people yet?'

'Sorry, no time, I'll do it when I go back to HQ.'

Ridpath nodded and thought for a moment before saying, 'Yesterday, we had a chat with Michael Carsley and the boy, Daniel. It strikes me there was something they were both hiding.'

'What do you think it was?' asked Chrissy.

'I don't know, but Mrs Carsley – Irene McMurdo as she calls herself now – was scared of Carsley. So scared she didn't want to go to her own child's funeral. Chrissy, did you check up on him? Anything in his past.'

'I got onto a friend at Police Scotland. Apparently, three years ago, Carsley was charged with assaulting his line manager at a warehouse in Falkirk. Eventually, the line manager withdrew the complaint and the Scottish Procurator Fiscal decided not to press ahead with the court case.'

'Wasn't that before the family moved to Manchester?'

'It was. Hang on, there's more. Two incidents of police being called to the Carsleys' on account of domestics. Neighbours filed a complaint about noise. When the police got there they both accused each other of assault. Nobody was arrested but Michael Carsley was cautioned.'

'So let me get this straight, both complained about each other?'

'That seems to be it. He was issued with a formal warning over his behaviour the second time.'

'Sounds like there was a pretty toxic atmosphere in that household,' said Emily.

'What a place for kids to grow up.'

Ridpath remembered Mrs Challinor's words about not judging a situation until he knew everything. 'We need to find out more, Chrissy. See if you can talk to any of the coppers involved in the call-out.'

'They probably won't remember, Ridpath.'

'Have a go anyway.'

Chrissie made a note on her to-do list.

'As I said, I met Mrs Carsley last night.'

'How is she?'

'Fragile. Scared. Guilt-ridden. Blaming herself for what happened to her son. An emotion not helped by her interview with Turnbull.'

'I know the feeling,' said Emily. 'Is she at risk?'

'I don't know, but she needs help.'

'When I was the FLO, I met the social worker looking after the family. I'll give her a head's up.'

'Good,' Ridpath let out a long sigh, 'but not a lot of progress on my end, I'm afraid. After this meeting, I want to go to Chorlton Ees and check out the area where the body was deposited. There's a reason David Carsley was left in that particular area, we just don't know what it is yet.'

'I don't think Turnbull is even asking himself the question,' said Chrissy. 'I went to the case briefing yesterday. They're stuck and lacking ideas. They've got nothing at the moment. Everything has turned into a dead end. The only thing new is the witness, Jon Morgan, told him there was somebody else with him when he discovered the body.'

'Shirley Burgess.'

'How did you know? Turnbull's spitting nails, ready to throw the book at him, but I don't think he will. Too much at stake, not least to Turnbull's reputation. So now the mysterious woman is no longer part of the investigation and they have nothing.'

'It makes our work even more important,' said Ridpath. 'How did you get on, Chrissy?'

'Other than checking up on the Carsleys in Scotland, I found your Peter Davies. He's a lorry driver who went away to Poland on the day of the abduction. I checked with Customs and Excise and they confirmed he passed through Dover on the 21 July. He's back tomorrow so I left a message asking him to go to Wythenshawe police station and make a statement.'

'He's not our killer?' asked Emily.

Chrissy shook her head. 'Not according to Customs and Excise.'

Ridpath interrupted. 'How did you get on with Liverpool?'

'I called them and talked with the SIO on the murder of the boy. He's still convinced they've got the killer in custody, but he sent me over the case file and the autopsy report. It confirms the MO was different, Ridpath.'

'OK, Chrissy, I'll read them both.'

She passed over the files.

'Great work, Chrissy.'

'I aim to please.'

A knock on the door, followed by another slightly louder. Sophia was standing in the doorway. 'That was a friend of yours, Harry Makepeace, on the phone, Ridpath. I told him you were in a meeting, so he said to give you this message as soon as you were free.'

'Thanks, Sophia, what was the message?'

'It's pretty short.' She read from a note: '"I know you're up to something so I thought I'd let you know. Turnbull is planning to take Michael Carsley into custody at four o'clock this afternoon. He'll be taken to Wythenshawe police station to be interviewed prior to charges being laid."'

Chapter 40

Ridpath decided it was more important to continue the investigation than get involved in Turnbull's stupidities.

'There's no evidence of his involvement in his son's abduction. The whole idea is preposterous – Turnbull is fishing, hoping to put pressure on and get a confession.' Emily was incensed.

'We need to stay focused, continue our investigation, ignore Turnbull.'

Emily Parkinson shook her head. 'They are getting desperate. There are no other suspects so they're going for the ones nearest at hand.'

'Most murders are committed by close relatives or neighbours.'

'But for Michael Carsley to be the killer, it would mean he had sexually assaulted his own son.'

'It's a good motive for a murder.'

'What?'

'Cover up a crime. Perhaps David threatened to report him.'

'No way, Ridpath, I'm not buying it.'

'You don't have to. It's CPS and Claire Trent that Turnbull has to convince.'

They were standing in front of their respective cars. 'Let's concentrate on what we're doing. Sod Turnbull. You leaving your car here?'

'No chance. I'm not getting stuck like yesterday.'

Ridpath shrugged his shoulders innocently. 'You'd better follow me then.'

They split up to go to their separate cars. Emily had just started the engine when she received a call from Ridpath.

'I'm not sharing a car.'

'It's not that. I entered Chorlton Ees into the satnav.'

'So? You can follow me if you don't know the way.'

'It's only giving me two places to park, both south of the river.'

'Where?'

'Sale Water Park and a pub, Jackson's Boat.'

'There are no places north of the river. It's only on-street parking.'

'Follow me, let's check them out.'

Five minutes later they were both exiting the M60 onto Rifle Road, leading to the car park at Sale Water Park. The area was almost rural, with trees on either side of the lane and no houses. On the right, the tram line from the airport into the city centre ran parallel to the road. They stopped in front of the entrance and both of them got out of their cars.

The car park was large, with a camera filming the number plate of every car that entered. Signs pointed in the direction of the man-made lake and a boathouse. A few cars were parked in the bays closest to the lake but, other than that, it was quiet.

'This is too far away, Ridpath.' Emily pointed towards the north. 'If he parked here, he would have had to carry the body across the river to Chorlton Ees. It's a walk of nearly a mile. And he's not going to take the park-and-ride, is he?'

'I agree. You'd better request the footage anyway, Emily.'

As they stood there, a tram stopped at the station for a minute before accelerating quickly towards Central Manchester. Inside, a few lonely souls stared out of the windows, looking like mannequins in a shop window.

'The next parking area is down Rifle Road, in a pub beside the Mersey called Jackson's Boat.' Ridpath got back inside his car, driving down the road followed by Emily. A minute later they reached the end of a cul-de-sac, fronting on the Mersey. Ridpath turned left and parked beside the pub.

'Chorlton Ees is across that bridge and to the left,' said Emily, winding down her window. Even though it was summer, there was a bitter wind racing down the river. She shivered.

'How far?'

'I'd guess about half a mile. Still a long way to walk.'

'But if you were only carrying a child's body? Not too difficult. Plus nobody would be around early in the morning.'

'There's that, though.' Emily pointed upwards to a security camera on the wall of the pub, looking directly down into the car park.

'Good. On our way back, we'll ask the landlord for the footage.'

'Where are we going now?'

'To walk to Chorlton Ees.'

Ridpath strode towards the pedestrian bridge over the Mersey. It was only wide enough for two people and painted an industrial green. Emily followed, trying to keep up with him, pulling on her coat and feeling the ache in her calves from yesterday's cycling.

They reached the other side and came to a concrete path leading in two ways. The signpost had directions but Ridpath preferred to ask Emily, 'Which way?'

She pointed left. 'Chorlton Ees is that way. This path goes towards Didsbury.'

'You know the area well?'

'I used to go running round here. It can be a bit muddy after the rain but as you can see, it's quiet and never too busy.'

Ridpath looked around. It was peaceful. The gentle bubbling of water came from the River Mersey on his left, at the bottom of two high, steep banks. A few birds sang in the trees to the right but the whole area was devoid of people even though it was nearly one o'clock. 'Does it ever get busy?'

'Not really. At weekends, there are more people. Sunday afternoons there might be a crowd at the pub who go for a walk after lunch. But weekdays it's quiet, with a few occasional dog walkers.'

Ridpath strode along the path as it wound beside the Mersey until he reached a flight of steps leading down to a path through a water meadow.

'Chorlton Ees Nature Park is over there,' Emily said.

'Where was the body found?'

'In the trees to the right of the path.' She pointed down a bare, earthen track about 100 yards away with a large clump of trees off to one side.

Ridpath started walking with Emily trailing after him. He spotted the police tape easily, the fluorescent red and white clear against the green foliage.

'Not far from the path.'

'Slightly over twenty meters, according to the CSIs.'

'But far enough to remain undiscovered for a long time.'

'If the dogs hadn't spotted it that morning.'

Ridpath looked all around him, doing a 360-degree turn. 'Where did Turnbull set up his operation?'

'Back in Chorlton, on the green.'

'And where did the man who discovered the body park?'

'Near a school, also near the green over there, about 300 meters away.'

'Did Turnbull search south of the river?'

Emily shook her head. 'I don't think so. The search was concentrated in Chorlton. He saw the river as a boundary.'

'A natural assumption, but as we can see, it's not too far to walk. We did it in six minutes. We'd better check out the footage from the pub.'

'I'll ask the landlord.'

'Can you also find out when the trams start running?'

'Why?'

'If I remember from one of my other cases, they have a camera in the cab to film in case there is an accident. You never know, it might have picked up something.'

'OK, I'll check them out.'

Ridpath ran his fingers through his thinning hair. 'Coming here has told me one thing, though. The killer was the same as you, Emily.'

She frowned. 'What do you mean?'

'He's local, a runner maybe. Somebody who knows this area well. He hadn't just come from Scotland.'

Chapter 41

After they walked back to Jackson's Boat, Ridpath returned to the Coroner's Office, while Emily stayed to contact the landlord.

'Sorry,' he said, 'bloody thing hasn't worked for two years, never got around to replacing it.'

'Do you have any other cameras?'

'There's one in the bar.'

'Does that one work?'

He shrugged his shoulders. 'Sometimes.'

She checked it out. It didn't give any view onto the car park. 'Thanks a bundle,' she said sarcastically.

Getting back in her car, she drove to Wythenshawe to find the places where she had spotted CCTV yesterday.

The first shop said their camera was only a box with nothing in it. 'It's a deterrent, love, nothing actually works.'

'Does it deter thieves?'

'Not really. We were broken into last month.'

She left him with a suggestion. 'Perhaps if it was a real camera it would be more of a deterrent?'

'Nothing to do with me, love, I just work here.'

'Give me your name and address anyway.'

'Why?'

'In case we need to contact you. I'll send one of our security consultants to have a chat with you.'

'Don't bother. Like I said, I just work here.' He gave her his name anyway.

The second camera was working but the hard drive on which the images was stored wasn't. 'Give it to me anyway. Perhaps our techies can get something from it.'

'But if I give it to you, how do I record anything?'

'You're not recording anything now, are you? We might be able to get it working for you.'

'For free?'

'Part of GMP's customer service.'

'Great,' he said, handing it over.

The third was an ATM in the side of a convenience store. She went inside and found a man standing behind the counter. She flashed her warrant card and said, 'I'd like to see the footage from the ATM's camera.'

'Nowt to do with me. I get the rent for it being in my shop, plus it's a service for the customers.'

'So you've never looked at it?'

He shrugged his shoulders. 'Why would I?'

Why indeed? she thought. 'Do you own this place?'

The man shook his head. 'Rent it. The owner lives in Spain. Went for a couple of weeks and decided never to come back.'

Emily looked around the pokey shop. 'Can't say I blame him. And your name is…?'

'Matthew, Matthew Oram.'

'You live here?'

'Not far away, in Sharston.'

She took down the address. 'How do I get hold of the footage?'

Matthew Oram shrugged his shoulders. 'I dunno. There's a customer service number next to the ATM, you could call that.'

Emily walked outside to the ATM. Above the hole in the wall was a small plaque with a number in case the ATM wasn't working. She rang it and reached a call centre somewhere in India.

'I'm ringing about an ATM at a convenience store in Wythenshawe.'

'What's the machine number?' a bored voice said on the other end of the phone.

Emily looked everywhere but couldn't see anything. 'What machine number?'

The voice became even more bored. 'There's a code number on the top right of the machine.'

Emily checked and there it was, almost indistinct. 'It's 4768930 – 423.'

'OK, it's one of the older machines. What seems to be the problem?'

'This is DS Emily Parkinson of Greater Manchester Police, I'd like to access the CCTV camera next to the machine.'

'I don't think it's possible.'

'You don't understand, this is a murder enquiry and I need to access the footage on the camera.'

'I'll talk to my supervisor.'

Emily waited on the phone for five minutes, listening to some inane voice crooning 'My Way'.

Finally, the same person came back on the phone. 'I've spoken to my advisor. Accessing the camera is not possible. It's sealed.'

'I know it's sealed – I need to access the hard drive where the images are stored.'

'I'll have to speak to my supervisor.'

Again, a wait, shorter this time, but not much.

'Accessing the hard drive is not possible, it's sealed.'

'Can I speak to your supervisor?'

'Let me talk to my supervisor.'

Emily mouthed the words before the man had finished saying them. A minute later a woman came on the phone. 'Hello, how can I help?'

Emily went through the whole rigmarole again, desperately trying to keep the impatience from her voice. After being reminded that the unit was sealed for the fourth time, she had a brainwave, remembering a piece of advice from her dad. '*When*

dealing with jobsworths always ask them what the company policy is.'
She formulated the question in her mind. 'What is the company
policy for accessing ATMs with broken cameras?'

'Let me check the manual.' Five minutes later: 'We're
supposed to refer that information to our security department
in England.'

She punched the air. 'Can I have that telephone number?'

'Certainly, just a minute.' The supervisor seemed inordin-
ately happy to pass her onto somebody else. She came back ten
seconds later. 'The number is in the UK.'

Emily wrote it down, dialling as soon as she had rung off
from India. She was immediately put through to the head of
security, Brian Carter.

'My name is DS Emily Parkinson of Greater Manchester
Police, I'd like the footage from one of your security cameras,
number 4768930 – 423.'

'Why do you need it?'

She rolled her eyes. This was becoming annoying. 'It could
provide useful information for an investigation… a murder
investigation,' she added.

'No problem.'

'What?'

'No problem. What was the number again?'

'The camera is in a convenience store in Wythenshawe,
number 4768930 – 423.'

'OK. What do you need?'

'Footage from two weeks ago – 21 July, from one to two
p.m. On second thoughts, you'd better give me the whole day,
just in case.'

'OK. It's one of the older machines with a separate camera.
I'll download it from the hard drive and send you a link if you
give me your address. It's going to be a big file, so I'll compress
it and send it in different packets.'

Emily gave him her work email.

'It's probably easier if I send it direct to your techies, otherwise it might get stuck in your server.'

'I don't have their email now as I'm at the convenience store.'

'OK, I'll send you my email and you can forward me the address later.'

'That sounds too easy.'

'I used to be a copper myself. We get lots of enquiries for CCTV footage from the ATMs, I'm afraid it's not the best quality and the cameras are fixed.'

'Well, it's a long shot for us but if you don't look, you don't find.'

'You sound like my ex-boss. Good luck with the investigation.'

The phone clicked off.

Finally something was going right. Now she had to convince the techies to look at it without letting Turnbull know.

She crossed her fingers. Easier said than done.

Chapter 42

Ridpath met the new assistant coroner, Helen Moore, as he was going into the Coroner's Office and she was coming out.

'Hi there, I wanted to have a chat since our meeting, but I haven't seen you around much.'

'I'm on secondment from GMP, and still have to do work there. How are you settling in?'

'Not bad,' she smiled and leant in towards him, 'but between you, me and the lamppost, Mrs Challinor scares me a little, she's so stern. Does she ever let her hair down?'

'I'm sure she does, but not when she's at work.' He pointed up the steps. 'I need to get in, I'm late again.'

'I'm off for a coffee, do you want to come for one?'

'Perhaps another time, Helen, I really need to go in.'

'OK, no worries – but all work and no play makes Tom an awfully dull boy.'

Ridpath climbed the steps to the office. Was she flirting with him? Surely somebody must have told her about Polly? He shook his head. The last thing he needed at the moment was an entanglement.

Sophia was waiting for him. 'The man of my dreams… actually more like nightmares. We have a shitload of work to get through, Ridpath.'

'Great, set it up, Sophia, I'll have a quick chat with Mrs Challinor.'

He knocked on the office door and heard a loud 'Come.'

Mrs Challinor was in her usual position; sat at her desk, poring over a case file. 'Ah, Ridpath, the man I want to see.'

'I seem to be in demand at the moment.'

'I wanted to ask you how the investigation is going? You're due to report back to Claire Trent tomorrow?'

'That's why I wanted to update you. Our client, Michael Carsley, is going to be taken into custody for questioning.'

Her eyebrows rose, touching her grey hair. 'Really? I was told this morning that the undertaker had already removed the body from the mortuary and taken it back to his funeral home.'

'He's not been charged with anything yet, but apparently there are anomalies in his statement.'

'You've met the man, Ridpath, do you think he murdered his own son?'

He shook his head. 'I don't think so. There's something not right there. The pathologist found bruising on the boy's arms and the mother is scared of even meeting Michael Carsley, but I don't think he murdered the boy.'

'Will he be charged?'

'I don't know. There has to be enough evidence to convince the Crown Prosecution Service. I don't think Turnbull has the evidence.'

'Why interview Carsley, then?'

'It's a fishing trip. A chance to question Carsley at length, put pressure on him. They can hold him for twenty-four hours before he has to be released.'

'When's the funeral?'

'I don't know.'

'And what happened to the other son, Daniel Carsley?'

'I don't know that either, Coroner. I presume he has been taken into care by the local council. He's a vulnerable child.'

Mrs Challinor's face hardened. 'My agreement with Claire Trent was that you investigating this case would not jeopardise your work with our clients, nor would it compromise your commitment to represent the interests of the family in this difficult time for them…'

'I don't think that's fair, Coroner, I—'

She held her hand up to prevent his speaking. 'I honestly don't care what you think is fair, Ridpath. Your job here is to represent the interests of the dead and their relatives. Remember the manual, "to be an advocate for the dead to safeguard the living."'

'You don't need to remind me, Mrs Challinor.'

She stared at him unblinking. 'So do you think you are doing your job?'

'Yes,' he answered firmly. 'I need to make sure no other child suffers the fate of David Carsley. I can only do it by finding the boy's killer before he kills again.'

'But the difference between the Coroner's Office and the police is stark, Ridpath, and you know this. We don't chase convictions, we don't chase criminals, we don't chase promotions. We simply represent the families and we look for the truth. Who died? When did they die? How did they die? Who was responsible? That's our remit. Nothing more, nothing less.' She paused for a moment. 'You don't know what's happening with a vulnerable family and their child. If your investigation is getting in the way of doing your job, let me know.'

'The investigation is part of the job, Mrs Challinor. If I don't find out who did this, other children will suffer. This man will strike again, of that I am sure.'

She licked her lips and softened her tone. 'I understand the guilt you are feeling since the death of Polly...'

'You don't understand at all, Mrs Challinor.'

'Let me finish.'

He nodded.

'I'm willing to make some allowances, but your work with GMP must not be to the detriment of the standards of this office. I wonder if by investigating this case and also being the coroner's officer on it, you have compromised your position.'

'I disagree, Coroner,' Ridpath said firmly. 'In fact, I believe understanding the case has helped me do my job better.'

'How?'

Ridpath thought. 'I met Mrs Carsley, whom I wouldn't have known otherwise, and involved her in her own son's funeral. And I am sure Michael Carsley is innocent despite what others might think.'

'Have you become too emotionally involved in the case, Ridpath? We do our job best when we are dispassionate.'

'I am dispassionate about evidence but not about the victims of crime, particularly when those victims are seven years old.'

Mrs Challinor sat back in her chair. 'I want you to be on top of all our cases and inquests, Ridpath. No excuses, is that clear?'

'No excuses. Yes, Coroner.'

Her tone softened. 'To that end, I propose we postpone your official return to this office until next Monday. It would give you time to finish your investigation. I'm sure Sophia could carry the workload until then.'

'It would help, Coroner, thank you.'

'But, Ridpath, the decision must be yours. Are you still a police officer or do you work for the Coroner's Court?'

Before Ridpath could answer, there was a slight tap on the door.

Sophia entered. 'I think you guys should see this...'

Chapter 43

She walked in, carrying the afternoon edition of one of the local papers. 'I picked it up when I went for my coffee.' She opened it out to a centre spread, most of which was dominated by a well-dressed Claire Trent standing in front of the police sign at GMP HQ.

Sophia began reading it out loud.

TOP COP PLAYS FOR KEEPS
by Molly Wright

She could be the chief executive of a publicly listed company. Or a top international lawyer. Or even something senior in politics.

Instead, Detective Superintendent Claire Trent chose to become a copper. Now she is the head of over 50 detectives and civilian personnel on the Major Investigation Team at Greater Manchester Police.

'My family had no connection with the police at all. My father was an accountant and my mother a housewife. Her job was to raise the kids and look after the home, while my father went out to work at 7.53 on the dot every morning.'

She is sitting in her office, the sun streaming through the windows highlighting the natural blonde streaks in her hair, a steely-eyed determination imprinted in her eyes.

'I went to the University of Leeds and studied history, but I wasn't one of your student radicals. I was more the type to stay at home, study and have a cup of cocoa, rather than be out raving every night.'

She talks about her past in the same way she discusses her present; open, honest, straightforward and frank to the point of bluntness.

'I finished Uni and didn't know what to do with myself. Then I saw an ad for the Greater Manchester Police fast track scheme. I applied and was accepted.'

She states the last fact modestly, but the fast track scheme is restricted to the best and brightest, the future elite of Manchester police.

'The rest is history and a lot of hard work, long hours and being in the right place at the right time.'

Once again, her natural modesty shines through. In truth, she has displayed a forthright intelligence throughout her career which has helped her rise to the top, to join the cream of detectives. Lecturing gigs at Bramshill, the police college, have singled her out as one of the deepest-thinking cops of her generation, a go-getter and strict disciplinarian.

'I was brought into MIT to shake it up, bring it kicking and screaming into the 21st century. Being a copper these days is not about pounding the beat and nicking the bad guys. It's much more a management role; forming a mission, hiring the best people, setting the standards and letting people get on with their work. You know, the latest advances in DNA, CCTV, criminal profiling, computer crime, encryption, digital investigations, forensic analysis and managed resource allocation mean that the modern police force is so much more than a few coppers on the beat.'

Public opinion polls have shown that people want to see more policemen and women, for them to have a visible presence in their area.

She counters this with a simple answer. 'But is it the most effective use of resources? Politicians always talk about putting more bobbies on the beat, but how is having a policeman on the street going to stop computer crime? Or track a criminal's cell phone? Or analyse DNA from a crime scene? Or combat international drug gangs?'

Ever the disruptor, she asks the questions other police officers avoid. No wonder she is being fast tracked to run a major force in the near future. 'Has it been difficult being a woman in a man's world?'

She shakes her head vehemently. 'Not at all. In fact, it's an advantage. Being a woman, I bring a determination to get things done, to finish the job, not to take no for an answer.'

No wonder one of her heroes is Margaret Thatcher, along with Mata Hari, and Florence Nightingale. As eclectic choices as the person who made them.

Of course, one of her latest cases, the murder of David Carsley, enters the conversation. Despite not having any kids of her own, she cares deeply about children.

'They should feel safe and protected at all times. The Carsley case has been one where we have interviewed over 3000 witnesses, canvassed 1200 homes in the area, and gathered over 250 different pieces of evidence. It's an ongoing investigation which I'm certain will soon result in an arrest.'

Her eyes take on a steely gaze as she talks about her desire to find the man responsible in almost evangelical terms.

'This man will kill again if he is allowed to stay on the streets. The job, the vocation, of myself and my officers is to make sure he is taken down and put away for the rest of his natural life for this heinous crime.'

The kidnapping and murder of the seven-year-old boy from Wythenshawe happened over two weeks ago and an arrest still hasn't been made yet.

'A man will be charged soon.'

'You have a suspect?'

'We do.' She answers firmly: again the steely tone in her voice reminds me of the late Mrs Thatcher. This is another woman who's not for turning.

'This man already has form for attacks on his wife and children. My Senior Investigating Officer, DCI Paul Turnbull, is sure we have the right man. It's a question of collecting the evidence to prove his guilt conclusively.'

I ask whether it is somebody from Manchester or further afield.

Ever the discreet copper, Claire Trent shakes her head. 'That wouldn't be the correct procedure. We still need to gather evidence and make sure the Crown Prosecution Service agree with us there is a case to answer. But I can assure your readers and the general public, we will charge the right man in the near future.'

That is indeed great news.

And with Detective Superintendent Claire Trent in charge, Manchester is sure it has the right woman.

'It's a puff piece,' said Mrs Challinor. 'I didn't know you were so close to arresting somebody.'

'Neither did I,' said Ridpath, checking his watch. 'But I think it is going to happen soon. Unless I can do something to stop it.'

Chapter 44

Ridpath didn't wait.

He walked straight out of the Coroner's Office and down the steps, passing Helen Moore returning with her afternoon coffee.

'You're off out again?' she asked.

He ignored her and strode out to his car, slamming the gear in and accelerating away in a squeal of tyres.

He had to talk with Claire Trent, find out what the hell was going on.

She didn't seem surprised to see him when he turned up at her office.

'Come in, Ridpath, and sit down.'

'I'd prefer to stand, boss.'

'Please yourself.'

He got right to it, there was no point in pussy-footing around. 'What's happening? I saw the interview you did with Molly Wright.'

'News travels fast. I only did it this morning. I haven't even seen the finished article myself yet.'

He passed the newspaper across the desk. She picked it up and scowled. 'I don't like the photo. Makes me look like some harridan from a brothel in Cheetham Hill. We'll have to get them to change it.'

She scanned the article and nodded as she finished it. 'Molly is better than I thought. She has communicated the main points across that I wanted.'

'You're going to charge Michael Carsley?'

'Paul Turnbull has already taken him to Wythenshawe nick. He seems sure the man will confess as soon as he is confronted. The evidence is beginning to stack up, Ridpath.'

'The man is innocent.'

The smile vanished from her face. 'How do you know that? What evidence have you brought me, Ridpath?'

She waited for his answer.

'I'm still working – we haven't finished yet.'

'But Turnbull is close to charging him.'

'You said I had till Saturday.'

She shrugged her shoulders. 'Things change in an investigation, you should know that.'

'You knew about the problems the Carsleys had in Scotland?'

She shrugged her shoulders.

'But you didn't see fit to tell me.'

'I wanted to see if your investigation was thorough. I told you as little as possible because I wanted you to check everything. Understand?'

He softened his tone. 'You didn't tell me you were planning to charge Michael Carsley?'

'I didn't know we were going to charge him when I briefed you. Something new came to light.'

'Like?'

She rolled her eyes. 'I'm not obliged to tell you anything, Detective Inspective Ridpath.' She stared at him for a long time, her eyes boring into him. 'But as you have been involved, however tangentially, I will let you know. We discovered new evidence.'

'What new evidence... boss?' The last was added by Ridpath in a deliberate attempt to at least appear to be contrite.

'Police Scotland have confirmed that Michael Carsley was arrested but not charged for child abuse.'

'What?'

'Teachers noticed bruises and a bump on the head of his son and reported it to Child Services. They called the police and he was arrested and charged. But, due to the nature of the crime, the Procurator Fiscal decided not to proceed with the case.'

'When was this?'

'Right before the family came to Manchester. It was probably the reason they left Scotland. He had earlier been cautioned for an assault at his place of work and on his wife, Irene Carsley. It seems the man has a problem with his temper.'

'Hang on, which son are we talking about? David Carsley would have been too young to go to school at that time.'

'Correct. The charges were for an assault on Daniel Carsley.'

Ridpath sat down, his eyes darting from left to right as he tried to process the information. Was that why Mrs Carsley was so scared of her husband? Had she been unable to protect her children? But why leave them with him?

'There are other factors as well.'

He looked up at his boss.

'Carsley was seen leaving the house by a neighbour at one thirty on the day of the murder. That's why we brought him in to question him. He admitted leaving the house but wouldn't say where he went.'

Ridpath was stunned. 'Why didn't this witness come forward before?'

Claire Trent's eyes rolled upwards. 'She didn't think it was important. And there's more…'

Ridpath waited for the kick to the teeth Claire Trent was going to deliver.

'The CSIs re-examined the boy's clothes again, stacked next to the body. There was no DNA anywhere, but there was a fingerprint on the big toe of a sock. It belonged to Michael Carsley.'

'They've just found out?'

'They used a technique called Vacuum Metal Deposition. Apparently, it can show prints on fabrics. Luckily, somebody at the lab had the good sense to use VMD on the boy's clothes.'

'The fingerprint could have come from touching the boy's clothes in the past. Dressing him the morning of his disappearance.'

'That's possible but would it have survived for so long on the sock? After two days the print would have disappeared with normal wear and tear. It was still fresh when they found it.'

'Convenient,' Ridpath said under his breath.

'What did you say?'

'Nothing, boss. Has Carsley confessed?'

'No. Paul Turnbull is interviewing him now at Wythenshawe nick. He reckons with a bit more pressure, he'll cough to the murder.'

'He didn't do it, boss.'

'What?'

'He didn't kill his son.'

'Where's your evidence, Ridpath?'

Ridpath tapped his fingers together. His mind flashed back to the happy picture of Michael Carsley and his sons on the mantlepiece. 'I don't have any. But I don't think he did it.'

'Another one of your hunches?'

Ridpath didn't answer.

'Did you find anything wrong with Paul Turnbull's investigation?'

'No, boss, there were a few minor things; he seems to have covered most of the bases. But it still—'

'Did he make any major errors? Miss possible evidence? Miss witnesses? Not follow proper procedure?'

'No, boss.'

'Did you discover anything?'

'Not really – we've only had three days.'

'Well, now your time is up, Ridpath. I'm reassigning Emily Parkinson and Chrissy back to Paul Turnbull. He'll need all the help he can to prepare the case for the CPS.'

She stood up. 'And now, if you'll excuse me, I'm off to tell the chief constable the good news. The fact that we've found the man responsible will be a weight off his shoulders. He may even be congratulated in the press for once.'

She strode toward the door.

'Oh, and Ridpath – you're off the case. I had a chat with Mrs Challinor a few minutes ago. Apparently, you have been neglecting your coronial work. I've told her you will no longer be working on the Carsley case.'

'But, boss, he's innocent.'

'Read my lips, Ridpath: you're off the case.'

'What about my report? You wanted to see it.'

She thought for a moment. 'Give it to me tomorrow at nine a.m. Afterwards, you can go back to work for the coroner. At least she will be pleased to see you.'

Chapter 45

Ridpath went outside HQ to get some fresh air. The usual groups of smokers were assembled around a standing ashtray, cordoned off like lepers from the rest of society.

For a second the familiar craving for a cigarette flooded his tastebuds as he smelt the secondary smoke drifting towards him.

Why did it always remind him of lavatories?

Perhaps that was where he had first started. Stealing a couple of cigarettes from his mother's packet, sneaking off during the morning break with Mark and Terry to the bogs and inhaling their first coughs. All the time listening out for any teachers who were prowling the corridors.

His youth. A long time gone and an age away. At least, it felt like that. In truth it had been little more than twenty-five years ago. How he would like to pick that young teenager up and shake him by the collar, saying, 'Don't be an arse.'

But at that age, he wouldn't have listened.

Why was he thinking about his past? Was he avoiding thinking about what had happened with Claire Trent?

Out of the corner of his eye, he caught Emily Parkinson striding towards him. He tried to walk away, but she was onto him too quickly.

'I presume you heard, Ridpath?'

'Yeah, Turnbull was quick.'

'Apparently, he's been planning it for the last few days.'

'What?'

'The information from Police Scotland came in before Claire Trent briefed you. They kept it hidden from everyone. Too many leaks…'

'Until they decided to leak it themselves.' She had set him up. She didn't want him to investigate properly, just check whether there had been any cock-ups in Turnbull's investigation, covering her own arse.

Ridpath bit his bottom lip, keeping his thoughts to himself.

'I rang the FLO who replaced me, DC Diana West, asking what happened to Daniel.'

In the nightmare of the case, Ridpath had forgotten about the boy.

'She told me he was taken into care by social services. There was enough concern about his well-being to warrant a care order.'

'No kid deserves that, to be separated from his mum and dad after he's lost his brother. Has anybody told Mrs Carsley?'

Emily shrugged her shoulders. 'Social services should do it.'

'Collateral damage.'

'What?'

'It's something Charlie Whitworth used to say. "In any investigation, there is always collateral damage. Our job is to limit it, so only the guilty are punished, not innocent victims."'

'I wish I'd worked with him more. Sounds like he thought about the job.'

'Charlie was a thug, but a damn good copper.'

They both were silent for a moment, Ridpath inhaling the secondary smoke from the cigarettes.

'If it's any consolation, I managed to get some CCTV from the day of David Carsley's abduction. The techies are looking at it now. There was nothing at the pub but I checked with Greater Manchester Transport. You know they have over 2000 CCTV cameras in the trams and on stations?'

Ridpath raised his eyebrows at the figure.

'The guy was helpful. He's sending me the footage from Sale Water Park station concourse for 23 July, plus he's digging up footage from inside the cab of the first tram that morning. It stopped at the station at 6.23.'

It was time to tell her.

'We're off the case, Emily.'

'What?'

'Chrissy's off the case too.'

There was a long pause. Emily Parkinson stepped closer to Ridpath and dropped her voice. 'I think Michael Carsley is innocent. He shouldn't be charged.'

'So do I.'

'Can't we keep going? I mean, without the bosses knowing? Chrissy's keen.'

Ridpath shook his head. 'We're off the case.'

'So you're going to give up?' She raised her voice.

'I'm tired, Emily. I can't keep banging my head against a brick wall.'

'So, Ridpath's tired and an innocent man is going to jail, convicted of something he didn't do. Murder his own son.'

'Are you sure he didn't do it? The evidence is damning.'

'I'm sure. Remember I spent twelve days in that house with those people. I would have known if Michael Carsley had murdered his son.'

Ridpath checked his watch. 'I'm tired and I'm going back to my flat, Emily. I want to call my daughter.'

He walked away.

'Enjoy your time off, Ridpath. Some of us care about the truth a bit more.'

He stopped for a second and then carried on walking.

There was no point in answering because she was right.

Chapter 46

Emily Parkinson was left alone when Ridpath walked away.

Inside she was seething. How dare he give up just like that? Hadn't he been the one lecturing her about responsibility and duty?

Gritting her teeth, she made a fist. Well, she wasn't going to give up. She knew Michael Carsley was innocent despite what Turnbull, Ridpath or anybody else said.

She pulled her jacket closer around her body, suddenly feeling cold.

But where to start?

She thought for a long time before working out what she needed to do. It was the only option available to her.

Going back to the MIT floor, she tried to avoid people. Luckily Turnbull and most of his new detectives were still at Wythenshawe nick. The floor was quiet, with only Harry Makepeace tapping away in the corner and Chrissy in her section.

She sat down at the desk and logged onto her computer. The message from Greater Manchester Transport was already there with links to the footage.

On seeing her, the civilian researcher came over.

'Where's Ridpath? I've been told we're off the case and I'm back helping Turnbull. He's got me checking with Child Services in Scotland.'

Emily looked over her shoulder to make sure Harry Makepeace wasn't listening. 'I just spoke to Ridpath, he's gone home.'

'How's he handling it?'

'Not well, he wants to give up.'

Chrissy frowned. 'But you don't?'

Emily leant forward and whispered. 'Michael Carsley is innocent. I know it.'

'What are you going to do?'

'Carry on. With or without Ridpath, for as long as I can.'

'But how? What do we have to work on?'

'I managed to get some CCTV footage from an ATM in Wythenshawe on the date of the abduction and a hard drive from a shop. There was a tram station close to where we parked at Jackson's Boat...'

'I know it well, lovely place for a quiet pint.'

'Anyway, Ridpath had the idea to check the footage from the day when the body was found. It's the only thing I can do right now. Have you heard from Turnbull?'

'Only to give me the new work. I don't know what's happening at Wythenshawe. It's being kept hush-hush.'

'What are you two ladies whispering about?' Harry Makepeace had crept up on them soundlessly.

Emily leant back in her chair. 'We were wondering if you'd heard anything from Paul Turnbull?'

He shook his head. 'Not a lot.'

She decided to be more direct. 'What have you heard?'

Makepeace smiled. 'Not a lot. It's on a need-to-know basis and Turnbull has specified that you two, and me, don't need to know.'

'Thanks for the heads-up before.'

'We have to stick together against the idiots. We're being frozen out, Emily. I'd start packing your boxes if I were you.'

He smiled once again at both of them and sauntered back to his desk.

'Can you find out, Chrissy?' said Emily under her breath.

'I'll try – a few of them owe me favours. What are you going to do?'

'Spend the rest of my evening sitting next to somebody who sweats and is desperate to get into my knickers.'

'Sounds interesting.'

'I wish.'

Twenty minutes later she went up to the techies' floor while Makepeace was away from his desk – Nerd Central, as it was called by the less enlightened members of the force, but in modern policing, it had become a vital resource. It was here that data on mobile phones was extracted, computer codes cracked, and most importantly for her, CCTV images analysed.

Phil Reynolds was the techie head of CCTV, sitting in his own private edit suite built from taxpayers' money. She knew he fancied her and wasn't above using that fact to ensure her work received priority. Now she had to face spending a whole evening together without even a glass of wine for solace.

'Have we got anything, Phil?' She sat down, feeling him tense up beside her.

'Hiya, Emily, the data from Daniel Carsley's phone hasn't come in yet. The lads are stuffed working on a county lines drug case, trying to break encrypted messages. Rather them than me.'

'When can we get the times off the mobile towers?'

He shrugged his shoulders. 'Your guess is as good as mine.'

'Not very useful, Phil.'

The techie blushed. 'I have more bad news. The hard drive you gave me from the shop is totally fried. I don't know what they've done with it but it looks like it's spent the last six months at the bottom of the Mersey.'

'Nothing you can do?'

'We could sell it for scrap and make a couple of bob, but I'm guessing you wouldn't be too keen.'

She smiled briefly. 'Right. How about the footage from the ATM and from the trams?'

'Both look good. Which do you want first?'

'Let's do the trams, starting with the first one on the morning of the 23rd that stopped at Sale Water Park.'

'Righto – gone with the wind, coming right up.'

'*Gone with the Wind*?'

'A tram? Moving? Gone with the wind?'

She laughed dutifully. Techie jokes were always the worst.
'Let's start with the platform footage.'

'What are you looking for?'

'I haven't a clue.'

Chapter 47

'Hiya, Dad.'

Eve was bright and bouncy on his screen. Exactly the opposite of how he felt.

He stopped off in Greggs to grab a couple of Cornish pasties for dinner, eating them sitting alone at the kitchen table of the service apartment with a cup of tea. Next to him was his laptop. He had finished the report for Claire Trent earlier and was checking it for typos.

Of course, Polly was there by his side.

'Don't take it so hard, Ridpath. It's just a job like any other. You win some, you lose some.'

He stared straight at the face of his dead wife. 'I seem to be losing a lot, recently.'

She laughed out loud. 'Oh dear, we are enjoying a pity party today.' She pretended to cry, rubbing her eyes like a baby. It was the same way she used to tease him when he came home from work with a grumpy face. 'Boo hoo, poor Ridpath, he's been taken off the case. What is he going to do? Roll over and give up?'

'I don't ever roll over and I don't ever give up.'

'So why are you doing it this time?'

He looked away and when he looked back, she had vanished.

He threw the half-eaten pasty in the bin and called up his daughter. He always missed her voice, missed her brightness.

'Sorry about ringing so late last night, I was on a case.'

'Which one?'

'You know I'm not supposed to talk about it.'

'I know, but I won't tell anyone. Anyway, there's only Paw Paw and Ah Kung here and they spend their lives watching Hong Kong television.'

'Sorry, still can't tell you and anyway, I'm off it now.'

'That doesn't sound good.'

'It doesn't feel good either. I'm sorry, thinking about myself all the time. Living with Grandpa and Grandma, it's not great for you, is it?'

'It's not so bad. They mean well, but they're from a different generation. Their idea of fun is to watch the news in Cantonese.'

'You know they love you, don't you?'

'I know.' A long pause. 'When are we going to get back together, Dad?'

'Soon, when I'm more settled, more in control.'

'But when will that be? Give me a date, a time?'

'I don't know, Eve.'

'You said it would be when the case finished. Well, it's finished now, you said you were off it. So can I come home?'

'Not yet, but soon, I promise.'

She pursed her mouth but finally nodded. 'Promise me something else.'

'Anything, Eve.'

'We're going to put flowers on Mum's grave on Sunday. Promise me you'll come too.'

'I'll try...'

'Trying isn't doing, Dad.'

'When did you become the little philosopher?'

'Since Mum died, one of us has to. And don't change the subject...'

Ridpath closed his eyes for a second. Polly's face appeared in his mind as he remembered her when they first met on St Patrick's Day, with her bright green hair, like an Irish leprechaun dancing to a wild reel. Except she wasn't Irish but Chinese and the music was by Maroon 5 and Destiny's Child.

'Dad?'

He heard Eve's voice as if it were coming from the end of a long tunnel. 'I'll try,' he finally whispered.

Chapter 48

It was close to ten p.m. when she finally discovered something.

The footage from the platforms had been worse than useless. Sale Water Park wasn't a busy stop. Hardly anybody got on or off before nine a.m. There were only three or four people, all of whom worked in the park's cafe and restaurants.

The footage from inside the trams had been just as bad. The early images had a few travellers looking like zombies going to a wake and then, after seven, the carriages began to fill up, and despite the necessity for social distancing, becoming as packed as cattle cars when the suburban herds began their daily trek to the feeding grounds of the city. She stopped viewing after ten a.m., reasoning the boy's body had been found by then.

The footage from the front of the tram mostly showed the track stretching in two parallel iron lines into the distance. As the first tram moved away from Sale Water Park station, however, she caught a glimpse of a white car going the other way, from Jackson's Boat to the M60.

'Can you get any tighter on that car, Phil?'

She leant across him to prod the screen on the left.

'I'll have a try but these cameras are for road traffic accident use, not anything else.'

She heard him click the keys of a keyboard. The image of the car appeared bigger on the screen. 'I'll try and enhance it.'

More clicks and the car became slightly sharper.

Emily stood up and leant closer to the screen, staring at it. As if moving her body closer would make it bigger. Instead, all she saw was the lines on the screen becoming clearer.

'It's actually better to step back and look from further back.'

She did as she was told. Phil Reynolds was right. The car was clearer.

'Can you discover the make of the car?'

'You remember my little box of tricks?' On a third screen, he brought up side views of a range of cars, each one rapidly changing as the computer scanned them against the image it had.

Finally it stopped.

'We don't have a lot to work with, I'm afraid. But the computer says it's either a Hyundai i20 or a Vauxhall Corsa.'

'How correct is that?'

'With the image we've got? My guess is 80 per cent correct.'

Was it a white Hyundai or a white Vauxhall? Or something else? She stared intently at the screen. There was a distinct shadow on the image. A single man behind the steering wheel?

'I suppose there's no chance of making it even clearer.'

'I could have a go, but it'll take a while. Is that what you're looking for. A white car?'

'It might be. Before you clean up this footage, could we take a look at the images from the ATM on 21 July?'

'Your wish is my command. Abracadabra…'

Emily realised that Reynolds was probably a big movie buff – even worse, he was possibly a Disney movie buff. She could imagine him singing along to the music from *Frozen*. Let it go, she thought, laughing to herself.

The footage from the cash machine appeared on the screen.

'It's not great. I think the last time they cleaned the lens was the Ice Age, but we'll be able to see the images at least.'

'Can you fast forward to between one p.m. and two p.m.'

'Will do, milady.'

The time clock on the footage accelerated for a minute, then slowed.

13.00.01.

13.00.02.

13.00.03.

The street in front of the ATM showed cars going down the road and the occasional pedestrian walking in front of it.

'Can you go at double speed? We should still be able to see everything.'

The pictures began to move faster but no little boys walked in front of the ATM. They stopped three times for white cars, but it was easy enough to see they were different makes.

They carried until the counter reached two p.m., then stopped.

'Nothing so far, what do you want to do?'

'Let's start much earlier, around eleven a.m.'

Reynolds glanced at the clock on the wall. 'It's already eleven thirty on a Friday night.'

She put her hand on his shoulder and looked him in the eye. 'You wouldn't leave me here on my own, would you?'

He checked his watch. 'I can give you one more hour. I have to go home and feed the goldfish.'

There was no answer to that so she didn't bother.

Phil ran the footage at double speed. She watched as bodies crossed in front of the camera, and the tyres and bottom of cars raced along the street.

Her eyes were closing and she was about to give up and go home herself when he said, 'What's that?'

'What?'

'See, a boy in front of the camera on the pavement.'

He stopped and rewound the footage, playing it at normal speed. A young boy stopped in front of the shop. He stood there looking around, walked one way and then another. A white car drove past, reversed back, the door opened and the boy said something, shaking his head. Then the boy got into the car, the door closed and the white car drove away.

'Is that David?' shouted Emily. 'Play it again.'

He rewound the ATM footage and they both watched it closely. 'It must be David Carsley, the description of the clothes matches.' She pointed to the screen. 'See, the boy is wearing a United shirt. Play it again.'

On the third viewing, she noticed something new, her hand going to her mouth.

'It can't be,' she whispered.

Chapter 49

Molly Wright stared at the empty bottle of Rioja in front of her and thought about opening another.

The interview with Claire Trent had been particularly successful. It had been an easy sell to one of the editors. An in-depth look at the woman in charge of the search for David Carsley's killer. The fact it was a woman was the key selling point – they wouldn't have been interested in another bloated, middle-aged man.

She thought at one time she'd over-egged the pudding with her effusive compliments about the woman and her job. But the editor had been happy with the angle while GMP's PR person, Sarah something-or-other, had rung her to say how pleased they were and could they just change the photo.

She pretended to try and then rang back saying the newspaper was looking for a better shot.

Vanity, vanity, thy name is woman.

That evening, she rang her source in MIT. He could give her little information except that Michael Carsley was in Wythenshawe nick being questioned. Was he the guilty man Claire Trent had hinted at?

If he was, this case could be explosive. She could hear the ker-ching of a till ringing up ever larger numbers.

After a moment's thought, she planned her line of attack. The interview she had arranged the next morning with Irene Carsley would be the first step. The woman had been reluctant at first but a guaranteed payment of £1000 had convinced her.

This money had come out of Molly Wright's own pocket, something she resented immensely.

'You have to be in it to win it,' she said out loud, walking to the kitchen for another bottle of wine.

If Michael Carsley was charged then an interview with the wife would be gold dust for any tabloid. Molly saw the headlines now.

WIFE OF KILLER REVEALS HER LIVING NIGHTMARE by Molly Wright.

MY LIFE OF TERROR: IRENE CARSLEY TELLS THE TRUTH AND NOTHING BUT THE TRUTH by Molly Wright.

And for the *Sun*, I SLEPT WITH A KILLER.

If she could get family photos of the Carsleys, particularly of Michael and his son, that would be the icing on the cake.

She opened the bottle and poured herself an extra-large glass. She also needed single pictures of the surviving son, Daniel Carsley. She knew he'd been taken into care, but didn't know which home he was in.

Never mind, she would find out. She always found out.

Life was finally looking pretty good for Molly Wright. She could ride this story all the way to a columnist gig with one of the tabloids. Or, if it went as well as she thought, a broadsheet might come knocking at her door.

And then it hit her.

A book.

An exposé of the dark heart of a marriage in modern Britain. An evil unleashed on a child. A shocking tale to thrill the quiet suburbs.

It could be her Norman Mailer moment. Or even her Truman Capote *In Cold Blood*.

She drank the glass of Rioja and poured one more.

This could be good, extremely good.

Chapter 50

Ridpath ended his call with Eve and spent the next three hours watching television. He couldn't remember which programmes he watched, just that there was a series of flickering pictures in front of him.

The news came on. More Covid horror stories, followed by the local news. There were tighter lockdowns in Oldham and Blackburn, but nothing about David Carsley. The PR people were obviously keeping a lid on the case, but not for long. Once it leaked out Michael Carsley was being questioned regarding the murder of his son, all hell would let loose. Journalists and television cameras would be camping out in front of the police station in Wythenshawe, waiting like hungry vultures for their story.

He wouldn't put it past them to doorstep the children's home where they were keeping Daniel. The poor lad would be under immense pressure, having lost his brother and blaming himself, and now hearing his father was the man responsible.

And what about the mother, Irene? Had anybody told her? Hopefully, they wouldn't know where she lived. Should he ring her?

Another voice answered him.

'You're off the case, Ridpath, remember. You've been told to go home.' Polly had returned and was sitting opposite him.

'What am I supposed to do, Poll? You always said don't get too emotionally involved.'

'Well, it's too late. You are involved whether you like it or not.'

His mobile phone rang. He looked at the screen and saw Emily's name.

'Are you going to answer it?'

'It's Emily. She's going to rant and rave, criticising me for giving up the case.'

'She'd be right, wouldn't she? Answer your phone.'

Wearily, Ridpath picked up his mobile. 'Emily, it's past midnight. What do you want? If you're going to give me an earful, then don't bother, I'm too old and too tired.'

'We've got something, Ridpath. I'm in the CCTV suite with Phil Reynolds...'

'What are you doing there so late?'

She carried on speaking, ignoring his question. 'We were going through the footage I found from the convenience store ATM. We've got pictures of what looks like David Carsley getting into a white car.'

'What?' Ridpath sat up straight. 'It's him on tape?'

'Actually on hard disk, but I'm pretty certain it's him, the clothes and the description match. The CCTV images aren't great. Phil is trying to clean them up as we speak. There's one problem, though...'

'What's the problem?'

'The pictures are from one hour earlier. Twelve thirty.'

'What? What did you say?'

'The pictures show David Carsley getting into a white car at twelve thirty.'

Chapter 51

Mother was snoring.

He watched her from the corner of the room. The television was still on, the pictures flickering but the sound down.

She liked to watch television before she slept. It soothed her, calmed her, she said.

She never knew the feeling wasn't coming from the box in the corner but from the Valium he mixed in with her supper, adding a soupçon of diazepam as a little treat.

He enjoyed going out occasionally after work. Mother, of course, never left the house. Being in lockdown meant little to her; life carried on as normal or what passed as normality for her.

There was a new film on at the cinema in Parrs Wood that evening. He liked going to the movies. Sitting there in the dark was like sitting in the cellar when he was young with his imaginary friends. Except now they were up on the screen, not in his head.

He'd taken the tram, sitting in one of the seats, checking out the other passengers while they studiously avoided looking at him.

A young boy had come aboard. At first, he couldn't believe his luck. The boy was perfect; the big eyes he liked topped by a shock of blond hair. For a second, he imagined combing the hair, parting it so a curl reached down over the forehead, highlighting the eyes. He would wait until the boy alighted then follow him, seizing the right moment to pounce.

He didn't have his car so he couldn't take this one home to play. He would have to enjoy him on the street. It wasn't as satisfying as taking his time at home, but beggars couldn't be choosers, as his mum always said.

He wasn't a beggar and he always chose.

Then an adult swayed into the compartment from another carriage and smiled at the boy, going over to sit next to him. He listened to their chat. The man was a neighbour, just his luck.

The boy was spoilt now, though, blemished by knowing the other man.

They stayed on the tram when he stepped off at the stop for the cinema. As he exited, he looked back, catching the boy's eyes. The innocence was there for all to see.

What a shame. He would have loved to own that innocence.

He walked to the cinema where his imaginary friends had come to him in the dark.

'You must hunt again.'

'Time to enjoy yourself. The prey is out there. Waiting.'

'Time to hurt.'

They all had Northern voices, the strong accents of Yorkshire with their long, rounded vowels, encouraging him to act, to be another Sutcliffe.

He knew then, he would act soon. All he needed was the right opportunity. He never planned these things, they just happened.

Seize the day.

Seize the child.

Like the boy with the United shirt. Now, that was a bit too close to home but he couldn't resist the opportunity.

Another one would happen soon, he was sure of it.

The voices told him it would and they were always right.

On the Fifth Day

Saturday, August 9

Chapter 52

They'd arranged to meet at a cafe close to Police HQ at eight a.m. that morning. Emily Parkinson had sent the footage to Ridpath after Reynolds had finished cleaning it up.

Ridpath watched it again and again and again.

Every time the door of the car opened, Ridpath leant forward, trying to see the interior. But it was dark and the man's face was constantly in shadow.

Did David Carsley know the man in the car and that's why he got in?

Was it the same man as in the park?

Or was it only a chance encounter?

From the footage, it could be any of these three things.

'What are we going to do, Ridpath?' asked Chrissy. She had also seen the footage.

'Only one thing we can do,' said Emily. 'We need to show this to Turnbull straight away.'

Ridpath spoke for the first time. 'Emily's right, but there's no point showing it to him. I need to get it to Claire Trent.'

'But she took you off the case yesterday, she's not going to be happy.'

'Her happiness is the least of our concerns. I'm supposed to present my report this morning at nine a.m.' He paused, thinking of the next steps and not looking forward to the meeting.

'What time do they have to charge Michael Carsley?'

Ridpath answered. 'The twenty-four hours are up at four p.m. today. If he doesn't confess, Turnbull will probably apply for an extension. In a case like this, a superintendent, Claire Trent, can authorise another twelve hours, but if they want longer they would have to find a friendly magistrate.'

'Not hard in the murder of a child.'

'More time to put the screws on…'

'Is there anything else on the ATM footage, Emily?'

'I've been through it from eleven a.m. to two p.m. and this is the only useful image. I sent you the footage from the tram. A similar car was in the area where the body was deposited at 6.23 on 23 July.'

'Can we narrow down the make and model of the car?'

'Not at the moment. Phil Reynolds reckons it's a Hyundai i20 or a Vauxhall Corsa.'

'Can you go back and check the rest of the footage from the ATM? See if we can narrow it down?'

'Will do. It means buttering up Reynolds once more, but I think he'll do it.'

'And Chrissy, can you get on to DVLA in Swansea and check how many Hyundai i20s and Vauxhall Corsas are registered in the Greater Manchester area?'

'It could be a lot…'

'It doesn't matter. It's the only real lead we have.'

'One thing is still bothering me. Both Michael and Daniel Carsley said the boys left the house at one p.m. But here we have footage showing David Carsley getting into a car thirty minutes earlier. Were they both lying?' asked Chrissy. 'Or did they get the time wrong?'

'Daniel Carsley remembered they left when the news was starting…'

'It doesn't make sense. Why lie about the time?' asked Emily.

'What about Daniel's mobile phone? We could get the time from the data on the mobile towers.'

Emily Parkinson shook her head. 'The techies are backed up on a county lines case. They don't know when they are going to get to our phone.'

Ridpath slammed his fist on the desk, causing the waitress behind the counter to stare at him. 'It's not good enough, Emily, we need that information.'

'I know but...'

'There's one other way of checking,' said Chrissy.

They both looked at her. She had a smile across her face, as if Manchester City had just scored five against Liverpool.

'Go on,' encouraged Ridpath.

'Nobody's ever asked the other kids.'

'What?'

'The other kids in the park. Nobody asked them what time they played basketball.'

Ridpath and Emily stared at each other.

'Can you get the addresses, Chrissy? I'll go to see them this afternoon.'

'You forgot – you're off the case, Ridpath.'

'Not any more.'

Emily stared at the footage on her laptop. 'This clears Michael Carsley, doesn't it? I mean, he doesn't own a car. Turnbull isn't going to be a happy bunny.'

Chapter 53

'You're off the Carsley case, Ridpath, I thought I made that clear yesterday. So you can leave your report and I'll read it when I have time.'

'You did, boss, but something's come up and you need to see it.'

'If this is another attempt to undermine Paul Turnbull's investigation then I'm not interested.'

Ridpath was about to say that it was Claire Trent who had briefed him to investigate the case – if anybody was undermining the DCI's investigation, it was her. But he didn't, instead biting down on his tongue and saying, 'It's still important you see this footage, boss.'

She waved him into her office. He placed his laptop on her desk. 'What you're about to see are images taken from the camera of an ATM located on a road close to the park.'

He played the footage, seeing David Carsley again in his United shirt, the white car stopping, both talking for a moment before the boy entered the car and it drove off.

'Play it again,' Claire Trent ordered.

Ridpath replayed the footage.

'Is this David Carsley?'

'We think so, boss.'

'You think so or you know so?'

'The clothing matches the description given by his father and his brother, later found beside the body. The video isn't so clear on his face but I'm certain this is David Carsley.'

'But the timecode on the video says twelve thirty. David Carsley didn't leave the house with his brother until one p.m.'

'I know, boss, I don't understand it either. But Turnbull needs to see this.'

'You haven't shown him yet?'

'I thought it best to show you first as you asked me to check the investigation.'

'Where did the footage come from?'

'An ATM mounted on the outside wall of a convenience store.'

'How did we miss it?'

'I don't know, boss, but there's more.' Ridpath clicked on the next clip. 'This is taken from the front cab of a tram going into the city centre at 6.23 on the morning the body was found.'

He played the footage.

'It looks like the same white car.'

'That's what we thought, boss. We're trying to narrow down the make and model.'

'Where was this footage taken?'

'South of the river, close to the Sale Water Park tram stop. There's a pub with a car park at the end of the road, next to the river.'

'Jackson's Boat.'

'You know it?'

She nodded.

'It's on the opposite side of the river to where the body was found at Chorlton Ees, but there's a bridge next to the pub and it's only a five-minute walk along a quiet riverside path to the place where the body was dumped.'

Claire Trent's eyes widened. 'But the boundary of our search was the river...'

'Exactly, boss.'

'Have you checked CCTV in the pub's car park?'

'It's not working.'

'Just our luck.' She thought for a moment before leaning forward and depressing the button on her intercom. 'Angie, can you ask Paul Turnbull to come and see me?'

Chapter 54

'You've got to be shittin' me.'

Turnbull was not happy, the deep blue vein in his bald head was throbbing. Ridpath could almost feel how angry his blood was.

'I am not "shitting" you, DCI Turnbull. I asked DI Ridpath to take a look at the investigation, see if there was anything we'd missed.'

'You got him to check up on me?'

Claire Trent was silent for a while, staring down at her blotter, before looking up again, the steely determination in her eyes noticed by Molly Wright plainly evident. 'Your investigation had stalled, DCI Turnbull...'

'I had—'

She held up her hand to stop him speaking. 'I wanted someone who hadn't been involved to look at it with a fresh pair of eyes. DI Ridpath had been away...'

'On sick leave,' Turnbull sneered.

'Yes, on sick leave. He was coming fresh to the investigation and has turned up two interesting pieces of evidence which you missed.'

'That...' he said, pointing to the laptop, 'a fuzzy video with a child who may or may not be David Carsley getting into a car. A video which I'd like to remind you has a timecode thirty minutes before our victim left his house. How do you explain that, DI Ridpath?'

Ridpath hesitated before finally saying, 'I can't.'

'Because if this is David Carsley, which I doubt, it means both Michael Carsley and Daniel Carsley are lying about the time the boys left the house. Why would they both lie? Tell me that, Ridpath?'

'I don't know.'

'And as for the same white car being seen in the vicinity of the place where the body was dumped, it could be any white car. Somebody could have gone for an early morning jog or they could have been dogging in the pub car park. That area is miles away across the river.'

'It's not miles away, it's a five-minute walk.'

'You still have to cross the river. Why do that when you can park on the street like all the other walkers?'

'Because the man knows the area. He knows the dog walkers in Chorlton Ees park on the street and he's aware it's only a five-minute walk from Jackson's Boat to our dump site. It's also no coincidence that Sale Water Park and Wythenshawe Park are on the same tram line.'

'Now you're clutching at straws. Half the suburbs of Manchester are on that tram line.'

'Did you look south of the river in the area of the pub?'

'Well, no. Why would we? The river is a natural barrier.'

'Not if there's a bridge across it.'

'Don't take that tone with me, DI Ridpath, I'm still your superior officer.'

'Enough,' Claire Trent suddenly shouted. 'You two will have to learn to work together. We have a murder we need to solve. Is that clear?'

'Yes, boss,' said Ridpath.

Turnbull stayed silent.

'Well, Paul?'

'I still think Michael Carsley did it. Last night, he was close to confessing, I could feel it in my water.'

'When do you have to release him?'

'At four p.m. this afternoon.'

'I'll authorise an extension if I have to, but only if it is totally necessary.'

'I'm sure he'll confess soon. The evidence against him is mounting up. Now I have to ask him why he lied about the time... if he did lie.'

'OK, keep the pressure on. I'd like a confession before four if possible. Ridpath, I want you to follow up on what you've discovered...'

'But I'm the Senior Investigating Officer, and I should be—'

Once again, Claire Trent held up her hands to stop him speaking. 'Nothing has changed, Paul, you are still the SIO. Ridpath is following alternative lines of enquiry, that is all.'

'But...'

'I've made my decision, Paul.' She dismissed him by turning to Ridpath. 'We have only one day left to resolve this. What's your plan?'

He thought for a second. 'Re-look at the footage, go and see Daniel Carsley's friends and check their account.' He scratched his head. 'There's one thing I can't get out of my mind. Why did HOLMES highlight the attack in Liverpool? It's been puzzling me for the last couple of days.'

'That was discounted by the pathologist. Two different MOs, two different causes of death. Therefore two different killers,' argued Turnbull.

'So close to each other? Liverpool is a mere thirty-five miles away.'

'I do know where Liverpool is, Ridpath,' snapped Claire Trent.

Turnbull stood up. 'I've had enough of this crap. Michael Carsley did it and I'm going to prove it.'

He stormed out of the room, slamming the door behind him.

'I don't think he's a happy man,' Ridpath said to the still shivering door.

'Watch yourself, Ridpath. Paul Turnbull is not a man you should cross.'

'I think it's a bit late for that.'

Chapter 55

'Right, Chrissy, do you have the addresses of the friends of Daniel Carsley?'

'The ones he played basketball with?'

'Exactly.'

She logged on to the computer. 'Hang on, they are on the list of witnesses from the day David Carsley disappeared.' There was the sound of tapping keys and then the whirr of the printer beside her desk. She handed him the paper with five names on it. 'You want me to keep looking for the Hyundai and the Vauxhall?'

'Yeah, keep hassling DVLA, we need the information, particularly if any of the car owners live in the vicinity of the tram line.'

'Right.'

'And get on to Liverpool. See if you can arrange for me to meet the SIO on their investigation.'

'DI Fitzgerald?'

'That's the man.'

'I'll have a try, Ridpath, but I don't know how keen he'll be to have somebody looking around a case he's already closed.'

'And book a time with their pathologist, if you can. Do we have the report?'

'It's on file.'

'Could you send it to Dr Schofield? I'd like his opinion on it.'

'Isn't this a bit of wild goose chase, Ridpath? The case is done and dusted. They have their perp.'

Ridpath shook his head slowly. 'There's something about it that bothers me, Chrissy. Two child-killers living within thirty-five miles of each other and killing at the same time? What are the odds? And I don't believe in coincidences.'

'Well, that's what it could be.'

Ridpath turned round and stared across a sea of empty desks on the MIT floor.

'Where's Emily?'

'With the techie nerds. She's going through the footage again.'

'Right, I'll find her.'

On the way out he was accosted by one of the few detectives on the floor, Harry Makepeace.

'I see you've pissed off our glorious leader, Ridpath.'

'What did Turnbull say?'

'Well, it wasn't that clear between the swear words. Something about going behind his back and stabbing him in the front. I'd avoid him if I were you. He's smoking downstairs before heading back to Wythenshawe nick.'

'Thanks for the heads–up, Harry.'

'No worries, you do have a habit of getting up his nose. Rather you than me – he's not somebody I'd cross.'

Ridpath pushed through the doors heading to the tech floor. He found Emily still viewing the footage. 'Anything new?'

She shook her head. 'Nothing. The only thing we have is the twelve thirty footage.'

'OK, you're with me.'

'We're back on the case?'

'For the moment, but I think we've pissed off Turnbull.'

'About time, he's a pompous prick,' Reynolds said loudly.

'And there speaks the voice of reason,' said Emily, patting his shoulder. 'What about the footage?'

'Don't worry, I know what you're looking for, I'll go through it with a fine-tooth comb and try to clean up what we have.'

'You're a star, Phil.' She kissed him on the side of the head and the man blushed a bright beetroot red.

'When you two have finished the mutual admiration society, we have a case to work.'

Emily put on her jacket. 'Where are we going?'

'To see the lads who played basketball with Daniel. Everybody seems to have forgotten about them.'

Chapter 56

At some time during the night, his mother died.

He discovered her in the morning, still sitting in front of the television. Her body was cold and her eyes closed.

It was probably the larger dose of diazepam that finished her off. He had mixed it into her cocoa as she watched Strictly.

Why did he do it?

He'd finally had enough. Yesterday, she accused him of not caring for her as well as she'd cared for him when he was young.

He supposed that had sent him over the edge. Anyway, it was done now.

She was dead.

He spent the morning tidying her up; putting on her make-up and eyeliner, ensuring her lipstick was a perfect cupid's bow and tidying her clothes.

He didn't intend to move her.

She would sit there with him, watching the telly like she always did. But silent now, finally.

He'd read about Dennis Nilsen, of course. Keeping those he had killed with him because he wanted company. He supposed it would be the same with his mother. She would be there for him in death as she had never been in life.

After he'd finished arranging her clothes, he stepped back and stared at her. He'd better get some air freshener from the supermarket. In this weather, she'd start to smell pretty quickly. He would keep the air conditioning on high just in case.

It did mean he no longer had to worry about bringing prey back to the flat. It was time he found something new to play with now that Mother was gone.

He stroked the cold cheek feeling the clammy skin beneath his fingers.

He would miss her, but at least he was free now.

The butterfly has left the cocoon.

Chapter 57

Ridpath pushed open the garden gate and walked up the path. This detached house was substantial and set back from the road, on the other side of Wythenshawe Park. It was an age and a class apart from the council estate.

He rang the bell and a middle-aged woman answered. Her hair was rigid and dry, stacked up in a beehive like something out of the 1960s.

'We'd like to speak to Tony Greene, please.'

'And you are?'

'Detective Inspector Ridpath and Detective Sergeant Parkinson from Greater Manchester Police. It's about the disappearance of David Carsley.'

'The police were already around here about two weeks ago. I told them I was out that day and saw nothing.'

'It's not you we'd like to speak to but your son Tony.'

'Tony's done nothing wrong.'

'We didn't say he had. Could we have a chat with him?'

She thought for a moment and then opened the door wider. 'You'd better come in. Wipe your shoes, please.' She indicated the mat in the hall.

Dutifully, Ridpath wiped his shoes, going that extra mile to make sure they were clean.

'I'll get him for you. He's doing his homework at the moment. He's at the grammar school, you know.'

She went upstairs, returning two minutes later with a young boy, tall for his age.

'Hi Tony, my name's Detective Inspector Ridpath. I'd like to ask you a few questions about the day David disappeared.'

The boy stayed silent.

'Can you answer a few questions for me?'

The boy shrugged his shoulders.

'Can you tell me what happened when David disappeared?'

'We were playing basketball... then Daniel realised his brother was missing so we went looking for him but couldn't see him anywhere.'

'You were playing basketball with the boys from the estate? I thought I told you never to mix with them.' Mrs Greene's voice could shatter cut glass.

Her son stayed silent.

'That's great, Tony, we just want a few more details about that day. How did you guys meet? Was it by chance?'

Tony glanced at this mother and then shook his head. 'I texted Daniel. I was so bored at home and Mum had gone out.'

'I told you to stay in that day and read. Why—'

Ridpath interrupted her. 'So you texted Daniel. What time was that?'

'About noontime. I also texted the other guys and we agreed to meet up at one p.m. in the park near the basketball court.'

'Are you sure of the time, Tony?'

He nodded.

'Are the messages still on your phone?' asked Ridpath.

He nodded again.

'Can you show them to me?'

'My phone's upstairs.'

'Go and get it, please.'

They sat in the lounge room, listening to a clock tick on the mantlepiece. Finally, Mrs Greene blurted out, 'He's a good boy, I told him never to pal around with those boys from the estate. They're a bad lot, you mark my words.'

'He's not in trouble, Mrs Greene, and they're not a bad lot. They were just playing basketball together.'

Tony returned with his phone and showed Ridpath the messages. The first was timed at 12.05.

> Wanna meet for a game?

The reply came a minute later from Daniel.

> Yeah, stuck in house. Right minging. Dad's watching telly and brother's a pain.

> Mint. I'll text the others. Meet at one?

> I'll try, need to work on my dad lol.

> Dad says OK but have to take me bro

> Gr8

'So you'd done this before, arranged to meet?'

Another glance at his mother. 'Yeah, it's no fun stuck inside.'

'So you went out and met the Carsleys?'

'Yeah, saw them at the playground. Dan's brother was playing on the swings.'

'What time was this?'

'A little after one. One of the guys was late. So maybe ten past one.'

'Are you sure?'

Tony Greene frowned. 'Yeah.'

'About the time, I mean.'

'Yeah, about ten past one.'

'And Daniel's brother was with him, playing on the swings.'

'That's what I said.'

Ridpath glanced across to Emily. What the hell was going on? It couldn't have been David Carsley on the tape, then. But the description matched perfectly.

It was Emily who asked the next question. 'What happened next?'

'We went to play basketball.'

'What about David?'

'He stayed in the playground.'

'On his own?'

Tony Greene nodded. 'Daniel didn't like his little brother hanging around with us so he told him to stay there while we played.'

'So how many others were on the court with you?'

Tony counted on his fingers. 'Altogether six of us. Me and Daniel, the Cassidy twins, Mike Murphy, and Fred Simpson, but Fred was called away by his mum after a couple of minutes. Right narked he was.'

'Not easy to play basketball with only five people.'

'It's easy, we played attack vs defence. Three defenders versus two attackers.'

'But that means you just used one basket, right?'

'Yeah, you only need one.'

'Which one? The one closest to the playground or the one furthest away?'

'The one furthest away. The basket at the other end has a hole in it.'

'Who played attack?'

'I did with Daniel. We're the best.'

'So let me get this right. If you're playing at this end, your back would have been towards the playground, right?'

'Yeah.'

'So when did Daniel notice the man was speaking to his brother?'

'What do you mean? What man?'

'Daniel told us he noticed a man talking to his brother and ran to tell him to stay away.'

Tony Greene frowned. 'I don't remember that. We played all the time. When Daniel noticed his brother wasn't in the playground, we all ran with him to look. We'd had enough anyway.'

Ridpath stared at Emily Parkinson.

She took up the questioning. 'Are you sure, Tony? This is important. Did Daniel ever leave the game to run back to his brother?'

'No, he was with us all the time. You can ask the others if you want.'

Chapter 58

Ridpath stood outside the house trying to work it all out.

'I don't understand what's going on,' said Emily. 'I could have sworn that was David Carsley on the CCTV monitor in the ATM, but it couldn't have been him. Tony Greene has confirmed David was with his brother in the playground at ten past one.'

Ridpath ran his fingers through his rapidly thinning hair. 'The way I see it, there are two possible scenarios. It was him on the ATM CCTV and the man in the white car picked him up and dropped him back at home.'

'But both Daniel and the father said they were at home all morning. The tweets suggest they are telling the truth. Plus to get in the white car and then be taken home means he knew the man. But Turnbull asked if they knew anybody with a white car and they said no.'

'The second scenario is it wasn't David but somebody else.'

'I don't buy that. The clothes matched and he looked like David. I had Phil Reynolds run the facial recognition software and it came back as an 87 per cent match. He can't be in two places at the same time, it doesn't make sense.'

Ridpath stared down at his feet, realising he hadn't polished his shoes in ages. They looked ugly and uncared for. 'And we have an even bigger problem,' he finally said.

'What?'

'Daniel Carsley has been lying to us. Tony Greene said he never left the basketball court all the time they were playing...'

'…So he couldn't have warned any man to stay away from his brother.'

'We don't even know whether the man exists or not.'

'But he gave us a detailed description of him. We've had it in every newspaper for the last two weeks.'

'Perhaps he created the man from something he had seen at school or on TV.'

'But why would Daniel lie to us?'

'I don't know, but it's probably time to ask him, don't you think?'

'Do we have time for lunch?'

Ridpath checked his watch. 'It's just after noon now. Let's grab a sausage roll from Greggs and eat it on the way.'

'The last of the healthy eaters, Ridpath.'

'You can grab one of the vegan sausage rolls if you're worried about your health. I hear Piers Morgan rates them.'

'Thanks a bundle.'

He opened the car door and stopped, staring into mid-air.

Emily had already fastened herself into the passenger seat. 'Hello, Earth to Ridpath. There's a sausage roll calling your name, but we have to drive there.'

He slipped into the car slowly. 'I've had an idea. There is a third scenario – a way David Carsley can apparently be in two places at the same time.'

He slipped the car into gear.

'Sorry, Em, no time for lunch, we need to get moving.'

'Where?'

'Back to HQ first and then to see Daniel Carsley.'

Chapter 59

Molly Wright was doorstepping Wythenshawe police station. It was one of the ugliest buildings she had ever seen, looking more like a brick barn than a bastion of law and order.

The photographer standing next to her was eating a Holland's Meat and Potato Pie.

'Is that all you ever eat?'

'Nah, in the morning I have bacon butties.' As he spoke the crumbs of the pie tumbled from his mouth. 'Best start to the day is a bacon butty. I like mine with a couple of slices of black pudding and a good slather of butter between two doorstops of white bread.'

'Sounds like a heart attack waiting to happen.'

'Nah, healthy it is. Full of vitamins and iron. A doctor told me that once. We were doorstepping Liam Gallagher and I went down the pub. Met the doctor there and we had a long chat.'

'The doctor was in the pub? What time was this?'

'In the afternoon – Liam didn't usually wake up till six so we always got a few pints down our necks before we started in the evening.'

Molly was tempted to ask him more but decided against it. This was one of those conversations she was always having while waiting for something to happen – for Godot to arrive or Estragon to realise he was never coming.

There was movement at the front of the nick. She elbowed the photographer, who stuffed the remaining lump of pie in his mouth and reached for his cameras like a gunslinger going for his six-shooter.

Paul Turnbull, the SIO, had appeared in the doorway and was waiting for a car.

Molly Wright walked up to him, the photographer trailing in her wake.

'Hello, DCI Turnbull, anything to say regarding the Carsley case?'

He looked at her down his long nose. His bald head was shinier than normal. Either he had recently shaved it or the sun was at the correct angle to highlight its smoothness.

Either way, it annoyed Molly. She hated men with bald heads almost as much as she hated other reporters.

'No comment, Molly.'

'Don't be like that, Mr Turnbull, you must have something to say.'

'Oh, I do, Molly, but not to the likes of you.'

She didn't like that sneer, not one little bit. 'We hear you've brought Michael Carsley in for questioning?'

'Have I?'

He was going to play that little game, was he?

'Yeah, you have. And you've got till this evening to charge him otherwise you have to let him go. But he's not singing, is he, Mr Turnbull? Doesn't know your tune, does he? My readers are going to be wondering, is he the bad man who killed his son or are the police looking for a convenient scapegoat?'

Turnbull faced her. 'And what do you think, Molly?'

'I haven't decided yet, Mr Turnbull.'

A car squeaked to a halt in front of them, forcing the photographer to jump out of the way as he took his shots.

'But when I do, I'm sure my articles will help the readers make up their minds. It could go either way.'

'Bye, Molly, I have work to do.'

He stepped down and opened the car door.

'Which way would you like it to go, Mr Turnbull? I think your boss, Claire Trent, has already made up her mind, don't you?'

At the mention of Claire Trent's name, he stopped for a moment and then sat in the back seat, slamming the door. The car raced off out of the main gate.

Molly Wright smiled to herself.

The case could go either way, Mr Turnbull, but for you a conclusion has already been decided.

You're toast.

Chapter 60

Back at Police HQ, Ridpath went to see Chrissy first. Luckily Turnbull wasn't there but still at Wythenshawe nick putting the screws on Michael Carsley.

'Did you get hold of Liverpool?'

'You're meeting with a DI at their HQ at eleven a.m. tomorrow. He's on duty this weekend but off for a week to Llandudno from Monday. I know it's Sunday but I thought...'

'You did well, Chrissy.'

'At two p.m., the pathologist can squeeze you in for half an hour. Now, he was defensive and didn't want to meet, I had to push hard. I've sent the results of his post-mortem to Dr Schofield.'

'Great. I have one more job for you. I need to interview Daniel Carsley this afternoon.'

'If he's in the care of social services, that could be tricky, Ridpath.'

'He hasn't been returned to his mother?'

'Apparently not, I don't know why. I'll have a go at persuading them but I ain't promising anything.'

'I know you'll manage somehow.' He turned back to Emily Parkinson who was opening a file on her desk. 'We need to go to see your friendly house-trained techie and check that footage once more.'

'Not again, Ridpath. I've seen it so many times now, there's nothing new on it.'

'I've got an idea.'

'You keep saying that.'

'Do you have a street map of Manchester, Chrissy?'

'There's one here,' said Emily, holding up her Manchester A–Z.

Ridpath walked over to her desk and was joined by the civilian researcher, still wearing her City scarf despite the heat.

'Can you find a map of the Wythenshawe area?'

Emily found the right page.

'Now, can you mark on it the position of the ATM?'

'I already did it. Here.' She stabbed her finger on the page.

'Can you add in the position of the Carsleys' house?'

She took a red pen and marked an X. 'It's here.'

He traced both marks with his finger on the page. 'If you follow the roads from the park to the Carsleys' house, one of the routes takes you past the ATM.'

'So you think David was walking home when he was picked up by the man in the car?'

'Exactly. I think he got bored waiting for his big brother to finish playing basketball and he knew he wasn't wanted on the court, so he decided to go home.'

'It's the sort of impulsive thing a seven-year-old would do,' Chrissy said. 'I remember my daughter, Molly, deciding to walk to her brother's nursery, rather than come straight home from school with her friends. Luckily, she was found by a stranger who brought her home. All those hours memorising her address had paid off. I was never so worried in my life. The worse thing was I didn't even know she was missing.'

'There's a big problem with your theory, Ridpath.'

'What's that?'

'The timing. David Carsley was picked up at twelve thirty.'

'Was he? I want to look at the footage one more time.'

They went to the techies' floor. Phil Reynolds sat behind his bank of monitors as if he were cemented to the chair and hadn't moved in the last week.

'Hi, Em, good to see you again.'

They walked around and saw he was looking at a robbery.

'Two armed thugs held up a post office in Little Hulton. Got away with fifty quid and a box of Twix. We're sure they'll strike again.'

'Could we ask a favour? Could you call up our ATM footage again?' asked Ridpath.

'There's nothing else on it. Myself and Em have been over it a thousand times.'

'It'll only take five minutes to satisfy a little itch I have.'

'There's a cream for that, Ridpath,' said Phil Reynolds, but he typed a number into his keyboard and after the rattle of keys, the image of David Carsley walking past the ATM appeared on one of the monitors. They watched the whole sequence; the car stopping, them chatting, the door opening and the boy getting in the car before it drove off. In the top right-hand corner, the timer counted up.

12.31.24.

12.31.25.

12.31.26.

All the way to when the sequence ended at 12.32.08.

'Is there any way the timer could be wrong?'

'Shouldn't be. The ATM would be linked back to the bank's mainframe over a secure line. Banks operate to accuracies of milliseconds. They have to.'

'But it's not the ATM we're dealing with, it's the CCTV. Was the camera integrated into the ATM?'

Emily imagined the scene in her head. 'No, it's separate. One of those globe type cameras mounted on the wall.'

'What would happen if it wasn't part of the ATM but a separate system?'

'It wouldn't be linked to the mainframe.'

'When you talked to the head of security, Emily, what did he say?'

'He said it was one of the old machines with a separate camera which records on hard disk.'

'What if the time was wrong? What if it was, for example, exactly an hour behind?'

Reynolds shook his head. 'But that's not possible. The only time that happens is when they forget to readjust the clocks forward for British Summer Time...'

There was a long silence in the room, broken only by the whirr of electric fans keeping the machines cool.

It was Reynolds who spoke again. 'The machines haven't been properly maintained, have they? The timer is one hour out. When it says twelve thirty, it's actually one thirty.'

'There's a quick way to check,' said Emily.

She pulled out her mobile phone and rang Brian Carter, the head of security, praying he would pick up.

He did. 'Carter.'

'Hi there, it's DS Emily Parkinson from GMP. We're looking at the footage you sent across from the ATM.'

'ATM? Oh, I remember – the abduction of the boy. I hope it was useful.'

'It was indispensable, but I have a question. The timer, is it accurate?'

'Of course.'

'But could it be one hour out?'

The man chuckled. 'Sometimes, the older machines don't switch over automatically after we put the clocks forward for BST. It would only update the time if it was switched off and rebooted. The maintenance team should have done it, but sometimes they cut corners to save time.'

'So it could be one hour off?' Emily crossed her fingers.

'If it wasn't rebooted recently, that's more than likely. I can get them to run a diagnostic on it, if you like?'

Emily punched the air. 'Please could you check and send me an email with your findings for our records?'

'No worries. I hope you find the bastard.'

'Oh, we will – and with your help, we're getting closer.'

Chapter 61

'Shall we update Claire Trent?'

'Not yet, let's interview Daniel Carsley first.'

Back on the MIT floor, Chrissy had both good and bad news for them.

'Give us the good news first.'

'The social workers will allow you to interview Daniel Carsley.'

'That's great news,' said Emily.

Ridpath scratched his head. 'Why do I feel there's a big "but" coming now.'

'But, as Daniel was taken into care after an Emergency Protection Order of the Children's Act, 1989, I had to apply for an interview under Section 44, subsections 6–9.'

'What does that mean?'

'It means we will have to follow the government best evidence guidelines to the letter, including conducting the interview in the Care Home, videotaping the interview, a social worker being present all the time, a written interview plan with questions being presented before it takes place and if Daniel, or the social worker, decide the interview stops, it must end immediately.'

'Anything else?' asked Emily.

'I forgot, they're only giving you one hour.'

'Jesus,' Emily said under her breath.

'Good, it's the right way to do it. We'd better start the preparations. Can you operate the video camera, Chrissy?'

She lifted up her damaged arm. 'This is feeling a lot better since I came back to work.'

'Good. This could be the most important interview of this case.'

'There's one other thing,' said Chrissy, 'Turnbull has applied to Claire Trent for an extension to hold Michael Carsley for longer. She has granted him just four hours.'

'Not twelve hours?'

Chrissy shook her head. 'He's not a happy bunny.'

'Are they going to charge him?'

'The word on the street is yes, but he hasn't confessed yet. The extra time is for Turnbull to get his ducks in a row with the CPS. The reporters have caught wind of it and a couple of them are already camped outside Wythenshawe nick.'

'Molly Wright?'

'And her photographer.'

'Once it gets out, the whole place is going to be besieged,' said Emily.

Chrissy threw another paper down on the table. Irene McMurdo's pinched face stood out from page three beneath the headline MY CHILD WAS MY LIFE and Molly Wright's byline.

'Looks like we need to work quickly,' said Ridpath, picking up the recording equipment. 'Before Michael Carsley is hung, drawn and quartered in the pages of the national press.'

Chapter 62

They parked outside Ford Avenue children's home at 3.45.

For a moment, Ridpath took a deep breath, wrapping his arms around himself and tapping his fingers on either shoulder.

'Shall we go in?' asked Emily Parkinson.

'Just give me a second.'

'Are you OK?' Chrissy Wright leant forward from the back seat. 'I have to go in and set up before we start at five p.m.'

'I know the time, you don't have to remind me,' Ridpath snapped.

'Hey, you need to calm down, you can't interview a child in this sort of state,' said Emily, placing her hand on his arm.

'I know, I know. Give me a second. You two go in first and set up. I'll be there in a tick.'

Emily raised her eyebrows at Chrissy, and they both got out of the car, Chrissy extremely gingerly with the cast on her leg. Emily went round to the boot to get the camera and recording gear they had borrowed from Phil Reynolds.

Ridpath sat alone for a moment. Why was he so tense about this interview? They normally never worried him. There was a pattern for questioning co-operating witnesses they had all learnt years ago.

Establish rapport.

Ask the interviewee to explain the event in their own words.

Drill down on the details.

Close the interview and explain the next steps.

Every interview was the same and yet everyone was different. It was exactly as he'd been trained at Edgeley Park, and refined on the job by Charlie Whitworth.

And Charlie was the best interviewer in the business.

So why did this one feel different? Was it because it was a child? The same procedures were in play whoever was interviewed. Obviously with children and vulnerable adults, you had to be far more careful with language and the way questions were framed, but the procedures were still the same.

Establish rapport.

Ask the interviewee to explain the event in their own words.

Drill down on the details.

Close the interview and explain the next steps.

'Get yourself together, Ridpath.'

He took three deep breaths, filling his diaphragm and then letting the air out through his mouth. He instantly felt warmer, calmer, more controlled. He wished he'd known about these coping techniques far earlier in his career.

'Time to make it happen,' he said out loud.

He got out of the car and walked up the path leading to the front door. After being checked in by security and going through the usual Covid-19 precautions, he was led to a large room off the lobby. Here, Chrissy had already set up and Emily Parkinson was sat next to a tall woman with short hair and a black leather jacket.

She held out her hand. 'I'm the social worker, Ruby Grimes.'

'DI Ridpath from GMP. I presume you've already met my colleagues.'

'Actually, I know Ruby socially, Ridpath, we've met a few times.'

It was on the tip of his tongue to ask more details, but he guessed this was neither the time nor the place. Instead, he reached into his bag and pulled out the interview plan he had written with Emily that afternoon.

Ruby Grimes flicked through it, taking in the details. 'I can keep this for our files?'

'Of course.'

'And who will be leading the interview today?'

'Emily... DS Parkinson will lead as she has already established a rapport with Daniel. I will jump in occasionally when needed. Chrissy is here to operate the camera and the recorder.'

'Good. I don't have to remind you of the ground rules. If Daniel wants to stop the interview, it will cease immediately. Or if I feel Daniel is being put under too much stress, I will call a halt. Understood?'

'Agreed. What's his demeanour been like since coming to the home?'

'Not good, I'm afraid. He's fluctuating between being totally uncommunicative to shouting and swearing that he wants to go home.'

'Not the best time to interview him.'

'No, the circumstances of being separated from his father have not been good for him.'

'What about the mother?'

'We assessed her living environment and decided it would not be a safe place to put a vulnerable child. We asked Daniel and he was vehement that he didn't want to live with her.'

'Why?'

'He didn't say and I didn't ask.' She glanced at the time. 'Shall we begin? We agreed you would only have one hour.'

Ridpath nodded.

The social worker and Emily Parkinson went upstairs to fetch Daniel.

Chrissy and Ridpath were left alone in the room with the civilian officer fiddling with the controls on the video camera and adjusting the levels on the mike.

Three minutes later, Daniel appeared at the door, recognised Ridpath and stared at Chrissy, before being asked to sit down in a chair beside the desk.

He sat awkwardly, his head staring down between his knees at the floor.

'Before we start, Daniel, do you want me to call you Daniel, or Dan like I used to when I was in your house?' asked Emily.

'Dan's fine,' he answered without looking up. The accent had a soft Scottish burr to it, as still untainted by the whine of Manchester.

'Good, Dan it is then. As I was explaining upstairs, this is a more formal interview; that's why we've got Chrissy here to record it.'

'I've already given lots of interviews.'

'I know, Dan, but we need to understand what happened to David on the day he disappeared.'

'Dave. We called him Dave, not David.'

'OK, Dave it is. We're going to start taping, if that's OK with you.'

'I suppose I don't have much choice, do I?'

The social worker leant forward. 'That's untrue, Dan. If you want to stop the interview, you can right now.'

'But you want to help us understand what happened, don't you? It's important, isn't it?'

For the first time, he looked up. 'Will it bring my father back from the cop shop? He's been gone a day now. They didn't even let us say goodbye.'

'I know how you feel, Dan, it's not easy being separated from your dad. But this interview is to help us understand better.'

'So he's going to be released soon?'

'Honestly, I don't know what's happening with your father, Dan, but as soon as I do, I promise we'll let Ruby know and she can tell you. Alright?'

The boy nodded, looking down again.

'Can we start now?'

He nodded again.

Chrissy started the tape machine with a loud click. Daniel looked up and smiled for the first time. 'It's a bit old, ain't it?'

'Yeah, we're old-school in Greater Manchester. One day we'll drag ourselves kicking and screaming into the twenty-first century,' said Chrissy.

Ridpath stared at her – she was supposed to be silent.

'You're a City fan too?' He pointed to the scarf around her neck.

'Yeah, since I was your age. Been through ups and downs with that lot, I can tell you.'

'Dad says he'll take me to a match one day when he gets his job back. Pep's mint, ain't he?'

'He's better than that, but he's still got a job to do in the Champion's League.'

'Yeah, but this year is our year, I reckon.'

'Me too.'

'You guys can talk about football afterwards but let's get the interview finished first, OK?' interrupted Emily. 'So you know who everybody is, Dan. Your City fan operating the video camera is Chrissy Wright, a civilian officer with Greater Manchester Police. DI Ridpath is also with GMP...'

'I thought you were with the coroner?'

'I'm with both, seconded to the coroner for a while,' answered Ridpath.

'Seconded?'

'Like a footballer, I'm out on loan to another club for a while.'

'I get it.'

Emily continued. 'Ruby Grimes is a residential social worker for Manchester Children's Services and I am DS Emily Parkinson. It's 4.05 p.m. on the afternoon of 8 August 2020. Before we go on, I'd like to say if you don't understand any of my questions, Dan, let me know and I'll ask them in an easier way so you do understand. Also if you can't remember, say "I don't know" or "I don't remember". We want to know what happened, that's all. Do you understand?'

'I get it.'

'And there's one other thing. You do know the difference between telling the truth and telling a lie, don't you?'

For a moment, his eyes flickered and he looked down again. 'I think so,' he mumbled.

'It's important you tell me the truth about things that have happened to you, Dan. Before we begin, I want to make sure you understand the difference between the truth and a lie.'

He lifted his head.

Emily continued, almost sounding like somebody from children's television. 'Let me tell you a story about John. John was playing with his ball in the kitchen and he hit the ball against the window. The window broke and John ran upstairs into his bedroom. John's dad saw the broken window, and asked John if he had broken it. John said, "No, Dad." Did John tell a lie or the truth, or don't you know?'

'John told a lie.'

'What do you think he should have said?'

'He should have told his dad he broke the window.'

'Because if he lies, somebody else might get into trouble, right?'

He nodded slowly.

'Good, I knew you'd understand, you're a smart cookie who always beats me at Warcraft.'

He laughed. 'That's because you're a noob.'

She laughed along and answered, 'Tell me about it.' After a few seconds, she composed herself and said, 'I'd also like you to tell me about the day your brother, Dave, disappeared. Take your time and try to remember as much as you can.'

He started haltingly. 'We'd been in the house all morning, me and Dave, watching TV and playing games. Dad had made us pancakes for breakfast. He makes good pancakes, but his porridge is crap, he puts salt in it. Then I asked him if I could go to the park. He said yes as long as I took Dave too. So we got ourselves ready and went out. We went over the road to the park and played on the swings for a while, before I met some friends who were going to play basketball. There's a court not far from the playground...'

'What did Dave do?'

'He wanted to stay at the playground.'

Ridpath looked across at Emily Parkinson. She had learnt her lessons well in Interview 101. Her body language was exactly mirroring that of Daniel; sat back in the chair, shoulders slumped, most of the time looking down but occasionally looking up, her hands by her side.

'So you went to the playground. What happened then?'

'I played with the others, defence and attack. I kept looking over to Dave to check he was OK. Dad had told me to look after my younger brother. One time, I looked across and a man was talking to Dave, so I stopped playing and ran back to the playground. The man was still there so I told him I would call the police unless he left Dave alone.'

'What did the man do?'

'He ran away sharpish, like he was afraid.'

'So what did you do?'

'I ran back to finish the game because the other lads were calling me. When I looked around again Dave wasn't there. So I went back to the playground and started looking for him, shouting his name, but he didn't answer.'

'What did you do next?'

'I thought he could have run home. I ran back across the road and asked Dad, but he hadn't seen him. We started looking then, meeting a copper on horseback in the park. Big hoss it was too, much bigger than me. The copper spoke on his radio and I heard it squawk but I couldn't hear what they were saying. Anyway, we carried on searching and then Dad rang the police again and they came out to look.' A long pause. 'That's it.'

Ridpath had been taking notes all this time. Everybody was looking at him as his pen scrawled across his pad.

Finally, Emily said, 'Would you like something to drink, Daniel, after such a long time talking? Shall we take a break for five minutes?'

'OK, I wouldn't mind going to the bathroom.'

'I'll take you,' said Ruby.

As they left the room, Ridpath's phone buzzed with a message.

> Michael Carsley going to be charged with the murder of his son at eight p.m. this evening.

Chapter 63

I was out yesterday but I didn't find anybody. There were a few children I could have taken but none had the innocence I was looking for.

What is wrong with this young generation? Why do they all look like they know everything and have seen it all? Perhaps it's the internet? Or YouTube? Or video bloggers?

I came back depressed and lonely. I thought about going to the other house but I didn't want to be alone, not tonight.

Mother sits there, not saying a word, but I know she's angry with me.

Time to find somebody.

I hope he's as good as the boy in the United shirt. I remember clearly his last words as he lay on the bed. 'Please leave me alone, please.'

I decided to kill him then.

He took a long time to die and I had to finish him off with a chokehold.

I'll keep the next one for longer.

He'll be my friend.

Chapter 64

Ridpath ran out of the interview room and past the surprised security guard as he dialled Claire Trent's number on his phone. 'What the hell's going on?'

'I'll remind you not to use that tone of voice with me, Detective Inspective Ridpath.' The voice at the other end of the phone sounded like a knife being scraped across a whetting stone. 'As Senior Investigating Officer, DCI Turnbull has decided, in collaboration with the Crown Prosecution Service, to charge Michael Carsley with murder at eight p.m. this evening.'

'But it's bullshit. Where's his evidence?'

'He obviously feels he has enough and the CPS agrees with him. A press release will be going out later this evening.'

'But we have video evidence confirming Michael Carsley wasn't involved.'

'What? Why didn't you tell me earlier?'

'We need to get confirmation from Daniel Carsley. We're halfway through the interview when I received a text saying Michael is going to be charged.'

'Who released the information? Everyone has been ordered to keep it under wraps.'

'That's not the point, boss, Carsley is innocent.'

He heard a long sigh down the end of the phone, followed by 'I want to see this evidence, Ridpath, now.'

'I need to finish the interview with Daniel Carsley first. We still have thirty minutes left with him.'

'Right, finish and be in my office at five thirty with your evidence that Carsley is innocent.'

The phone rang off abruptly. Ridpath stared at the empty screen for a second before returning inside to the interview room.

Emily was still sat in the same place. Chrissy was checking the footage she had shot in the first part of the interview.

'Well?'

'It's true, Emily, he's going to be charged.'

'What am I supposed to do now? I promised Daniel I would let him know as soon as I heard anything about his father.'

Ridpath made the decision for her. 'Tell him as we conclude the interview.'

'Not straight away?'

'No.'

'Is that an order, DI Ridpath?'

'No, it's an instruction, Emily. And I will tell him.'

As they spoke, Daniel Carsley came back in the room, drinking a coke and eating a bag of cheese and onion crisps. He sat in the same place and Chrissy readjusted the focus on his face. She switched on the tape machine with another loud click.

Daniel Carsley smiled at her.

'We are now ready to resume the interview with Daniel Carsley at 4.29 p.m.' Emily's voice had changed. It was harder now when she spoke into the microphone, not as soft as before. 'Right, Daniel, are you ready to begin again?'

'Yeah, I'm getting hungry, though,' he said through a mouthful of crisp.

'Your evening meal is at six,' said Ruby Grimes. 'I think it's fish and chips tonight.'

'I like fish and chips.'

'Daniel,' began Emily, 'I'd like to dig a little deeper into your statement, ask a few questions to clarify the details. Would that be OK?'

The boy nodded. 'OK.'

'Now right at the beginning you said you asked your dad if you could go to the park. Is that correct?'

'Yeah.'

'What time did you ask him?'

'Dunno, nearly one o'clock I think.'

'Why did you ask him then?'

Daniel thought for a moment. 'Me and me brother were bored and there was nothing on the box except stuff about antiques and doing up houses.' Then he seemed to remember something. 'And Tony Greene texted me saying they were going to the basketball court so it seemed a good time to ask Dad.'

Emily glanced across at Ridpath. Daniel was telling them everything, he just needed prompting to remember the details.

Ridpath remained as stony-faced as ever.

'So you went to the park. What time was it when you left the house?'

'I dunno.'

'Had the BBC News started?'

'I think it had. I remember hearing that rotten music as we were going out the door.'

'So you went to the park, crossing the main road with your brother...'

'Yeah, I held his hand like my dad said and waited for the green man.'

'Perfect, that's exactly the right way to cross the road. What did you see when you walked to the park?'

'What do you mean?'

'Did you see anybody? Hear anything?'

Daniel closed his eyes, obviously reliving the walk. 'There were a couple of men fixing one of the fairground trucks and there was the smell of cut grass everywhere. I remember Dave sneezing, he hated that smell.'

'So you arrived at the park and went to the playground. Why there?'

Daniel frowned. 'Sorry, I don't understand.'

'Why did you go to the playground? It's a big park, you could have gone anywhere.'

Daniel smiled as he understood the question. 'Dave wanted to play on the swings and it's where we always met up with Tony Greene.'

Once again, Emily glanced across at Ridpath. He carried on writing in his notepad, not returning her look.

'Good. When did Tony Greene and your friends arrive?'

'I dunno.'

'Was it five minutes or ten minutes after you were in the playground?'

'I dunno, not long, though. We weren't there long.'

'So you met them. What did you do next?'

'Like I said, we went to the court to play basketball.'

'Leaving Dave on the swings.'

'Yeah, he wanted to carry on in the playground.'

'It must be a bit of a pain having a younger brother trailing around you all the time,' said Ridpath.

Daniel smiled. 'Yeah, it is,' he answered quickly before remembering and changing his response. 'Yeah, it was.'

Emily pushed a sheet of paper and a marker pen across the table to Daniel. 'Could you do me a favour? Could you draw the park, putting in the basketball court and the playground?'

Daniel seemed glad of the change, giving him something to do. Ridpath glanced at the time: 4.45. He saw the social worker, Ruby Grimes, had seen it too.

Daniel finished drawing and held up the paper. 'Here's the court and here's the playground. The path we took here leads to the main entrance.'

'Aren't there a few trees between the court and the playground? Could you draw them for me?'

He quickly drew a couple of trees in a child's style.

'Now where were the baskets? Can you draw them in?'

'Sure, they're at either end. But we always play this way because one of the baskets is broken and nobody's fixed it.'

'One last favour. Can you draw a circle to show where you were and the rest of the players, putting a name above each one?'

'But we were moving around all the time?'

'No worries, show me roughly where you were.'

'We were playing two attackers versus three defenders. I was an attacker.'

'All the time?'

'No, some of the time I played defence.'

When he had finished naming the players and their positions, Emily looked at the drawing and said, 'So when did you notice the man talking to Dave?'

Daniel looked down and mumbled. 'I don't know what time it was.'

'Make a guess. Had you been playing for five minutes? Ten minutes? Fifteen minutes?'

'I don't know.'

'Could it have been twenty minutes?'

'Daniel has already said he doesn't know, DS Parkinson.'

'And when did you run across to speak to the man?'

'I dunno.'

'Daniel has answered the question.'

Emily held her hands up. 'This is important, Dan. Remember what we said earlier about telling the truth?'

The boy looked like he had been caught in a trap.

'Because when we talked to Tony Greene, he said you never left the basketball court. You stayed there all the time playing the game.'

Daniel looked across at Ruby Grimes, then at Ridpath and finally at Chrissy Wright, none of whom reacted.

Emily asked the question. 'Did you run across to Dave?'

Daniel Carsley stared down at his feet and shook his head.

'I'm sorry, Dan, I've got to hear your answer.'

'No,' he said quietly.

'You didn't run across to talk to a man, did you?'

'No.'

'Did you see a man?'

'No.'

'Dan,' said Ridpath, speaking for the first time.

The boy looked up, his eyes full of tears.

'You mustn't blame yourself. You did nothing wrong.'

'But if I'd looked after him better, like my dad said, then he wouldn't be dead. He'd still be alive.' There were tears in his eyes. 'It's ma fault.'

Ridpath understood the emotions the boy was feeling. That overwhelming sense of guilt, that sat in the middle of the chest like a lump of concrete. When he spoke again, he knew the words were meant to reassure himself as much as for the boy. 'It's not your fault, Dan. A bad man hurt your brother, don't blame yourself.'

'I think it's time to end this interview, Daniel is unable to carry on.'

'One last question, Ruby... please,' asked Ridpath.

She nodded.

'Dan, why did you leave Scotland? Was your dad hitting you?'

The boy exploded. 'You don't get it, do you?' he yelled. 'It was my ma, my ma who was hurting me and Dave. She was sick and couldn't control herself. She kept hitting us. Dad took the blame but it wasn't him.'

'This interview is definitely over,' said Ruby.

Chapter 65

Ruby Grimes took Daniel back upstairs so he could dry his eyes before he sat down to dinner. The last thing she wanted was for the other residents to see he had been crying.

Ridpath, Emily and Chrissy were left alone in the room. The place was cold as if a shroud had been wrapped around it. In this case the shroud was a young boy's guilt.

Eventually, Ridpath broke the silence.

'Did you get everything on tape, Chrissy?'

'Yeah.' The answer was monosyllabic, almost sullen in its tone.

He checked his watch. 'I'll need it for my interview with Claire Trent at five thirty.'

'You want me to be in the meeting?' asked Emily.

Ridpath shook his head. 'Best if I handle this one alone. If Turnbull is there it could get nasty.'

'Do we have enough to prove Michael Carsley is innocent?'

'I think so. We know David went with his brother to the park and then he vanished. My theory was he got bored waiting for his brother and decided to walk home. He was picked up by the man in the white car outside the ATM. Michael Carsley doesn't have a car and can't even drive so that rules him out.'

'It had to be somebody David knew,' said Chrissy.

'Not necessarily. He was young and maybe he was starting to panic and felt lost. An adult stops and says he'll drive you home. What do you do?'

'You get in the car...' said Emily.

'At least, we know now why they left Scotland. I'll get onto Glasgow and find out everything about Irene Carsley.' Chrissy adjusted the City scarf around her neck. 'Poor woman, what made her hit her kids?'

'See if you can find out, it might help convince Claire Trent.'

'When are we going to tell Daniel his dad's going to be charged? I promised I would tell Ruby as soon as I knew anything. Well, I know something and we haven't told him.'

'He's in no state to hear that news now.'

'I agree, Ridpath, but can you imagine the state he'll be in when he finds out? Besides, I gave my word.'

'I agree, he must be told. Let me talk with Claire Trent, maybe I can convince her and Turnbull to release Michael Carsley.'

'And if you can't?'

'I'll come back here and tell him. He has to find out this evening. I'm sure it will be plastered across the newspapers tomorrow morning.'

'It may be on the evening news…'

'I'll take that chance.' Ridpath stood up. 'I'm going back to HQ, do you want a lift?'

They both nodded.

'Ridpath…'

'Yes, Chrissy.'

'I don't want to do this again.'

'Do what?'

'Be present at an interview. I just want to do my work in the office. In fact, I don't ever want to leave there again.' She paused for a moment, regarding both Emily and Ridpath. 'I don't know how you do what you do. It's like you are…' She searched for the words, '…vultures feeding on carrion. No disrespect meant.'

'None taken, Chrissy.'

'The interview made me feel dirty. How do you sleep at night?'

'With difficulty, sometimes, Chrissy. I take a long hot bath to wash away the sins of the day,' answered Emily.

'And you, Ridpath?'

Ridpath stood there, eventually answering, 'I don't.'

Chapter 66

Claire Trent was waiting for Ridpath in her office. Paul Turn-bull wasn't there.

'Where is he?'

'I thought it better that he stayed away until I heard your new evidence. He's convinced that Michael Carsley is guilty; no alibi, the domestic abuse of his wife and kids, and there is another reason why he was finally arrested this afternoon. Turnbull got a warrant to search the house, finding the underpants David was supposed to be wearing hidden in the bedroom.'

'What was Carsley's answer?'

'He said David must have changed them before he went out.'

'Why would he do that?'

'Exactly Turnbull's response. So what's your evidence, Ridpath? It had better be bloody good.'

He had spent a long time on the drive back to HQ thinking about the sequence of events and how best to present the evidence to Claire Trent. His theory that the boy had decided to walk home on his own was only that, a theory. But it did explain the video footage and the timeline.

He decided to show Daniel's interview footage first to give a better context for everything else.

'You've just shot this?'

'We concluded the interview not long ago, at slightly before five p.m.'

'Get on with it, then.'

Claire Trent sat through Daniel's interview, not a glimmer of emotion appearing on her face. 'So you only got two things from Daniel; he'd arranged to meet the boys in the park and he didn't go back to check on his brother.'

'It means we have to discount the story of the man in the playground. He made it up.'

Claire Trent's mouth soured as she thought of all the newspaper articles and wanted posters adorning lampposts, shops, police stations and post offices throughout Manchester, not to mention the press conference and interviews she had given on television, her newly cut hair and brilliant white teeth on prominent display.

'Why would he do that?'

Ridpath stared at the top of her desk. The wood wasn't real, but a cheap veneer over MDF. 'Guilt, probably. His dad had told him to look after his brother and he let his dad down. Guilt drives people to do strange things.'

'In this case, to waste thousands of hours of police resources and manpower chasing somebody who didn't exist. I should charge him for wasting police time.'

'You can't charge a ten-year-old who's just lost his brother.'

Claire Trent nodded. 'More's the pity. This interview was well done, Ridpath – congratulate Emily Parkinson for me, she has a talent for getting information. But none of it contradicts any of Turnbull's evidence.'

'You're wrong, boss. I asked Daniel a question after the social worker said stop the tape. Luckily, Chrissy kept rolling.'

Ridpath played the question about why they had left Glasgow, and the boy's reply; that it was the mother who beat them, not the father.

'This is merely the assertion of a ten-year-old. It wouldn't stand up as evidence.'

'But it gives the real reason why they left. Plus I understand now why Daniel refuses to live with his mother.'

'Still…'

'Chrissy is going to check with Child Services in Glasgow.'

Claire Trent frowned. 'OK, you've probably got a chance of removing one of Paul Turnbull's planks of evidence, but you have to remember it was Michael Carsley who was given a warning, not his wife.'

'I think it's the reason the Procurator Fiscal didn't proceed with the case. There wasn't enough certainty about who was responsible for the abuse.'

Claire Trent frowned again. 'Get Chrissy to check it out. What else do you have, Ridpath?'

Ridpath pulled out the street map of Wythenshawe showing the park. 'It's my theory that David Carsley got bored waiting for Daniel to finish the game so he decided to walk home alone...'

'Any evidence for this?'

'None, but it fits with the facts. The ATM camera is on the route from the park to David's home.'

'You've showed me the footage already, are you bringing it up again?'

'It's the key to the case.'

She sighed loudly. 'Show me the footage again, Ridpath.'

He pressed play on his laptop, crossing his fingers as he did.

Detective Superintendent Claire Trent stared intently at the images on the screen. 'You still have the problems Paul Turnbull pointed out. The timing is an hour wrong and we don't have a positive ID of David Carsley.'

'We checked with the owners of the ATM. The camera time is supposed to be adjusted manually during maintenance. Apparently, they forgot. So when the time is actually one thirty, it displays twelve thirty. We're getting a sworn statement from their head of security who is an ex-copper.'

'At least that makes sense, but you then have another problem.'

'What's that?'

'If the timing is wrong, the video evidence is inadmissible in court. You can't use it.'

Ridpath thought on his feet. 'That's true, boss. We can't use it to confirm the time, but we could use it to confirm an identification.'

'Hmm,' was all Claire Trent answered, sitting back in her chair.

'The other evidence is a similar white car was seen close to the disposal location of the body. We captured the footage from a tram.'

'This is still pretty weak, Ridpath. We're not even certain if it's the same car.'

'But the coincidence is strong, boss.'

'Coincidence is not evidence, Ridpath, you should know that by now.'

She sat forward and closed her eyes, resting her head on her elbows and running her fingers through her thick blonde hair. Ridpath could see the dark roots close to her scalp.

'Let me understand this. We have a witness who admits he has been telling us lies and wasting our time. And we have a video with the wrong time which may or may not have pictures of David Carsley getting into a white car. Plus we have footage of a white car in the area where the body was disposed of, which may or may not be the same model and make. Have I summed this up correctly?'

'You've forgotten one thing, boss.'

'What's that?'

'We are about to charge a man for the murder of his son who didn't commit the crime.'

Chapter 67

The need, the hunger was growing inside him like a cancer, possessing his body, dominating his soul.

The voices in his head were shouting now.

Do it.

Do it.

DO IT.

At work, he went through the motions, pretending all was OK, as polite and subservient as ever.

Inside, he was ready to explode.

He must act soon.

We must act soon.

Chapter 68

Claire Trent raised her head, staring directly at Ridpath. 'Leave everything with me.'

'What are you going to do?'

Detective Superintendent Claire Trent thought for a long time before finally answering. 'You don't have enough here to stop the arrest of Michael Carsley yet...'

'But you saw for yourself. A man in a white car abducted the boy.'

'A man in a white car apparently gave a lift to a boy who looked like David Carsley...'

'At the same time and in the same area?'

'You don't have the right time.'

'I'm getting a statement from the head of security of the ATM company stating the machine was one hour out.'

'That will help... And the identification of David Carsley?'

'Only two people could do that. Michael or Daniel.'

'So your next steps are...?'

Claire Trent was leading him to a conclusion. 'I need to show the video to either of them and confirm the ID.'

'But Turnbull probably won't let you near Michael Carsley, so...'

Ridpath sighed. 'I need to interview Daniel Carsley again.'

'When?'

'This evening, if I can.'

'If you get a positive ID from Daniel Carsley, I will persuade Turnbull and CPS to postpone charging Michael Carsley, pending the review of your evidence.'

'Docs persuade mean order, boss?'

'No, it means persuade, but as you know, Ridpath, I can be very persuasive when I want to be. And Ridpath, you might want to ask Daniel about the underwear.'

'Why?'

'Because if there is a reason why the underwear was hidden in the bedroom, then all of Paul Turnbull's evidence has vanished.' She begins to count off her fingers. 'One, we have a positive ID of a man in a white car picking up David at the time he disappeared. Michael Carsley doesn't drive. Two, I'm sure Chrissy will find evidence that it was the mother, not the father, who was abusing the children. And three, the only thing left is the underwear in the house. Not enough to justify an arrest for murder. In the absence of other evidence, the defence would be able to explain it away easily.'

Ridpath frowned. 'You told me before there were two other pieces of evidence against Michael Carsley. Leaving the house at one thirty and a fingerprint on the clothes.'

Another long sigh. 'Carsley has admitted he left the house at one thirty. He says he went to buy the kids some chocolate as a treat when they came back from the park.'

'You've confirmed it's true, haven't you?'

'He paid with a debit card as he didn't have any cash. The receipt shows he bought chocolate at 1.40. He just forgot.'

'And the fingerprint?'

She put on an officious voice. '"The lab cannot confirm or deny the presence of a fingerprint on item 22/47." Apparently, there was a mix-up in the chain of evidence. They're saying they can't get the staff.'

'So… if I can get Daniel to ID his brother…'

She raised her eyebrows.

'…There's only one problem. I don't think I can get in to see Daniel again tonight. He was pretty upset at the end of the last interview and you heard the social worker at the end of the tape.'

'It's time for you to be persuasive, Ridpath.' She checked the time. 'It's already six thirty. I'd get a move on if I were you?' She went back to reading her file.

Ridpath moved towards the door, then stopped, turning back. 'How do you do the job you do, boss?'

She paused in her reading and looked up. 'Because you can't go charging at every obstacle that gets in your way, Ridpath. Sometimes, you have to look up and work out a way to go round and still achieve what you want. That's my job. You should consider it one day.'

Chapter 69

On the MIT floor, Chrissy and Emily Parkinson were waiting for the news.

'What happened? Is she going to release Michael?'

'Not yet. We have to get Daniel to confirm the ID of David Carsley.'

'What?' Emily's mouth dropped open. 'You're going to ask a ten-year-old boy to watch footage of his brother being abducted?'

'That's about it.'

'An abduction which he blames himself for allowing to happen?'

'If he doesn't confirm the ID, his father stays in detention.'

She walked away and then turned back. 'This is fucked up, Ridpath, really fucked up.'

'And besides,' added Chrissy, 'Ruby Grimes won't let you anywhere near him tonight.'

'That's what we're going to find out.'

Ridpath pulled his mobile phone from out of his pocket and dialled the number on her business card. The call was answered after three rings.

'Ruby Grimes,' she said brightly.

'Hi there, it's DI Ridpath.'

Immediately, the tone changed. 'Yes, what do you want?'

'I have a favour to ask.'

'If it's about work, I don't do favours.'

'I need to show Daniel some footage this evening.'

'No.'

'But you haven't heard me out yet.'

'The answer is still no. You got him worked up earlier. I've spent the last hour calming him down and he's now eating his dinner. Afterwards, he'll watch television with the other boys before lights out.'

'Listen, we promised we would keep him up to date on any news about his father...'

'Yessss.'

'Well, he will be charged this evening at eight p.m. with the murder of David Carsley.'

'What?'

'The father will be charged—'

'I heard you the first time, Ridpath. How could they charge a man for the murder of his own son?'

'They believe they have enough evidence. The only way we can get GMP and the CPS to back off is to present evidence that Michael Carsley didn't abduct his son.'

Her voice sounded suspicious. 'How are you going to do that?'

Ridpath took the plunge, crossing his fingers. 'We've found footage from CCTV of David Carsley on the day of the abduction. We need Daniel to confirm it is his brother.'

'No, definitely no. You can't show footage from the day of the abduction. Daniel is going through enough trauma without having to suffer more.'

For a moment, Ridpath saw Polly opening the door, the flash of a gun muzzle, the sound of the shot, Polly falling backwards, another shot, Polly lying bleeding on the hall floor, her life oozing from her chest.

'I understand, Ruby, but it's the only way we can get them not to charge Michael Carsley. If there was another way, believe me, I would use it.'

'Ask Michael himself, he could identify his own son.'

Ridpath stayed silent.

The penny dropped for her. 'You can't get in to see him, can you?'

'He's being questioned at the moment...' Ridpath let his voice trail off.

'So Daniel is your last hope if you want to release Michael Carsley?'

'That's it, in a nutshell.'

'Damned if I agree and damned if I don't. I'm stuffed either way.'

'If there was another way of doing this, I'd use it, but there isn't.'

There was another long silence at the end of the phone.

'How soon can you get here?'

'Thirty minutes. Sooner if we can.'

'Right. Seven thirty it is. I'll warn Daniel you're coming.'

'Please don't say anything about the reason.'

'Why?'

'We can't be seen to be leading a witness in any way. We must only show him the footage and film his answer. We can't be seen to be giving him any inducement.'

'The possibility of his father being released and not charged is an inducement?' Her voice rose at the end of the sentence.

'The courts might see it that way. We can't take the risk.'

He could hear her sighing at the other end of the phone. 'OK, I won't tell him and we'll do the interview at seven thirty.'

'Thank you, Ruby.'

'Ridpath?'

'Yes.'

'How do you do what you do?'

It was the same question he'd asked Claire Trent only fifteen minutes ago.

Unlike her, he didn't have an answer.

Chapter 70

They set up quickly in the same room in the children's home as before.

Despite her previous disquiet, Chrissy had agreed to come with them. 'He's a City fan, you have to support your own.'

They decided this time Ridpath would ask the questions and Emily would take notes.

Daniel was brought into the room by Ruby Grimes at exactly seven thirty. 'I've told him you want to ask a few more questions. If at any time he wants to leave and go back to watch television, all he has to do is tell me and I will immediately stop the interview.'

Daniel eyed them suspiciously before sitting in the same seat as before in front of the camera. 'I've already answered your questions, why do I have to be here again?'

Ridpath smiled tentatively. 'I'm sorry, Dan, we need to clarify a few matters and give you some news.'

'What news? Is it about my dad? Can I go home?'

'Let's just ask a few questions and then I'll let you know, OK?'

Daniel nodded once and looked away.

Ridpath indicated with a wave of his hand that Chrissy should begin recording. Again, the machine started with a loud click and a whirr. 'Sorry, same old police, same old machines.'

'It is exactly 7.30 p.m. on 9 August, and we are back in Ford Avenue children's home to interview Daniel Carsley. This is the second recorded interview of this witness today. In the room are myself, Detective Inspector Thomas Ridpath, Detective

Sergeant Emily Parkinson, the residential social worker, Ruby Grimes, and a police civilian support officer, Chrissy Wright, operating the recording equipment.' A second's pause as Ridpath caught his breath. 'Now, Dan, I'm going to show you some footage and I would like you to tell me who is on the tape. Do you understand? For the record, I am now going to show Daniel Carsley a video on my laptop.'

On the way down to the children's home, Chrissy had quickly edited the footage from the ATM just to show the time when David was in front of the ATM, cutting out the later footage of the white car.

Ridpath pressed play and Daniel leant forward to look closely. 'That's Dave. Where did you get this?'

'Are you sure it's David Carsley?'

'I know my own brother. Where did you get it?'

Ridpath ignored the question. 'Would you like to see it again to be sure?'

Daniel nodded.

'I am now showing the witness the same footage again.'

Daniel leant even further forward. 'That's my brother. He's wearing the same clothes as the day...'

His voice trailed off as he realised where the footage came from.

Ridpath pushed on, not wanting to lose momentum. 'I'm now going to show a second piece of footage, marked as item 2. Dan, do you recognise the car in this tape?'

Ridpath pressed play, revealing the footage from the tram taken on the day David's body was found.

Daniel shook his head. 'We don't have a car in Manchester. Dad doesn't know how to drive. Mum drove all the time when we were in Scotland.'

'You don't recognise it?'

'Nah, never seen it before. Why? What is it?'

Ridpath continued. 'One last question and then we'll be finished.' He pressed a key on the laptop and a picture came up. 'These are Dave's briefs. You told the police earlier he was wearing them on the day he disappeared.'

'Yeah, I remember seeing them.'

'The police found them in your house, earlier today. How could they be in the house if he was wearing them?'

Daniel's eyes moved left and right as he considered the question. 'He must have taken them off.'

'Why would he take them off?'

'Dad.'

'What do you mean?'

'Dad was always telling Dave off for not changing his underwear, but there was never any clean ones. We used to take them off and hide them to wash later ourselves. Same with our socks. Dad never had the time.'

'Did you see him take them off?'

'Why would I watch my brother get changed?'

'I mean, did you know he had taken them off?'

'No.' He turned to Ruby Grimes. 'Can I go now?'

The social worker looked at Ridpath who nodded his head, saying, 'The interview ends at 7.40 p.m. on 9 August.' He waved at Chrissy to stop the taping. 'Just one more thing, Dan, before you go.' Ridpath took a deep breath. 'I have to tell you your dad, Michael Carsley, may be charged with murder this evening.'

'Murder? Why? Who did he kill?'

Ridpath took another breath. 'He may be charged with the murder of your brother, David Carsley.'

'But that's impossible. Dad loved Dave.' Pain was etched on his face. 'You've got it wrong, Dad would never hurt Dave. Dad was at home all the time.'

'I think we should go now, Dan.' Ruby Grimes took his arm and gently stood the boy up.

'You're wrong, Dad would never hurt Dave.'

'I think you're right, Dan, that's why we're going to do our best to make sure your dad is not charged.'

'I don't believe you, I don't believe you!' He was struggling now as Ruby Grimes tried to take him out of the room. 'You're lying, you're all lying. The police are liars.'

The door opened and another social worker rushed in to help Ruby. Together, they managed to usher Daniel out and up the stairs.

All the time he was shouting. 'You're lying, you're all lying! My da wouldnae hurt Dave. You polis are lying, you're all liars.'

Chapter 71

They could still hear the boy shouting and screaming as he was carried upstairs until the sound was gradually swallowed up by the thick walls.

Inside the room, nobody said anything.

Ridpath picked up his mobile phone and rang Claire Trent. 'Daniel has confirmed the boy in the ATM footage is the murder victim, David Carsley.'

'Are you sure?'

'We have the confirmation on tape.'

'Right.' A pause followed by, 'The underwear, did you confirm that David Carsley took them off himself?'

'Daniel didn't see him taking his underwear off, but he said they used to do it all the time. Their dad didn't wash them often enough so they did it themselves.'

'Right.'

'We also showed Daniel footage of the white car. He didn't recognise it, said he hadn't seen it before.'

'OK.'

'What's going to happen?'

There was a long silence on the other end of the phone, before Claire Trent spoke again. 'I am going to order Paul Turnbull to release Michael Carsley pending further enquiries.'

'Thank you, boss. Can I tell the social worker?'

'Yes, he will be released this evening.'

Ridpath smiled, giving a thumbs-up to Chrissy and Emily Parkinson. 'Great, I'll let them know.'

'I wouldn't be too happy, Ridpath.'

'Why, boss? It's great news.'

'It means we have a child-killer out there who, according to the criminal profiler, is going to strike again — and, after two weeks, we don't have a clue who it is. We will have a team briefing tomorrow morning at eight a.m. Be there.'

The phone went dead in Ridpath's hand.

Chapter 72

Molly Wright was typing furiously on her laptop. The police had given her a wonderful opportunity. Releasing Michael Carsley after interviewing him for over a day was a godsend.

The gloves were off now.

She could kick Trent and Turnbull and Ridpath and all the rest of them from here to Southern Cemetery.

Her source had told her they were scrambling. Desperately trying to find new angles to investigate. After more than two weeks they had nothing.

No suspects.

No leads.

No lines of enquiry.

All they had was a white car that may or may not have been involved in the abduction.

Pathetic.

She checked over what she had written. The tone was just right; a mixture of restrained fury and articulate sadness.

The editor would lap it up and come crawling on his belly for seconds. With a bit of luck, she could keep this going long enough to make enough money to tell them all to fuck off. The book about the murder would be the icing on the cake. Of course, she would make sure she was the star. After all, it was her story as much as anybody else's.

Publishers would be queuing up for the inside story of the hunt for a child-killer. Now, if she could also meet him? A tingle went down her spine. You had to be talking about a bestseller; book tours, TV interviews, the Richard and Judy book club, even morning TV with Piers Morgan or Kay Burley. It was all there for the taking.

What this article needed was a good headline. She could wait for the subs to do it or she could help the process along and give them a narrative to work with.

She finished off the glass of Rioja and poured some more. Time to go easy on the sauce tonight. She needed to get this done and dusted. Her deadline was only an hour away.

She read through her last paragraph. She wrote angry extremely well. Perhaps because it was always bubbling up inside her, ready to explode. Now she had an excuse to let it roam free with all its savage verbosity.

And then it came to her. The one word headline she needed:

INCOMPETENCE

English was a beautiful language.

Chapter 73

'You did well today, Ridpath.'

He was back at home, a cup of cold tea in his hand, sitting in the living room.

Polly was in front of him on the couch, her black hair dyed a deep green, exactly the same as the day they had met all those years ago. It was 17 March, St Patrick's Day, and he and some friends had gone to a Chinese restaurant to line their stomachs with some stodge before a night out in town on the lash. Polly had been their waitress. On an impulse, Ridpath had asked her to meet them later at One Central Street followed by a trip to Nick the Greek's. For some reason, she had turned up and the rest was history.

'Did I? It doesn't feel like it. I interviewed a young boy who didn't know his answers could possibly send his father to jail for life.'

'But the answers didn't, they helped clear his father.'

'And next time? Will the next boy I interview help convict his father?'

'You always said it was part of the job, remember? "Find the truth", you used to say to me.'

Ridpath grimaced. '"The truth is out there." Wasn't that the tagline of some awful TV series you used to watch.'

'*X-Files*. And Mulder and Scully weren't awful, they were simply confused.'

'Like me, you mean?'

'You're not confused, just a little obsessive.'

'My obsessions cost you your life.'

'Don't blame yourself. You didn't pull the trigger. You didn't shoot the gun. You did your job and stopped a man from killing seven people. A woman who couldn't accept the fact her son was a killer pulled the trigger.' She pulled aside her white shirt to reveal an unblemished chest. 'See? The wounds have healed.'

'Mine haven't.' A long pause. 'I don't know if I can keep doing this, Polly.'

'What else would you do?'

The truth was he didn't know. He had been a policeman working for GMP or working with the coroner for so long, he could think of nothing else. Finally, he said, 'I could be a teacher like you.'

She laughed. 'The first stroppy teenager who gives you some lip, you'd slap the cuffs on and charge them with insubordination.'

He smiled. 'Teachers can do that, can't they?'

'Seriously, Ridpath, you know what you have to do now.'

He nodded. 'Find the killer.'

'Got it in one. But before you do that, you'd better ring Eve. Remember you're supposed to lay flowers on my grave with her tomorrow.'

'Shit, I'd forgotten.'

'She hasn't. She never forgets.'

Chapter 74

The FaceTime call was answered almost immediately. 'Hi Eve.'

'Hi Dad, I was waiting for you to call.'

'I guessed. Sorry, it's a bit late again.'

'That's OK. I checked on Ah Kung and Paw Paw and they are fast asleep. Ah Kung is snoring so loud he could wake King Arthur beneath Alderley Edge.'

'How do you know that story?'

'We learnt it years ago, Dad. There's an army sleeping beneath Alderley Edge led by King Arthur. If England is ever in great trouble, Merlin will wake them and they will ride to our rescue.'

'Do you believe it?'

She laughed. 'Not really, but it's a good story and we all have to have something to believe in, don't we? White knights, castles, maidens in distress, all that stuff.'

'You're reading about King Arthur and the Knights of the Round Table, aren't you?'

She laughed again. A high, unrestrained laugh. 'How did you guess? Ah Kung and Paw Paw leave me alone when they see me reading.'

There was a silence for a moment before Ridpath said, 'I have something to tell you.'

'You can't make tomorrow, can you?'

'How did you guess?'

'I'm a detective's daughter, remember?'

'I have to work.'

'Your case? Are you back on it?'

'I think so. Can we go another time? I'd *really* like to go with you and see Mum.'

'OK, we can go midweek when it's quiet and there's nobody there.' Another pause. 'Dad, do you often think of Mum?'

'Every day, sweetie.'

'Same here. I suppose we'll never stop thinking about her.'

'I hope we never do, Eve. We'll keep her alive in our hearts and our memories for ever.'

'I like that idea.'

'And remember she's always part of you.'

'At least half of me.'

'So she lives on. You just have to make her proud. We both have to make her proud.'

'We will, Dad.'

'I'll call you tomorrow.'

'OK, and Dad…'

'Yes…'

'Be careful, won't you. I don't think I can handle losing both of you.'

'Don't worry, I will.'

The screen faded to black.

'How did I do?'

'Not bad,' answered Polly from the couch. 'I don't think you need me any more, do you?'

'I don't know.'

'Bye, Ridpath.'

'Poll, don't go…'

But she had already vanished.

On the Sixth Day

Sunday, August 10

Chapter 75

The following morning Ridpath drove to Police HQ. He'd spent a night tossing and turning, his mind in turmoil, searching for possible angles he had missed.

Even though it was Sunday, the Situation Room on the MIT floor was packed when he walked in. For today, the regulations concerning social distancing seemed to be forgotten. He looked for a place to sit but they were all occupied, so he walked to the back and leant against the wall, pulling out his notebook.

A sharp clap and Claire Trent was standing at the front. Next to her, a subdued Paul Turnbull was sitting upright. Even from where he was standing, Ridpath could see the blue vein on the man's bald head throbbing.

'Listen up, everyone,' she began, 'we're going back to basics on this investigation. To bring everyone up to speed, last night we released our one and only suspect, Michael Carsley, after we were made aware of new evidence.'

Ridpath heard the passive voice in her statement and wondered what it meant.

A hand went up from the middle of the detectives. 'What new evidence, boss?'

'We'll get to that in a minute. For the moment, let us just say that the evidence made it pretty clear that Michael Carsley was not responsible for the abduction and murder of his son.'

'Have you seen the papers this morning?' It was the PR person assigned to the case, Sarah Hampson. She held up a raft of local and national newspapers, each of which had the case on their front pages.

POLICE INTERVIEW AND RELEASE MICHAEL CARSLEY from the *Guardian*.

FATHER OF DEAD BOY RELEASED by the *Manchester Evening News*.

GREATER MANCHESTER POLTROONS in the *Express*.

COCK-UP OVER CARSLEY from the *Sun*.

The worst was from the *Mail*:

INCOMPETENCE by Molly Wright.

'Sorry, I tried to stop these headlines but once a story goes viral and a narrative sets in, it's hard to stop.'

'Change the bloody narrative, then,' snarled Turnbull.

The PR person went bright red. 'These attacks in the press won't stop until you make an arrest. It's even knocked Covid off the front pages.'

'Thank God for that, if I have to read another article about wearing face masks and washing my hands, I'll throw a wobbly,' said Harry Makepeace.

'Don't bother, mate,' said a voice from the back. 'Just drive to Barnard Castle to check your eyes.'

Claire Trent held her hands up to stop them talking. 'Sarah is right. These attacks won't stop until we find the man respons-ible for this murder... until you find the man responsible.' She pointed at the assembled detectives and paused to let her message sink in.

Ridpath noticed Emily Parkinson sitting down at the front, taking notes. She hadn't looked in his direction once. Chrissy was leaning on the wall opposite; she saw him watching her and waved.

Claire Trent continued. 'As I said at the beginning, we're going back to basics. I want every assumption questioned, every witness statement examined, every piece of evidence we have tested under a microscope. By this evening, I want to meet again with a full list of facts on this case plus a series of steps we need to follow moving forward.' She turned to face Turnbull. 'Paul, you will be in charge of the re-evaluation.'

He nodded once, the vein in his head still bright blue.

'Once we have questioned everything, I believe it will open up new lines of enquiry which we can pursue.'

A hand went up. 'You said there was new evidence, boss?'

'I'm coming to that, Julie.' She paused. 'Yesterday, we had to release Michael Carsley because three new pieces of evidence were discovered.'

Ridpath noticed the passive voice again. They were obviously not going to be credited. Emily looked around for the first time, noticed him standing against the wall, and turned back quickly without acknowledging his existence.

Claire Trent switched on her laptop and connected it to the television. A still picture of Daniel Carsley appeared on the screen. She pressed play, adjusting the volume. Daniel and Emily's voices came over loud and clear as he described inventing the man.

'Because when we talked to Tony Greene, he said you never left the basketball court. You stayed there all the time playing the game. Did you run across to David?'

Daniel Carsley stared down at his feet and shook his head.

'I'm sorry, Dan, I've got to hear your answer.'

'No,' he said quietly.

'You didn't run across to talk to a man, did you?'

'No.'

'Did you see a man?'

'No.'

The video stopped and Claire Trent looked across the assembled heads of the detectives of MIT.

'But that means all the work with the photofit, splashing it across newspapers, going door-to-door was a waste of time?'

Claire Trent glanced at Paul Turnbull. 'Yes, it was, Harry.'

'There was no man? The boy made it up? Why?'

'I think it was because he felt guilty at letting his father and his brother down. He invented a story which made it appear as if he was less culpable.' Ridpath spoke for the first time.

'And wasted two weeks of police time,' grunted Turnbull.

Claire Trent ignored him. 'Explanations or justifications for what he did don't matter any more. It happened, we need to move on. Understand?'

The detectives nodded.

Claire Trent returned to her laptop. 'The second piece of evidence was captured from an ATM at a convenience store.' She played the footage of David's abduction, ending the tape by freeze-framing on the white car. 'This occurred at the same time as David disappeared. We believe this is footage of the abduction.'

Another question came from Alan Parker. 'Are we sure this is David Carsley?'

'The ID was confirmed last night by his brother.'

'The same brother who had lied to us previously...' said Turnbull, '...and yet we believe him this time.'

'Having seen the footage, I believe he is telling the truth,' said Claire Trent. You could cut the tension between the two with a blunt knife. It was Turnbull who looked away first.

Claire Trent stabbed the screen of her laptop with an elegantly painted nail. 'We need to find this white car, people. Harry, I want you to work with Phil Reynolds in CCTV. This is priority. It takes precedence over everything else.'

She played the footage from the tram. 'This was taken at 6.23 on the morning of 23 July near the tram station at Sale Water Park. David's body was discovered on the other side of the river in Chorlton Ees. We believe it is the same car as the one on the abduction tape.'

'But we didn't search across the river.'

'Exactly, Julie, that's why I want you to expand the search area to include the Mersey, the area around Jackson's Boat and Sale Water Park.'

'But... but... It's been two weeks, boss, and that area is immense.'

'It has to be done, Julie. Make it happen.'

'Yes, boss.'

'The observant among you will notice that both Sale Water Park and Wythenshawe Park are on the same tram line to the airport in one direction and the City Centre in the other. Does our perp take the tram to work? Or use it regularly? Tomorrow we will question every commuter on the line between seven and nine a.m. asking them if they noticed anything unusual. I've also asked Greater Manchester Passenger Transport Executive for help. Alan, you will co-ordinate this work.'

'Yes, boss. Resources?'

'The uniformed branch will provide and there's no problem with the overtime.'

An unknown voice from the back said, 'The plods will be happy.' This was followed by laughter.

'This is not a matter to joke about,' snarled Claire Trent. 'We have a seven-year-old child who has been abducted and murdered and his body dumped in a park. Worse, the criminal profiler is convinced the killer will strike again.' She paused, taking two deep breaths and regaining control. 'After more than two weeks' work, we don't have a single suspect.'

She let her message sink in then continued, 'We are on our last legs, people. The powers that be have given us three more days to sort this out and find our perp. If we don't, they're gonna bring in some "specialists" from the Met and the National Crime Agency to "assist" us. We all know what that means. I'm not having some wankers from London coming here telling me how to do my job. I've promised our bosses I'll have this sorted in three days.' She paused again, standing up straight and staring at each detective individually. 'You all know me, I don't make promises easily. Right, you know what to do. Get out and do your jobs. We meet again at six this evening to regroup. Ridpath – in my office. Now.'

She walked towards the door and then stopped in the entrance. 'I want this perp caught. Understand?'

'Yes, gaffer,' came the instant reply from the detectives.

Chapter 76

He'd finally worked out what to do. He couldn't wait for an opportunity to arise any longer, the need was too great inside of him.

A hunger, a terrible hunger, needing to be sated.

The visit to the cinema earlier in the week had given him the idea. On Sundays there would be plenty of families there but not too many. The social distancing rules were still in place.

He had scouted the area yesterday. There was somewhere to park the Corsa within easy walking distance of the cinema. If somebody asked, his son was feeling sick and needed to go home.

He'd checked for CCTV. There was none in the parking area. Workmen were digging up the street nearby but they weren't likely to be working on a Sunday. He'd take a quick look around to make sure.

It meant he wouldn't have as much control over the victim as he'd like but beggars couldn't be choosers, as his mother used to say.

He wouldn't rush his time with the boy, whoever he was.

There was no need to rush.

Not any more.

Chapter 77

On his way to Claire Trent's office, he was accosted by Paul Turnbull, who had obviously been lying in wait to ambush him.

'Don't you ever cut me off again like that, toerag.'

'I just did my job – you should have done yours.'

'You should have done yours, sir.'

'Of course… *sir*.'

Ridpath found himself pushed against the wall, looking down at the bald head of the smaller man. 'You're not fit to lick my boots. You should have come to me with your new evidence.'

'You wouldn't have believed it.'

'Wouldn't I?'

Ridpath shrugged him off. 'You were too convinced that Michael Carsley was guilty.'

'He was guilty. He *is* guilty, I know it.'

'You're right, he is guilty. He took the blame for something his wife did in Scotland and he's guilty of being unable to bring up his family in Manchester. But you know what…'

'I'm sure you're going to tell me.'

Ridpath jabbed his finger in Turnbull's chest. 'I'd rather have ten of him than one of you. And one more thing, if you ever touch me again, I'll have you up before Professional Standards quicker than a Manchester bus goes back to the depot.'

Turnbull stared back at him. 'I'm going to get you, Ridpath. It won't be today, it might not be tomorrow, but one day, when you're least expecting it, I'll grind you down till there's nothing left but a couple of hairs on your chin. Everybody feels sorry for you because your wife was murdered, but I don't care. I don't like you, I don't like the way you work and I don't like your attitude. Now, piss off and see your fancy woman. I know you two have a past, and I'm going to find out what it is sooner or later. When I do, I'm warning you, I'll take both of you out.'

He adjusted his tie, smoothed down his non-existent hair and walked away. 'Remember, one day...'

Still gritting his teeth, Ridpath knocked on Claire Trent's door. He'd have to think about Turnbull later. The last thing he needed was a senior officer determined to make his life miserable.

'Come,' he heard, and entered.

'Sit down.' She pointed to a chair in front of her. He sat down and she continued.

'As you can guess, Paul Turnbull wasn't too chuffed when I showed him your evidence last night.'

'I know.'

She raised an eyebrow. 'Oh, how?'

Ridpath wasn't going to grass on a senior officer even if the man was an arsehole. 'It doesn't take a detective to work it out.'

She frowned. 'Nothing else?'

He shook his head.

'Right, well I would steer clear of him for a while.'

'I intend to. Listen, boss, I'd like to go to Liverpool today if that's OK with you?'

'Liverpool?'

'HOLMES flagged up a link to the murder of a young boy there six weeks ago.'

She frowned again. 'I remember, Turnbull checked it out. The MO was completely different – the boy in Liverpool was stabbed – plus the Scousers already arrested somebody.'

'I want to check it out. I can't believe there are two separate child-killers operating less than thirty-five miles apart, at the same time, both dumping their bodies in a park.'

'The Liverpool victim was dumped in a park?'

Ridpath nodded. 'The body wasn't posed like David Carsley, though.'

'Another difference?'

'I know, but I still think it needs to be checked out.'

'I was going to ask you to supervise the Situation Room, co-ordinate any new info that comes in. You have a knack for making links when they are not obvious.'

'Emily or Chrissy could do the job just as well, boss, probably better. I still want to go to Liverpool.'

'Very well, but I want to see you back here before six for this evening's meeting. I'm sure it's like Peter Sutcliffe; we have the answer somewhere in our files, we just haven't made the links yet.'

Ridpath stood up. 'I'd better get going.'

'You're sure you don't want to tell me anything about Paul Turnbull?'

'Quite sure, boss.' He placed his middle finger on top of his index finger. 'Me and Paul, best mates.'

Claire Trent sighed, returning her gaze to the cost sheets spread out on her table. 'Let me know if you find out anything in Liverpool, Ridpath. Remember, no surprises, OK?'

'Last thing I'd ever do, boss, is surprise you.'

'Unfortunately, you have form, Ridpath. Heed this warning. No. More. Surprises.' She enunciated each word slowly and distinctly.

Claire Trent was the second person who had given him a warning in the last five minutes.

He wondered if the universe was trying to tell him something.

Chapter 78

Ridpath arrived in Liverpool just over an hour after he left Claire Trent, parking in front of a dour brown brick building on the waterfront beside the docks. As ever in Liverpool, despite it being summer, a bracing breeze was racing in from the Irish Sea across the city. Ridpath pulled his jacket around him and ran from the car park to the building.

After going through the usual Covid-19 formalities he was taken up to the third floor and placed in a meeting room. The furniture was the same MDF specials found in any police station in any district of England. He felt immediately at home.

'I'm DI Fitzgerald, but most people call me Fitz.' The detective stuck out his hand and immediately retracted it to touch elbows. 'How the world has changed in only six months, hey.' He had a broad Liverpool accent, warm and friendly, so different from the Manchester whine, with the 'th' becoming a heavy 'd'.

'What do you mean? Two coppers from Liverpool and Manchester actually meeting and trying to shake hands?'

'Yeah, that as well. You're DI Ridpath?'

'That's me,' he said, handing over his card.

'Major Investigation Team? We have Matrix units here.' The irony was heavier than the accent.

'Same job, different words.'

'Tell me about it. The job never changes; we collect evidence, arrest the bad guys, and sit back while the courts screw up. Next year, there'll be new buzzwords to learn.'

Ridpath liked him, a man after his own heart and one who didn't waste time on small talk.

'You're here about the McCarthy murder?'

'A young boy found in...' Ridpath rechecked his notes, '...Festival Gardens. Where is that?'

'Along the river, south of here. The lad, Alan McCarthy, was found on 18 June at four p.m., stabbed twice through the heart. We think he'd been abducted about three hours before.'

'How?'

'His mum sent him out for some sweets from the local shop just before one o'clock. When he didn't return after an hour, she went out looking for him, checking with the other local kids. Nobody had seen him. They went frantic looking for him and reported his disappearance to us, at the same time as one of our patrols had been alerted there was a body in Festival Gardens.'

The coincidence of the timing set off alarm bells in Ridpath's head. Was this an opportunistic abduction or was it more planned? Did the murderer stalk the victims or was he acting on impulse?

He dismissed the thought for a moment and asked, 'How old was he?'

'Seven.'

Ridpath stared out of the window at the dock buildings beside the Mersey. They had once been trading with the world and were now tourist traps and high-end apartments for footballers.

'Why are you so interested in this case? We already found our perp. He's on remand in Walton.'

Ridpath tilted his head. 'The name came up on HOLMES...'

Fitzgerald laughed. 'Lots of crap comes up on that.'

He was an old-school copper. 'Sometimes, some of it is actually useful.'

'Tell me about it.'

'Anyway, the name came up as we were investigating the abduction and murder of another seven-year-old in Manchester.'

'The David Carsley case?'

Ridpath's eyebrows rose. 'You know about that?'

Fitzgerald laughed again. 'We're not actually backward in Liverpool. Some of us can read, too, joined-up words and even newspapers.'

'Sorry, that came out wrong.'

'Don't worry, we're used to it from Manchester coppers.'

'Anyway, there are similarities in the case.'

'Like?'

'The abduction and murder of a child, the location of the body in a park. A location close to the River Mersey.' Ridpath had just thought of the last one.

'True, but there are a lot of differences too. My child was stabbed, yours was strangled. Mine was found almost immediately and yours wasn't found for over a day. My body was dumped and yours was posed. You want me to go on? The biggest difference is we've caught our perp and he's confessed. Your guy is still on the loose and will probably strike again.'

Ridpath was impressed. The man had done his homework. But when he thought about it, it was exactly what he would have done in similar circumstances.

'How did you find your man?'

'He was sleeping rough in the park, still had the knife with the child's blood on it when we picked him up. He had a history of child sex offences. Open and shut case.'

'He confessed straight away?'

The detective shook his head. 'Said he found the knife at first, but changed his story later and coughed to the killing.'

'How did he move the child from the area around the sweet shop to the park?'

Fitzgerald smiled. 'Good question. It's the one thing we haven't worked out yet.'

'What did he say?'

'He said they walked.'

'How far is it?'

'Not far, less than a mile.'

'Any CCTV footage?'

'None, we don't have as many as Manchester.'

'Did anybody see them together?'

He shook his head again. 'Nobody has come forward. We even recreated the crime for the *Liverpool Echo* but still nobody remembered seeing them together.'

'Seems strange.'

'After Jamie Bulger people aren't so keen to say they saw a child and did nothing.'

Ridpath remembered the case. A young child abducted by two ten-year-olds and walked around Liverpool for nearly three hours. Thirty-eight people came forward to say they had seen them together but the ten-year-olds lied, telling them they were taking him to a police station, and nobody intervened.

'Could I see where the body was found?'

'Aye, you could. You want me to take you?'

'If it's not too much trouble.'

Fitzgerald stood up and began walking towards the door. 'Sure, why would it be any trouble. I only have three muggings, a stabbing and a security van robbery on my slate.'

'Look, I know what it's like, I'm a copper too. Somebody from out of town comes in and expects to be driven around. I'll grab a cab.'

Fitzgerald stopped. 'No, honestly, it's not a problem. If you don't mind eating lunch in the car, it's only ten minutes away. It's toad-in-the-hole day in the canteen and we can grab some Wet Nelly on the way back.'

'Wet Nelly?'

'It's a dessert, with fruit and nuts and custard. You've never had Wet Nelly before?'

'Not in Manchester. We're the land of Eccles Cakes, Holland's Pies and Vimto, remember?'

Fitzgerald took his arm. 'You're in for a treat, mate.'

Chapter 79

The strong scent of freshly mown grass filled the air. 'What is this place?' said Ridpath, looking for a bin to put his rubbish in. There didn't seem to be any nearby.

'This is the Festival Gardens. It was opened in 1984, after the Liverpool riots of 1981, to bring a bit of colour into people's lives.'

'Did you work during the riots?'

'I might look ancient but I'm not that old. Way before my time. Nah, I was throwing bricks at the coppers then. It was a part of growing up if you were a Scouser. That and supporting Liverpool, of course. Outside riots on the streets, in here a riot of colour. That was the joke in those days.'

Ridpath looked around at the derelict Chinese pagodas and dishevelled shrubs and trees. 'Doesn't look colourful.'

'I remember coming here then, it was actually quite well done, but, of course, there was no money to keep it going, so it was left to rot.' They were sitting on a graffitied bench. Fitzgerald spread his arms wide. 'This is after the council cleaned it up, too. Before it was the gardens, it was a rubbish tip. They discovered recently that most of the rubbish had simply been buried even deeper. These days, it's hardly ever used except as a fairground now and again. There's a plan somewhere to build houses on it, create a garden paradise. Pigs might fly, I think, before this lot gets built on.'

To Ridpath, it looked remarkably like Chorlton Ees. 'Where's the river?'

He pointed south. 'Over there. Quiet now, used to be buzzin' when I was a lid.'

'Lid?'

'Kid. Lad.' He changed his voice, mimicking received pronunciation with a Scouse accent. 'A child. When I was young.'

Ridpath stood up. He thought he could just see the river from here. The unmistakeable sound of seagulls squabbling raucously over a morsel of food came from that direction. He stared back at the trees. 'And the body, where was it found?'

'Back there, in the trees.' Fitzgerald joined him. 'Let's walk across. I think they took the police tape down a while ago, either that or it was nicked. People round here use it to decorate bedrooms.'

'Classy.'

They reached an area of denser scrubland. 'The kid's body was found in there by a man walking his dog.'

Another coincidence. 'You checked him out?'

'Put him through the wringer. Clean as a whistle.'

Ridpath looked at the stand of trees. Exactly like Chorlton Ees; they were close to the path, but once you stepped behind them, all was quiet and hidden.

'Lucky the body was found so quickly.'

'Aye, lucky for us, not so lucky for the parents. The mother tried to top herself last week. Husband caught her just in time. She blames herself. Well, wouldn't you if something like that happened?'

Ridpath stayed quiet and then said, 'I've seen enough, Fitz. Do you know Canning Place?'

'What do you want there?'

'I need to see the pathologist.'

'Dr Sewell? A good man. You'll like him. Detailed, efficient and conscientious. I wish we had more like him. I'll give you a lift to the Royal Ozzy, it's on the way.'

'It isn't really, is it?'

'Nah, but I'll drop you off anyway. Wouldn't want some Manc copper wandering round my patch and getting lost, would we? We can pick up the Wet Nelly on the way.'

Chapter 80

Fitzgerald dropped Ridpath outside the Royal Liverpool Hospital. The Wet Nelly had been interesting, in the same way being hit over the head with a sock full of cement was 'interesting'.

After fighting with the signage, he eventually found the mortuary.

Dr Sewell was waiting for him. 'You're late.'

Ridpath glanced up at the clock. It was 2.10. The doctor was short and officious with salt-and-pepper hair that stood out like surgical needles from his scalp.

'Sorry, I was out at Festival Gardens.'

'Checking the location where the body was found?'

Ridpath nodded.

'Discover anything?'

They were walking towards a big sign with the words 'Mortuary and Path Lab' printed on it. Dr Sewell opened the door.

'Not a lot. The location was similar to that of my victim in Manchester.'

'In Chorlton Ees?'

Ridpath looked surprised.

'I read your pathologist's report. Dr Schofield, wasn't it? Extremely thorough and detailed. A man after my own heart.'

'You two should meet up and chat about the latest dissection techniques.' Ridpath laughed light-heartedly. Mortuaries always made him feel light-headed. He never knew whether to laugh or cry.

'You're right, we should.'

The joke went over the doctor's head as he unlocked the door.

'Of course, the body has already been released back to the family, so I have nothing to show you. But we can access my original report and display it here.'

The mortuary was made up of a row of six stainless steel tables. The last two were occupied by the shapes of human bodies covered by white sheets. The whole place had a sterility and an anonymity to it that Ridpath hated. He hoped he never ended up in a place like this.

An image flashed through his mind. Polly lying on one of these tables, her body displaying the awful Y-section from her shoulder, down between her breasts and ending just after her belly button.

He quickly whispered his coping word, 'freedom', and concentrated on remembering the image of being on top of a mountain, the wind blowing through his hair, tired but happy.

'What was that?' asked Dr Sewell.

'Nothing,' Ridpath mumbled.

A technician was preparing the area for a post-mortem, placing the instruments in the correct order on a table next to the head of the body. 'Let me finish this, Mike, and then we'll get started.'

'No worries,' the technician answered. 'Whenever you're ready, Pete.'

The whole set-up was far more informal than Dr Schofield's in Manchester. They walked down to the end of the mortuary and through another door.

A small lab. Another technician, female this time, was placing a slide on the viewing ledge of a microscope. 'Got that gut cross-section for you.'

'Won't be a sec.'

Dr Sewell put his password into a computer and then entered another code for the McCarthy case. A standard pathologist's report appeared. He scanned the report, reminding himself of the details of the post-mortem. 'What do you want to know? I bet it's if there are any similarities between this murder and the one in Manchester?'

Before he could answer the question, the doctor continued.

'In post-mortem results, quite a lot of difference. Alan McCarthy was killed with a knife; two thrusts to the chest region, one of which penetrated the pericardium. The boy died instantly. Plus, unlike your case, there was no evidence of any sexual activity, either before or after death.'

'Was the body washed?'

The doctor checked his notes. 'It was. I found evidence of soap on the skin. A common or garden supermarket soap, Lifebuoy. Your body was also washed, I believe.'

'We think it was to remove all fibres or DNA traces.'

'True, there were no fibres or external DNA on the body.'

'Where?'

'Where what?'

'Where was the body washed?'

'We believe it was in a toilet in the Festival Gardens used by the homeless.'

'Why take the risk?'

'The risk?'

'Of being caught washing a body in a public toilet?'

The doctor shrugged his shoulders. 'You'll have to ask the killer, I'm afraid. Science doesn't tell us the motivations for any action, merely that it has happened. You can't "follow the science". You make a decision based on the evidence. All decisions are inevitably value judgements. Science doesn't make decisions, people do.'

Ridpath felt deflated. He had been hoping there would be more links between the two deaths. But other than both bodies being washed, there was nothing. All the evidence was inferential: the location of the body, hidden in woods close to the Mersey.

'Just a few more questions, Doctor. Were there any signs of violence on the body? Bruising or anything like that?'

Once again, the doctor checked his notes. 'None that I found.'

'Finally, you were the medical examiner called out when the boy was found.'

'I was.'

'Was the body posed in any way?'

'No, unlike your boy it was naked and thrown away as if in a hurry. Not posed at all.'

'Thank you, Doctor.'

'I hope I have been of help, DI Ridpath, but I fear I haven't. The only real similarity between these two deaths is that they both involved young boys.'

'That's it, Doctor. I can't believe two child-killers were operating at exactly the same time only thirty-five miles apart. It just doesn't make sense.'

'The science suggests otherwise, Detective.'

'But as you said earlier, Doctor, science doesn't make judgements, people do. And my judgement is that these two cases are linked.'

'Despite there being no evidence to support this claim?'

Ridpath tapped the side of his head. 'The evidence is in here, Doctor.'

Chapter 81

On the drive back to Manchester along the M62, Ridpath's mind went over every detail of the case again and again.

Nothing made any sense.

Were the cases linked?

Possibly, but there was no concrete evidence, plus Merseyside already had a suspect who had confessed to the crime.

In Manchester, they didn't even have a suspect. Turnbull's bullheaded insistence that Michael Carsley was guilty had wasted valuable days of work.

Daniel's statement that it was his mother who was violent towards them, not his father, was interesting. Could the mother have picked up David from the street? It might explain why the boy got into the car. But the idea of any mother killing her son was unthinkable. Nonetheless, he made a mental note to ask Chrissy about Irene Carsley. Perhaps he would have to pay her a visit again.

By the time he parked outside Police HQ back in Manchester, he had been through the case, backwards and forwards. The problem was he still had nothing to offer Claire Trent.

Upstairs, on the MIT floor, the detectives were gathering in the Situation Room. There was a distinct atmosphere of gloom over the place. Ridpath could smell it, that bitter aroma of failure.

The meeting began with Claire Trent taking the lead.

'Harry, what do you have on the car?'

'Not a lot, boss. Working with Reynolds, we've narrowed it down to one model. A Vauxhall Corsa manufactured between 2014 and 2019. This is one of the most popular models of saloons in the UK. There were 279,000 sold during this period. I'm still trying to find out how many in the North West.'

'It's too wide, can you narrow it further by version or year?'

Harry Makepeace shook his head. 'The pictures aren't good enough, boss, and we can't see the number plate on either of the CCTV images. It's the best we can do.'

'Right, Harry, keep going.'

'You want me to start building a database of the owners?'

'Yes, and cross-reference it against the Register of Paedophiles. Maybe we'll get lucky.'

'And if we don't?'

'You'll have to start contacting each owner individually, asking what they were doing on those dates.'

'We could end up being swamped, boss.'

'Start with the North West.'

'I'll need help – there are too many people to call.'

Claire Trent ran her fingers through her hair. 'I'll find the resources.'

'Maybe somebody with experience of running a contact tracing operation.'

'Then don't call Dido Harding,' said a wag from the back.

Everybody laughed at the weak joke. Ridpath could feel the collective release of tension. As ever with the police, black humour lurked just beneath the surface of even the most serious meetings.

'Thanks, Harry,' Claire Trent summed up as the laughter died down. 'Get started straight away.'

'Yes, boss.'

Sarah Hampson coughed. 'I think at this point I should let you know the nationals have doubled down on the story.' She held up the front page of the *Daily Mail*. Two words in big, bold, black letters dominated everything.

'This is going to be the front page tomorrow morning and this time they are not speaking about the government but about us.'

'Can't we do anything to stop these headlines?'

'Last time I looked it was a free press. We keep feeding them our point of view but when a narrative takes hold, it's difficult to shake.'

'Has the chief constable seen these, Sarah?'

'Not yet, Claire.'

'Anything we can do?'

Sarah Hampson shrugged her shoulders. 'Hope and pray another big story happens overnight. If it doesn't, this is what will run.'

'Something for me to look forward to tomorrow. Julie, any news from the search close to the Water Park and Jackson's Boat?'

'Twenty-three bags of rubbish and seventeen used condoms but nothing else, boss. It's been nearly three weeks.'

'Thanks, Julie. And Alan, anything from Greater Manchester Transport?'

'We won't interview most of the commuters till tomorrow morning, boss. No point on a Sunday. But the security for the trams are not hopeful. It seems most travellers are pretty much zombies in the morning.'

'Right, Alan, so nothing to report.'

Alan shook his head.

The mood in the meeting was even more deflated than at the beginning, if that was at all possible.

Claire Trent called on Paul Turnbull next.

'We've been through all the witness statements one more time, concentrating on those who live on the route David Carsley potentially took from the park to the ATM. We even went out this afternoon to re-interview them. But it's been three weeks now. People's memories have become even more vague. A couple of things. There definitely was a man with a dog, an Alsatian. His name is Peter Davies. He went into the station this morning and owned up to being in the park on 21 July.'

'Why didn't he come forward earlier?' asked Claire Trent.

'He's a lorry driver and went over to Poland on a job that afternoon. He has a watertight alibi for the time of the abduction. We've checked out footage of him at his depot in Sharston.'

'Bring him in anyway. I want every possible lead or suspect shaken down. Nobody, I repeat, nobody is in the clear until I have reviewed their statements. You said a couple of things?'

'We checked with the Procurator Fiscal in Scotland why Michael Carsley wasn't charged with child abuse or domestic violence.'

'And...?'

'There wasn't enough evidence of who was the perpetrator, him or his wife, so they let the case lapse, delivering a stern warning and placing both children under a care order.'

'Why did nobody follow up?'

Turnbull shrugged. 'The family had gone south to Manchester, so I guess they thought it was somebody else's problem. One less issue to deal with.'

'Right, Paul, keep going, there must be something we missed. Finally, Ridpath. You went to Liverpool today?'

'He's not still trying to link our case with the murder in Liverpool?' Turnbull's hand slammed hard on the desk. 'Why are you indulging his fantasies, Claire? It's a waste of our time.'

Just as Ridpath was about to speak, his phone rang. He looked at the screen and saw it was Mrs Challinor. What did she want? He wasn't due to return to the Coroner's Office until tomorrow. Was she trying to remind him? Not like her.

He answered, but before he could get any words out, she spoke.

'My grandson, he's gone missing.'

Chapter 82

'What?'

'My grandson, Ben, he's gone missing.'

The whole of MIT was watching him, including Claire Trent.

'How? When?'

'My daughter took him to the cinema as a treat for his birthday. They were waiting for the film to start when he announced he wanted to pee. She pointed to the toilet and asked him to go while she stayed behind to look after his sister. He went and didn't come back.'

'When was this?'

'About an hour ago. She's frantically looking for him and has just called me.'

'Right, let me get on it. Where is your daughter now?'

'Still at the cinema. She doesn't know what to do.'

For some unknown reason, Ridpath knew this was bad.

'What is it, Ridpath?' asked Claire Trent.

He held his hand up again to stop her speaking. 'We'll send a car to bring you here. I'll go to your daughter now.'

'What shall I do, Ridpath? I'm going to the cinema.'

'No, stay where you are until the car arrives. What's your daughter's number?'

Ridpath reached into his pocket to write it down in his pocket book as she spoke.

'Let me repeat, wait for the car to bring you to Police HQ. Do you understand, Mrs Challinor?'

'Yes.'

'I'm going to ring your daughter now.'

'She's out of her mind, Ridpath, not making much sense.'

'Don't worry, I'll handle it. Stay where you are until the car arrives.'

He rang off. Claire Trent was staring at him.

'Boss, we have a problem.'

Chapter 83

It had been easier than he thought.

He waited in the toilet of the cinema, pretending to wash his hands. He'd chosen that one specially. There were steps leading to an exit through a fire door. From there, it was a two-minute walk to the car.

The boy had come in on his own. His hair was freshly combed and he was wearing new clothes; a Harry Potter badge saying Gryffindor prominent against his pale t-shirt.

Perfect, he couldn't have asked for better.

He waited for the boy to finish and come to wash his hands. He watched the door all the time hoping nobody would come in, the possibility of discovery adding a frisson of danger, a spice of excitement.

'Why are you wearing gloves when you're washing your hands?' the boy asked him.

'Be careful, the water is extremely hot.'

The boy seemed satisfied with this answer, turning on the cold water so it flowed more strongly out of the tap.

When the boy reached out to put his hands under the running water, he grabbed them both with one hand, placing the pad soaked in chloroform over his mouth.

There was a short struggle, but he held the boy tight against his body until he went limp.

He covered the boy with his coat and picked him up, resting him on his shoulder as if he were carrying a sleeping child. Carefully, he checked outside the door.

The way was clear.

He rushed down the stairs, out through the emergency exit and onto the street, the boy's head still resting on his shoulder.

Hurrying past the empty digger that had been repairing the road, he entered the car park. His Corsa was parked in the corner near the exit.

He opened the boot, checked the area one more time. A couple were leaving their car and walking to the exit but they weren't looking at him.

Good.

Slowly and carefully, he placed the boy's limp body in the back. Taking out the hypodermic, he found a vein in the boy's elbow and injected his mother's drug into the soft skin.

He didn't want to damage the goods. Not after going to so much trouble acquiring them.

Well, not yet, anyway.

Chapter 84

Ridpath had put Sarah Challinor, the coroner's daughter, on speakerphone so the others could hear. She had been distraught and almost incoherent, alternately talking to him and to her daughter. 'It's my fault, I should have never let him go on his own. Where is he? What's happened? Keep up, Amy...'

'Where's Ben?'

'Don't ask, Amy, I'm looking for him.'

'Why are you crying, Mummy?'

'I've looked everywhere. Where has he gone? I rang Mummy because I didn't know what to do.'

Ridpath could hear her breathing as she rushed aimlessly around the cinema. 'Sarah, please take a moment and tell me what happened.'

She repeated the story Mrs Challinor had told. Ben had vanished after going to the toilet in the cinema. She'd checked the area, finding the Harry Potter badge she had given him that morning on the floor of the toilet.

'He would never have dropped his badge, he loves Harry Potter. Somebody's taken him.'

Ridpath covered the mouthpiece. 'This could be our man, boss.'

'Or it could be a child who's wandered off for an ice cream and got lost,' said Turnbull.

Claire Trent thought for a second. 'We can't take the risk.' She nodded at Ridpath.

He uncovered the mouthpiece and said, 'We're on our way. Please stay where you are.'

The detective superintendent immediately took charge.

'Ridpath, go to Parrs Wood with Emily and Harry Makepeace.'

'Yes, boss.' He handed the phone to Chrissy.

'Hiya, love, now just take a few deep breaths, the police are on their way. Where are you? Look around and tell me what you can see?'

In the Situation Room, Claire Trent was barking out orders.

'Alan, go to pick up the coroner.'

'Right.'

'Paul, you and I are organising the search from here. Get onto West Didsbury nick and get some manpower. Let Wythenshawe and Cheadle Heath know too. I want that cinema and the surrounding area locked down.'

'I'd like to go to Parrs Wood.'

'Not yet, we need you here.'

'Sam, notify PTU, we might need them.'

'Yes, boss.'

'John, get onto the traffic police, tell them to check all their cameras. We're looking for a white Vauxhall Corsa. Kingsway runs right past the area.'

'On it.'

'The rest of you get ready to move.'

She clapped her hands. 'Come on people, time to get this bastard.'

Chapter 85

Molly Wright was with a crowd of reporters outside the Carsley house in Wythenshawe. The police had beefed up their presence since his release. There was a squad car, a sergeant and two constables in front of the red-painted door.

She'd seen nothing of Michael Carsley since he'd arrived back at home yesterday evening. The curtains were drawn and the house was quiet. She knew he was in there, though. It was only a matter of time before he came out.

Until then, she would stand here patiently chatting to the other reporters and waiting for her chance. A couple of editors had already been onto her, looking for more on the Carsley case. It had really taken off since her piece in the *Mail*. All she had to do was keep the pot stirring and she was good for at least another two weeks. An interview with Carsley would be a great scoop.

Was he the innocent victim or the evil mastermind? She hadn't decided which yet but she tended towards the former. It was a much better read.

Her photographer waved a bacon-butty-stained hand from his car.

She ignored him. He probably wanted to skive off and take a shower after being there all night.

Sod him, she'd been here too and she wasn't going anywhere.

He waved again, more urgently this time, actually opening the car door and standing up to get her attention.

She wandered over to him as nonchalantly as she could. No point in letting the other ghouls know he wanted to speak to her.

'There's something going on.'

'What?'

'Dunno, but it's at Parrs Wood. My scanner is going bonkers.'

She bent down and listened to his police scanner on the front seat. It tracked GMP's radio calls to the police cars. There seemed to be a hell of a lot of activity around Parrs Wood.

'What's going on?'

'Dunno.'

And then she heard it, loud and clear, from a controller to a police car.

'Child missing in Parrs Wood. Look out for a white Vauxhall Corsa.'

Without waiting any longer, she took one look back at the gaggle of reporters clustered outside Michael Carsley's gate. 'I'm gonna get something to eat, waste of time here. See you lot later,' she said, and she got into the car.

She had to get away before they realised what was going on.

Chapter 86

They arrived at the cinema only twelve minutes after Ridpath had left the car park of Police HQ.

Racing down Kingsway, sirens blaring and lights flashing, Ridpath had forced the other drivers to pull out of the way, going into an oncoming lane at one point when one stupid old man refused to look in his rear-view mirror.

Emily Parkinson, with her usual coolness, took down the miscreant's number, intending to send him a warning about his driving.

Ridpath barely slowed down for red lights, looking both ways to ensure the traffic had stopped before stomping his foot on the accelerator and feeling the surge of the turbo kick in.

It was a joy to be behind the wheel of something more powerful than his usual car.

They arrived at the same time as a patrol from West Didsbury.

Emily stared at a text on her phone. 'Chrissy says Sarah Challinor is in front of a Wagamama.'

They spotted her straight away, carrying another young child in her arms, rushing towards them.

'Help me, help, I don't know where he is.'

She was crying and her mascara was smeared in dark streaks around her eyes. Ridpath put his arm around her shoulders.

'Take a few deep breaths and tell us what happened.'

'He went to the toilet and then the cinema went black and the film started.'

'He went on his own?'

She nodded. 'He likes his independence.'

'What happened next?'

'You've got to start looking for him.'

'Please tell us what happened next?'

She gasped twice, sucking in air. 'I knew he didn't want to miss the beginning so I took Amy and went to the toilet to find out what was taking him so long.' Another gasp for breath. 'But when I went there, it was empty. I found this on the floor.' She opened her hand to reveal a large, black badge with the word *Gryffindor* printed on it.

'Which cinema?'

'Screen Two. He wanted to see *Harry Potter* on the big screen. They are reshowing the films after lockdown and he's a big fan.'

'Harry, go and check the toilets. You two...' he pointed to the uniforms who were standing around, 'check out the other screens. You're looking for a six-year-old boy...'

'Ben's seven... today.'

'A seven-year-old boy,' Ridpath corrected himself, 'called Ben.'

He turned back to the distraught woman. 'What did you do when you saw the toilet was empty?'

'I went back into the cinema. I thought maybe I'd missed him somehow. But it was dark and I couldn't see properly so I called his name, but there was no answer. A few people told me to shut up and be quiet.'

More police arrived with flashing lights and sirens. A crowd had begun to gather, listening to the woman speak.

She started to hyperventilate and the child in her arms began to cry.

Ridpath touched her arm. 'Take a few deep breaths and then tell me what you did next.'

The woman inhaled slowly, holding her child closer to her body. 'I went out into the lobby but it was empty. I looked around for about ten minutes but I couldn't see him. I was getting frantic now. He never wanders around on his own.

Then I thought he might be with the cinema manager – children must get lost all the time. So I asked them and they knew nothing. The manager sent his people into each of the screens with a flashlight, shouting his name.'

'Still no response?'

'Nothing. I couldn't think of anything else to do so I called my mum.'

'Mrs Challinor?'

She nodded.

Harry Makepeace arrived back. 'The toilets are empty, Ridpath, but I found this beside the sink.' He held up a plastic evidence bag with a white handkerchief inside. 'The thing stinks of chloroform.'

'Is that good or bad?' asked Sarah Challinor.

Ridpath frowned. 'It's not good,' he finally answered. 'Make sure forensics check it for fingerprints and DNA, Harry.'

The detective inspector nodded.

Next to Ridpath, Sarah Challinor and her child both began wailing.

Chapter 87

The boy still slept.

Had he given him too much diazepam in the injection? He hoped not but with these young ones, it was always difficult to tell.

He was tempted to wake him up to play but he decided against it. A drowsy playmate was no fun. They didn't feel anything; no pain, no joy, no fear.

The voices wanted the boy to feel fear. They enjoyed that, feeding on it like a moth feeds on light. The boy might be afraid of Mother sitting there watching television. She still scared him even though he knew she was dead.

Should he cover her up? Hide her from sight?

No.

The boy had to meet her sometime. Today was as good as any other day.

He went back to the kitchen and stirred the saucepan of bolognese one more time. Let it cook for the next hour and it would be perfect. The boy should have woken by then and they could have something to eat together.

He enjoyed eating with people, he didn't do it often enough. He would ask the boy about his family and his school and his life, hinting that if he told the truth he would let him go.

It would be a little white lie, of course. But he had to give him some hope. What was anybody's life without hope?

This one would never leave him. He had decided to keep him forever.

Next to Mother in front of the television.

Chapter 88

The cinema manager wasn't happy.

'You need to close the complex,' ordered Ridpath.

'What? People have bought tickets. It's a Sunday – you can't close the cinema on a Sunday.'

'I'm telling you to do it. It's a crime scene. Do it now.'

Sarah Challinor and her daughter had been taken into the staff room of the cinema and given warm, sugary tea and an orange drink, while one of the coppers tried to calm her down. The manager had given Amy a big bag of popcorn which she was devouring by the handful.

Claire Trent had decided to come to the complex, bringing the coroner with her to be with her daughter. It was the least they could do as she obviously needed support. Ridpath hadn't asked about a husband and Sarah hadn't mentioned anybody. He would check with the coroner later.

Meanwhile the cinema manager was digging his heels in.

'I can't do it. The patrons would kill me.'

'What would you do if there was a fire?'

'We would clear the building immediately and block anybody from entering.'

Ridpath paused for a moment. 'Can you smell smoke, DS Parkinson?'

She cottoned on quickly. 'Now you mention it, I'm sure I can. A strong, pungent aroma. It could be dangerous, Ridpath.'

The cinema manager took the hint. Two minutes later the fire bells began to ring and people filed out of their films.

'Sergeant,' Ridpath shouted to a uniform in the lobby, 'make sure you take everybody's name and address as they leave.'

'How many people are in the cinema right now?' he asked the manager.

The manager checked his sheet. 'There are eleven screens and we've sold 329 tickets at the moment. Some people might not have turned up, though, if they bought online.'

'You know exactly who everybody is?'

The manager shook his head. 'Only if they bought and reserved online. They have to leave a name and credit card number.'

'So if you simply turn up, there's no record?'

'Not if you pay cash. We have a record if you pay by credit card.'

'I'll need those records.'

'Right. You think he came in this morning?'

'There's no way in except through the lobby?'

'All the doors are alarmed and can't be opened from the outside. We had somebody try this morning at 10.15, but they'd vanished when I checked it out.'

'Where was this?'

'At the bottom of the stairs leading out of Screen 2. I thought one of the kids was trying to let his mates in.'

'There's no other way in, right?'

The manager shook his head.

'And the doors don't have security cameras?'

'They're not necessary.' He thought for a moment. 'We do have them behind the cashiers', though. Do you think that would help?'

Chapter 89

Molly Wright arrived with her photographer as the police cars were blocking the entrance to the shopping mall.

'What's going on?' she asked a copper who was waving her car away.

'I dunno, but you need to get out of here.'

Another squad car arrived, sounding its siren to encourage her to move out of the way.

She checked the shopping mall. The police had set up a cordon around the cinema. People were slowly coming down the steps, complaining loudly about missing their film.

A crowd had formed, all craning their necks to see exactly what was going on.

'Park here, and let me out,' she ordered the photographer. 'Get as many shots as you can of this shambles, I'll call you if I need you.'

'Where are you going?'

'Inside.'

She jumped out of the car and joined the crowd behind the police tape. At the entrance, another police car had arrived, unmarked this time, and was let through the cordon.

Molly Wright watched as Claire Trent and that bald-headed thug, Turnbull, got out of the car accompanied by an older woman with white, curly hair, dressed elegantly.

Who was she?

'Claire! Claire Trent!' They hurried into the complex without looking across at her as she shouted at them.

She elbowed her way through the crowd to where a constable was pushing people back behind a barrier, showing her press credentials. 'I need to talk to Claire Trent.'

The constable stared down at her pass. 'Never heard of her. Nobody is allowed in.'

'She's your boss. A detective superintendent.'

'She's not my boss and anyway, nobody is allowed in. So please move along.'

'But I need to speak to her, it's important.'

'And it's also important you move back behind the barrier, otherwise I will arrest you for obstruction. Do I make myself clear?'

Molly glanced to her left and saw one of the restaurants was still open. She pushed her way through the crowd and rushed through the emptying tables to a kitchen at the back.

Outside a rear door, two chefs were taking the opportunity to have a break and smoke a cigarette.

'I'm lost, is this the way back into the cinema?'

One looked at his mate and smiled. 'There's a back stairs to take you into the lobby but no way into the cinema itself. We know, we've tried. The buggers have got all the doors alarmed.'

'Where is it?'

'Over there, next to the bins. But they've got some sort of fire drill going on…'

'Thanks,' she shouted over her shoulder as she rushed to the grey unmarked door, pulling it open. A short set of steps led up to another door. She dashed up, wrenched it open and stepped into the quiet of a carpeted lobby.

Now where was Claire Trent?

Chapter 90

The detective superintendent was standing in front of a bank of televisions, staring at the black and white images as they played in front of her.

Next to her, Ridpath leant on a desk and, on the other side, Emily Parkinson stood beside the cinema manager.

DCI Paul Turnbull was at the back, staring at the ends of his fingers, ignoring the screens.

They had already shown the coroner to the staff room, where she was comforting her daughter and her grandchild.

The manager was explaining in tortuous detail. 'The doors open at precisely 9.45 a.m. and the first film today was 10.15 on the dot. We've only just reopened after lockdown so there's not a lot of new films – that's why we're reshowing some golden oldies. The new generation have never seen the Harry Potters or the Lord of the Rings and they are surprisingly popular.'

Claire Trent pointed to the screen, where a woman and a kid were standing in front of a glass barrier. 'So these are the customers this morning?'

'The two monitors on the right are walk-ins. The monitor on the left is for pre-bookings. They can pick up their tickets at this cashier. What are you looking for?'

The three detectives looked at each other.

'We don't know,' answered Ridpath.

Turnbull coughed from the back.

Ridpath ignored him, remembering the criminal profiler's description. 'Perhaps a single white male, aged over thirty?'

The images continued to flash on the screen as customer after customer stepped forward and chose their seats.

'Shouldn't be too many of those, but you'd be surprised how much the Harry Potters and the Lord of the Rings cross the generations.'

A single man came forward and selected a seat, paying in cash.

'Can you freeze it here?' ordered Ridpath.

The manager stopped the picture.

Ridpath leant in closer. Was this him?

'I can print out the image if you want. We've got a video printer as part of the kit,' the manager said proudly.

Ridpath nodded.

The other screens carried on rolling as the sound of the video printer echoed through the small viewing booth.

'Stop. Stop it now.'

Emily Parkinson was pointing to the screen. 'I know this man.'

Chapter 91

They sat down to the meal he cooked.

The boy had woken up ten minutes earlier, confused, not knowing where he was or how he had got there.

The wonders of modern drugs.

He explained that the boy had fallen ill and he had brought him home. They would just have something to eat and then he would take the boy back to his parents.

'I don't have any parents. I have a mum, though.'

'Same as me. I have a mother too.' He pointed to the woman sat watching the television.

'Can I go home now?'

'Let's eat first and then I'll take you home.'

'Mum will be worried about me.'

'She won't. I rang her to let her know where you are and that I'll bring you home after we've eaten. Aren't you hungry?'

The boy nodded but then said, 'It's my birthday. We were supposed to see Harry Potter and then eat some cake and ice cream. Mum promised.'

'Of course, you will. She's arranged it all. But you have to eat your birthday lunch first and then you can go.'

'All of it?'

'Every last spoonful.' He rolled the spaghetti around his fork. 'See, this is how you do it.'

'I know, Mum showed me.' The boy then swirled some spaghetti and sucked it up through his lips, trailing bolognese sauce everywhere.

The man took his handkerchief and wiped the boy's mouth, saying, 'You are a mucky pup.'

The boy ate another three spoonfuls, ingesting the drug the man had sprinkled on top with the parmesan cheese.

For a moment he stopped and stared at the woman sitting in the chair. 'Why doesn't your mum move?'

'Because she's dead,' answered the man truthfully.

Chapter 92

'What?'

Both Claire Trent and Ridpath spoke at the same time.

'I know who it is. I interviewed him when I was checking out the CCTV. He's the owner of the convenience store close to the park.'

'Are you sure?'

Emily Parkinson stared at the screen again. 'Certain. David Carsley was standing outside his shop on the footage before he was kidnapped. I've got his name somewhere.' She reached into her jacket, pulling out her notebook. 'Here it is. Matthew Oram. That was his name.'

'He's buying tickets for the same cinema as our missing boy. Screen Two.'

'The toilet where the boy was abducted, how do you get to it?'

'The only way is through the cinema. Funny, there's a door at the bottom of the steps. The alarm went off this morning.'

Ridpath was on his phone in a flash. 'Chrissy, we need an address immediately. Matthew Oram, we know he owns a convenience store in Wythenshawe.'

'No problem.' Ridpath heard the tap of computer keys. 'It's not a common name. I'll check the electoral register. Yeah, here we are. There's just one listed. He lives in a house not far from the park in Sharston. It's 168, Winman Street. There are only two registered occupants, himself and a woman, Marjory Oram. Could be his wife or his mother.'

'It's the same address he gave me,' said Emily Parkinson.

'Paul, get onto the Police Tactical Unit, I want a team ready to go into that house in twenty minutes.'

'On it, Claire.' Turnbull seemed animated at last, immediately diving for his phone and striding out into the lobby.

'What about the shop? He might be there.'

'Ridpath, go and check it out. Take Emily and a squad car with you.'

Turnbull was back. 'The PTU is set and on its way, ready to go on your orders, boss.'

'Good, Paul, you're with me. I want to get this bastard.'

They all strode out into the lobby. Ridpath shouted, 'Won't be a moment.'

He ran to the staff room and stuck his head around the door. Mrs Challinor was sitting in the corner with her daughter's head resting on her shoulder, gently smoothing Sarah's hair as she sobbed. At their feet, Amy played with what remained of the popcorn.

'We've got a lead to where he could be. I'll let you know as soon as I can.'

Mrs Challinor lifted her head. 'Thank you, Ridpath.'

In the lobby, Molly Wright came out of the shadows and strode directly towards Claire Trent.

'Claire, can you tell me what's going on?'

'No. You shouldn't be here. This cinema is cordoned off.'

'Don't be like that, Claire, tell me what's going on.'

Claire Trent stared at her for a second and then spoke directly to the sergeant at the door. 'Get rid of her. She shouldn't be in here.'

The sergeant took the reporter's arm.

'You won't hear the last of this, Ms Trent. I can build you up and I can take you down.'

'Come along, miss.' The sergeant tugged on her arm.

'You won't hear the last of this,' she shouted over her shoulder.

Ridpath ran back to join them.

'Be careful, you two,' were the last words he heard Claire Trent shout as he ran out of the lobby door and down the stairs, Emily Parkinson just a step behind.

Chapter 93

Molly Wright was fuming.

How dare that bloody jumped-up tart get rid of her? Who did she think she was? She would show her. It takes a lifetime to build a reputation but one article could destroy it.

You'd better watch your back from now on, Claire bloody Trent. One wrong step and it's going to be posted in every newspaper from here to Timbuktoo.

The sergeant let go of her arm, shoving her behind the police tape. 'Make sure she doesn't come back in,' he ordered a nearby constable.

She smoothed down her clothes and tidied her hair, imagining the vicious barbs she would write about the detective superintendent. Barbs to destroy the woman and her career.

As she did, Ridpath and the female police officer ran past her.

Where were they rushing to?

The detectives spoke to another sergeant and were immediately shown to a squad car, getting in the back. The car put on its siren and flashing lights, pushing itself slowly through the crowd lining the pavement, before zooming off down Kingsway. She saw her photographer still parked on the road where she had left him ten minutes earlier.

Thank God for stupidity, she thought.

She ran over to his car and wrenched open the passenger door. The photographer was still listening to his police scanner.

'Follow that car,' she ordered.

'Which one?'

She rolled her eyes. 'The one with the flashing lights and the bloody siren.'

He pulled out and sped away down Kingsway, seeing the police car in the distance.

Molly Wright shook her head. You can't get the staff these days.

Chapter 94

He carried the semi-comatose boy to the bedroom.

The meal hadn't gone according to plan – things started to go wrong when he had told him that his mother, the woman sitting in front of the television, was dead.

A slow realisation had dawned in the boy's eyes. A realisation that perhaps he shouldn't be there. That this wasn't a good man sitting next to him. That dead people don't sit in living rooms watching television.

'I'd like to go home now.'

'Finish your meal first.'

The boy threw his fork down on his plate, scattering bolognaise sauce all over the table. 'I want to go home now. I want to see my mum.'

Why did they always have to spoil it? Here they were having a wonderful meal, cooked by him, enjoying a little chat and some good food. But still they were not satisfied.

He tried one more time.

'You can go home after you've eaten your food. Doesn't your mother always tell you to finish your food because there are starving babies in Africa who would love a bowl of spaghetti?'

'No,' the boy shouted, flipping his plate up, spilling the food all over the table and on the floor.

'Look what you've done now,' the man said gently. 'Little boys need to be punished if they throw food. Didn't your mother tell you that too?'

The boy's eyes started to glaze over and defocus. The drugs were beginning to kick in.

'Now, I'm going to have to clean up before I punish you.'

There was no answer from the boy. His head lolled to one side and his mouth opened slowly, the tongue creeping out from between his teeth.

'You sit here while I tidy up. Please understand, you have been a naughty boy and you are not going to escape punishment. My mother,' he pointed to the body sitting in front of the television, 'punished me when I was naughty. I deserved it, I always deserved it. And so do you.'

Chapter 95

They cut the lights and siren when they were five minutes away from the shop, coasting to a stop a block away. The convenience store was at one end of a row of shops in a residential neighbourhood. Michael Carsley's house was only a few minutes' walk away and Wythenshawe Park was behind them.

'What are we going to do, Ridpath?' asked Emily.

'If he's just abducted somebody, he's unlikely to be working in the shop, he's probably at the other address. But we can't take any chances. You two,' he pointed to the two constables, 'go round the back and check out the rear alley. If he is in the shop, that's where he's going to run.'

'And us two?'

'We're going to walk straight in. You are doing some follow-up on your enquiries a couple of days ago.'

'If he's there?'

'We take him down and break his balls until he tells us where the boy is. Ready? You two go first. We'll give you a minute to get round the back and then we'll go in.'

The two constables left the car and ran down the alley behind the row of shops.

Ridpath got out of the car first, pulling down his jacket. Followed by Emily, he strode past the hairdressers and the Chinese takeaway, past the bookies and the knitting shop. They stopped for a second in front of the ATM and its camera.

'This is where you got the footage?'

She nodded.

'Strange that none of the other shops saw the boy.'

'It was lunchtime, many of them were closed.'

'Are you ready?'

She nodded again.

'You go in first and I'll watch your back. Remember, if he's there, you are just following up on the ATM footage.'

'And if he's not?'

'We'll play it by ear. The uniforms should be in position by now. Ready?'

She pushed open the door, hearing a bell ring above her head.

They didn't notice Molly Wright and her photographer watching them from the car across the road.

Chapter 96

Sergeant Trevor Hall was the head of the Police Tactical Unit. Claire Trent had worked with him before and knew him to be an efficient, dedicated officer.

His unit, Claire Trent and Paul Turnbull were standing behind a parked PTU van at the corner of the road, hidden from view of the house. Discreet cordons had already been placed eighty yards on either side of number 168. All the men were uniformed and carrying their Heckler & Koch semi-automatics, gathered round the rear of the van.

'I want to go in with your men, Sergeant. I'm firearm-trained.'

'I'm afraid not, Detective Chief Inspector Turnbull. There is possibly a child inside and we can't have extra people who've not trained with us as part of our team.'

'I insist, Sergeant.'

Trevor Hall glanced towards Claire Trent. 'You can insist all you like, Chief Inspector, but as long as I am in charge of this Tactical Unit, the only members of it are going to be people I know and trust. Clear.'

'Let's move on, gentlemen. Trevor is in charge of this entry, Paul. You will remain here with me.'

Turnbull reddened and turned away, muttering under his breath.

Sergeant Hall adjusted his bulletproof vest across his chest, pulling it down so it was more comfortable. Had he gone soft in lockdown? A few hours in the gym would soon clear up anything that resembled fat.

'Listen up, people, there are only two entrances to this house. The rear backs onto the garden of another house at 37 Dalgliesh Road. Jimmy is already in there with eyes on the back.'

'Any movement, boss?'

'None so far, Lenny. He'll report it immediately if he sees something.'

He pointed to the street map stretched out in the back of the PTU van. 'Here's the house. Team A will assemble here with Jimmy. When I give the order, they will go in the back over the fence.'

'How high is it, boss?'

'Four feet, three inches and wood-panelled. A pretty standard B&Q special with posts set in concrete. Even you should be able to get over it, Lenny.'

His men laughed nervously, relieving the tension that all of them felt.

'Team B will go in the front. Steve, you're going to be in charge of the big orange key. I want a clean one-strike entry like we practised. Team A will clear downstairs while Team B will go upstairs. Got it?'

They all nodded.

'There is the likelihood that a child is present. So be careful, everybody, the perp has killed before.'

'What's his name?'

'Why, you gonna write a letter to him, Tony?'

'No... I...'

'It's Matthew Oram. Little is known about him. Aged thirty-two, single, owns a convenience store near Wythenshawe Park. He's not on the Register of Sex Offenders.'

Sergeant Hall checked his watch. 'We go in two minutes, people. Team A leads off and we follow. Our entry time is... exactly 12.15. It is now... 12.10.'

They checked and adjusted their watches.

'All communications on Channel 7. Lenny, you're leading Team A and I'm leading Team B.' He turned to Claire Trent. 'Anything to add, Detective Superintendent?'

343

She shook her head. 'Be careful, a child could be inside.'

'Tony, you will be responsible for extracting the child. Clear?'

'Yes, Sergeant.'

'Right, let's get ready to move. Lead your team off, Lenny, and good luck.'

Without answering, Lenny and his team ran across the street, turning right into Dalgliesh Road.

Sergeant Hall assembled his men. As ever, the butterflies were fluttering in his stomach. He hated this time before everything kicked off. As soon as it started, he would be OK. The training would kick in and his one focus would be on the job at hand; gaining entry into number 168 and eliminating any threat inside.

Trevor Hall had no qualms about killing if necessary. It's what he had been trained to do in the marines and now in the Police Tactical Unit. Death was just part of the job. He didn't look forward to it or enjoy it, but he was damn sure if anybody was going to die that day it wasn't going to be him.

The Airwave squawked. 'In position on Dalgliesh Road. Still no sign of activity at number 168. Over and out.'

'Message received, over. Moving into position. Will give the order to enter in one minute, repeat, one minute. Over.'

'Message received, over.'

Trevor Hall raised his arm and instantly the five men in his team moved forward behind him, covering his every move. They were quick and silent, speed being the one element that gave them a tactical advantage.

Within forty seconds they were crouched down behind the low wall in front of the house. Hall brought the Airwave up to his mouth. 'Team B. Go.'

'Order received. Over.'

Through the Airwave he heard the sound of heavy feet, thudding across wooden floorboards.

He stood up and waved Team B forward. They advanced as one, with Steve running forward, carrying the orange enforcer to gain entry.

It was raised and came crashing down against the lock on the yellow door.

The door held.

Steve raised the enforcer again and crashed it down. The door swung open, smashing into the wall and coming off its hinges. Trevor Hall jumped through the door, his Heckler & Koch pointing forward.

He entered the narrow hall, seeing his doppelganger moving towards him. For a second, he thought he was looking in a mirror, until the man shouted, 'Kitchen clear.'

Hall raced upstairs, followed by his team. He went to the bedroom on the left.

Nothing but a made bed.

'Clear,' he shouted.

From other rooms both upstairs and downstairs, he heard shouts of 'Clear. Clear. Clear.' Followed by a shout from downstairs in Lenny's voice. 'Boss, you should come and see this.'

Trevor Hall shouldered his rifle and trotted downstairs.

'What is it, Lenny?'

'In here.'

Hall pushed open the door leading to the rear living room. His mouth dropped open. 'Jesus, what sick fuck did this?'

One entire wall was covered in pictures of naked boys, most of whom were less than eight years old.

Chapter 97

Walking into the convenience store, they saw the magazines on their left, facing a central aisle stocked with all the necessities of modern living: bread, milk, eggs, crisps and chocolates. Beyond the central aisle was half a wall of fridges filled with soft drinks and ice cream. The rest of the wall was made up of shelves of alcohol, most of it cheap and all of it extra-strong. Between the two was a solid steel door leading to an outside delivery area.

Against the far wall were more groceries and a green door with the red stencilled words 'NO ENTRY' printed in capital letters.

Matthew Oram certainly knew his customers.

A young man was standing behind the counter with a till on his right and a closed shelf of cigarettes behind him. He didn't raise his head from the MMA magazine he was reading.

There was nobody else in the shop.

'Hiya,' Emily said brightly, 'is the owner around?'

The young man finally lifted his head. 'No.' He then went back to reading his magazine.

Emily fished out her warrant card. 'I'm DS Parkinson. I talked to Mr Oram on Friday and I'd just like to follow up on a few things he said. Do you know where he is?'

The man's bottom lip came up over the top one. 'No.'

Emily glanced at Ridpath. She reached forward to close the magazine.

'Oi…'

'Now I have your undivided attention, where is Mr Oram?'

The man attempted to snatch back the magazine but couldn't take it from Emily's grip. 'I told you, I don't know. Sunday is his day off, that's why I'm here. He's probably cooking dinner for his mother. That's what he normally does on Sundays.'

Ridpath relaxed. He was at the address Chrissy had got from the electoral register, then.

'So he's not here?' Emily persisted.

The man took his magazine back. 'Look around. Can you see him?' He rolled his eyes as if to say *these people are so stupid*.

'Thank you for your time,' responded Emily.

She turned back to Ridpath but the man carried on speaking.

'He's probably upstairs. His mum lives in the flat above and she don't go out much. In fact, she don't go out at all.' He leant forward. 'She's a bit strange,' he whispered. 'Scares the hell out of me.'

Both detectives stopped. Emily turned back to face him. 'How do we get into the flat?'

'The stairs are through that green door. I can ring him and tell him you're coming if you want.'

'Don't bother,' said Ridpath, striding towards the door. 'We prefer to surprise him.'

Chapter 98

*He'd just finished cleaning the mess the boy had made when he heard
a noise coming from the back alley.*

*He looked out of the window to see a blue uniform ducking down
behind a low wall.*

*His Corsa was parked in full view, in the place they reserved for
deliveries to the shop, not in the garage. He'd wanted to move the boy
up to the flat as quickly and silently as possible.*

*The top of another policeman's head appeared briefly above the wall.
There were at least two of them out there.*

Were they onto him? Or just checking out the car?

*Another sound from downstairs. The bell ringing as somebody
entered the shop.*

It was quiet, too quiet.

*He walked to the bedroom, grabbing the baseball bat from behind
the door. The boy was still lying on the bed, his open eyes staring at
the ceiling.*

Should he finish him off?

*He heard the door from the shop open and footsteps coming up the
stairs.*

*He raised the bat above his shoulders, ready to bring it down on the
boy's head.*

The doorbell rang.

*Should he answer it? Brazen it out? They couldn't come into the
flat without a warrant anyway. He didn't want to kill the boy, not yet.
It would be such a waste.*

The doorbell rang again, more insistently this time.

'Coming, coming,' he shouted, 'keep your shirt on.'

Closing the bedroom door, he checked everything was OK in the flat.

It all looked fine. He would say Mother was sleeping and that's why they couldn't come in.

He walked to the door and checked through the peephole. It was the same female detective who had asked him about the ATM on Friday. Why was she back?

And there was somebody else with her. A taller, thinner copper he hadn't seen before.

The bell rang again.

'Hang on,' he shouted, placing the baseball bat out of sight and opening the door.

Chapter 99

Emily Parkinson smiled as broadly as she could. 'Hiya, Mr Oram, remember me?'

Matthew Oram stood in the doorway. He was dressed in a smart, casual outfit; a white shirt and blue slacks with a pair of brown, tasseled loafers on his feet. It was as if he was about to go on a Sunday afternoon date.

'Of course, you're the policewoman who was asking about the ATM footage. Did you get it in the end?'

'We did, thanks.' She tried to peer around him to see into the flat. 'I've just got some follow-up questions. I wonder if I could come in? It won't take more than a few minutes.'

Ridpath stayed quiet, staring at the man. Was this their killer?

'It's a bit awkward, I'm cooking afternoon lunch for my mother.'

'It won't take long.' Emily tried to push past him but he stood his ground.

'I'd like to ask you a few questions, Mr Oram.'

'I'm afraid it's not convenient now.'

Ridpath spoke for the first time. 'Perhaps you'd like to come down to the station to answer the quest—'

Before Ridpath could finish the sentence, Oram had a baseball bat above his head and was striking down at Emily.

The bat hit her with a dull thud where the neck joined the head and she fell forward into the flat.

For one second, Ridpath stood there staring down at the inert body of his colleague. Oram raised the bat once more, and

Ridpath, realising the danger he was in, threw himself forward, taking the man around the chest in a classic rugby tackle.

They both fell to the wooden floorboards with a heavy crack. Ridpath felt the air explode from his mouth as the handle of the baseball bat struck him in the chest. He lay there struggling for breath, his chest heaving, desperately searching for air.

Ridpath felt something hit him in the stomach.

Oram's knee.

He bent double, trying to grab the man's arm, but he wrenched it free. He was far stronger than he looked.

A fist struck Ridpath's temple.

Once.

Twice.

Three times.

His head went woozy and he thought he was going to black out. He tried to avoid the blows, throwing his arm up to cover his head. But Oram was on top of him now, striking downwards again and again.

Ridpath kicked out blindly, feeling his knee connect with something solid. Oram screamed in pain and, for a second, the blows on Ridpath's head stopped.

He kicked out again, trying to wriggle free from Oram, but the man was ready for him this time. The kick was blocked and the punches against his head came one after another, Ridpath feeling the man's hard knuckles strike his head again and again and again.

Ridpath blacked out for a second and woke up to feel the man's fingers around his Adam's apple. He felt them pressing in, squeezing ever tighter and tighter.

Ridpath couldn't breathe. He felt a weight across his chest, weighing him down. The pain was immense, getting stronger. The fingers tightening around his throat, squeezing the breath, squeezing the life out of him.

Words whispered in his ear. 'Can you feel the pain? Do you know what it's like to die?'

The pressure increased.

Tighter and tighter.

Hands gripping his throat. He couldn't cry out, couldn't breathe. His legs kicking weakly against the floor.

The pain grew less, as if it were being swallowed up by a whale. The weight on his chest became heavier and heavier. And now he was floating above his body, looking down at himself with Matthew Oram's hands around his throat, slowly squeezing the life out of him.

In his head, he whispered his last words. 'I'm sorry, Eve.'

Then there was a flash of bright light and the pain stopped.

Chapter 100

Molly Wright and her photographer followed the detectives into the convenience store.

What were they doing here? She hoped to God they weren't just getting cigarettes for Claire Trent. If they were, Molly had definitely chosen the wrong car to follow.

A young man was standing in front of a green door, staring up at a carpeted flight of stairs.

Molly could hear the noises of a fight coming from above.

At the same time, she could hear the sound of fists pounding on the back door of the store, desperate to get in.

She ordered the young man to open the door and climbed up the stairs, the photographer following gingerly behind her.

The sounds of the fight were getting louder; a gagging sound, feet being kicked against a wooden floor, whispered words.

The inert body of Emily Parkinson was draped across the doorway. She was still breathing but out cold.

Molly stepped into the living room.

A man was on top of the thin copper, his hands around the detective's throat, choking him to death.

Ridpath's legs were still kicking but she could see he was getting gradually weaker.

The man leant forward and whispered something in his ear.

The photographer took a shot, the flash going off. As the man raised his head, noticing them for the first time, Molly picked up the baseball bat and swung it wildly, connecting to something soft with a satisfying thud.

The man slumped backwards, blood pouring from his ear and temple.

Behind her, Molly could hear the pounding of heavy feet on the stairs, followed by, 'Jesus, what the fuck has happened here?'

Two Weeks Later

Sunday, August 23

Chapter 101

'Dad, do you believe in heaven?'

'Not really, Eve.'

'So you think Mum isn't in heaven, she's just here, buried in the ground?'

'I'm not very religious, Eve, I don't really buy into this heaven and hell stuff. But I think your mum is still with us, in our memories and in you and me.'

They were in Stretford Cemetery standing in front of Polly's grave. The green granite stone they had ordered from the mason was etched with these words:

Polly Lim Ridpath

1981–2020

Daughter, Mother, Wife, Lover

Taken from us far too early

It was Eve who had added the last bit about being a lover. 'Well, that's what Mum was all about. Love. For me and for you, Dad. So why can't we put it on her gravestone?'

He agreed with her. Polly was about love and so much more.

'I still miss her.'

'So do I, every day, but it's good to come here.' He looked around at the other graves arrayed in lines across the top of the hill overlooking the floodplain of the Mersey.

'Shall we go for a walk?'

'Where?'

She pointed to the river. 'There must be a path down there.'

'OK.'

They walked past some newly dug graves, finding a path leading towards the river. Many of the gravestones bore the Irish tricolour or the Gaelic harp, representing the country's strong presence in this part of Manchester.

'Dad, are you a hero now?'

'Definitely not, I just did my job.'

'But that woman says you're a hero?'

'Molly Wright? She's a reporter doing her job.'

'Telling the news?'

'No, selling newspapers. But she probably saved my life.'

'I should write and thank her.'

'That would be a good thing to do, a nice gesture. She's writing a book about the case.'

'You're going to be in a book, Dad?'

'Probably.'

'That's so cool. And how's Emily?'

'She's fine, back at work already.'

'Is she still wearing a bandage on her head?'

Ridpath laughed. 'Not any more. She's made of tough stuff, is Emily Parkinson, particularly her head.'

'She promised we would go riding together when she came out of hospital.'

'I'll let her know you're available, shall I?'

'I'll have to get my bike fixed first, the chain has come off.'

'I'll do it for you if you like.'

–

Across town, Molly Wright was enjoying a rather pleasant lunch with her agent in the Midland Hotel. She'd chosen a Chassagne Montrachet and a 2010 Château Palmer. Not the best year, but still far better than her usual Spanish plonk.

He was taking her through the marketing plans for the book she was writing on the Carsley case. 'We should be able to get you on Jeremy Vine and Radio 4. Piers Morgan is interested in doing a segment and Tiger Aspect are working on plans to film it. I think you were awfully brave, attacking the killer like that. You saved the copper's life.'

'How is he?'

'Ridpath? I've heard he's going back to work soon. Of course, we contacted him to tell his story. It would have sold well, but he's not interested, just wants to get on with his job.'

'Strange. And the other detective, Emily whatsherface?'

'She's fine too. Both are receiving commendations for their work on the case, but it was you who saved their lives. You must emphasise that aspect in the book. Please, no modesty, you are a hero.'

Actually, she was a heroine, but didn't say the words. 'Who's going to play me in the film? Somebody glamorous, I hope.'

'They are talking to Scarlett Johansson and Anne Hathaway.'

'They're both American. I was hoping for somebody younger.'

'It's still early days, I'm sure they'll find somebody… *suitable*.'

'I want to make sure I am portrayed correctly. The story is important to me.'

'As it is to us. Talking of the book, when do you think the first draft will be ready?'

'Soon,' she answered, without giving a date.

'The earlier the better. We should strike while the iron is hot.'

Molly Wright loved the way agents always spoke in clichés whilst admonishing their writers for using them. The truth was, she was finding the book hard to write, not usually a problem for her.

As if reading her mind, he said, 'We could find you a ghost if you need some help getting the words down on paper.'

A ghostwriter. Why didn't she think of that? It would take all the pressure off her. All she had to do was tell the story and let somebody else do the work of turning it into words on paper.

She raised her glass. 'I think that's an extremely good idea, when can we find somebody?'

–

On the other side of Manchester, the Carsleys were faring less well. Daniel was languishing in a police station, having been arrested for shoplifting at Primark. He was waiting for the social worker from his children's home to arrive before the police gave him a caution about his future behaviour.

Irene Carsley, nee McMurdo, was sitting in her bedsit staring at the four walls, having been forced to self-isolate. The scars on her arms showed evidence of self-harming but, as she never left her bedsit, nobody was aware of her mental condition. Her son, David, had been buried a week ago on Wednesday. She hadn't attended the funeral.

Michael Carsley was still in his living room, staring at the glowing TV in the corner. He had switched off his mobile phone. The only calls he received were either from reporters promising him a small fortune for telling his story, or from well-wishers saying he should be hung, drawn and quartered for what he did to his son. 'Despite what the police say, I know you were involved in his death,' was the usual refrain on the calls.

He was too numb to respond any more.

–

On 20 August 2020, Jon Morgan finally left his wife, the family home and his dog, and went to live with Shirley Burgess in a rented apartment in Whalley Range.

They had both decided that living for love was more important than living a lie.

They still strolled together every morning beside the Mersey and were thinking of getting a pair of Jack Russells to accompany them on their walks.

Matthew Oram was remanded under Section 35 of the Mental Health Act 1983 to Ashworth High-Security Psychiatric Hospital for evaluation. He is considering pleading not guilty to the murder of David Carsley, Alan McCarthy, Steven Protheroe and Peter McDonald, according to Section 2 of the Trial of Lunatics Act 1883.

He still hears the voices telling him to kill.

–

Margaret Challinor was packing up for the day after an inquest on a death at a building site. The jury had still to decide on a verdict of negligence or accidental death.

On her way home, she had promised to get the children pizza. Her daughter had moved back in with her after Ben's abduction. The boy seemed to be recovering well from his ordeal; there were no apparent after-effects. To be on the safe side, Mrs Challinor had asked a specialist in paediatric mental health to sit down for a few sessions with the boy.

Her daughter, on the other hand, was taking a lot longer to recover. The sense of guilt at what had happened appeared to be overwhelming the young mother. She couldn't sleep at night and constantly felt anxious. She was starting counselling next week after being persuaded she needed help by Mrs Challinor.

For the first time in many a year, the coroner was finally able to give her daughter the love, care and attention she deserved. She was glad her daughter had returned home but wished it could have occurred under better circumstances.

She vowed she would never allow them to become estranged again.

–

Eve had reached a stile leading to a path beside the river. Ridpath helped her over it.

'I like writing, Dad. You know, I think I'd like to be a reporter when I grow up.'

Ridpath kept quiet – it was far too early to pour cold water on her dreams. 'You'll have to study hard. When do you start the new school?'

'In September, if the virus lets me.'

'I'm sure it will.'

She thought for a moment, twisting her hair around her index finger. 'What's going to happen to the man?'

Ridpath felt the back of his neck. 'The one who attacked me? He's in hospital now. The Crown Prosecution Service are deciding whether to charge him.'

'He killed four children.'

'At least four children, but he may not be well enough to stand trial. He hears voices.'

'Do you ever hear voices, Dad?'

He looked at his daughter. Did she know about Polly? Since the day he fought with Matthew Oram, he hadn't seen Polly. It was almost as if she decided she didn't need to be around, once he no longer needed her. 'Not any more, Eve.'

'Good, I'm glad. When can I move back in with you?'

A pause as he climbed over the stile.

'I've talked it over with your grandparents and they've agreed you can move back next weekend before you start school. Your granny realises she can't take you there every day and it's too far for you to travel on your own. I've spoken with the coroner and Claire Trent. They've said I only have to work until three every day so I can pick you up from school.'

She jumped in front of him, a big smile on her face. 'That's great, Dad. I can't wait to come back.'

'We'll live in the service apartment.' He took a breath, waiting to tell her. 'I've decided to sell the house.'

She thought for a moment. 'I'll miss my room, but I understand, Dad. Too many bad memories.'

'Actually, too many good memories. I hope we can find a place soon, perhaps closer to your new school.'

'Sounds like a plan, Dad. Don't forget to take my BTS posters off the wall in my room.'

'Don't worry, I know how important they are to you. But one thing you have to promise...'

'What's that?'

'You should spend weekends and holidays with your grand-parents.'

'Dad...'

'It's the right thing to do, Eve. Imagine how much they are going to miss you.'

They stopped in front of the Mersey, its waters running fast between the high banks.

He went quiet for a second before saying, 'You know, it was my greatest achievement, being with your mum, I mean.'

'You've still got me, Dad.'

'I know.'

She looked over the river and then a small smile crossed her lips. 'Dad...'

'Yeah.'

'Before I start the new school...'

'Yeah...'

'I was thinking of dyeing my hair bright green. What do you think?'

She looked at him, trying to keep a straight face and then she couldn't maintain it any longer, collapsing in a fit of giggles.

He hugged her close. 'Smart arse, just like your mum.'

'I know, it's where I got it from.' She leant into him and stared down at the river below them. 'It's funny, Dad, but this river has been flowing here ever since the Romans. You know they built a road to Chester that crossed the Mersey over there?' She pointed back towards Stretford. 'That's how the town got its name. Mum taught me that. For thousands of years, this river has been flowing to the sea. Every day of every month of every year. It's never going to stop, is it?'

'No, it's never going to stop. Whatever happens, it just keeps moving on.'

'That's what it does.'

She pulled away from him. 'Shall we walk back?'

He nodded and she walked back up the path, turning back to look at him as he stood on the path overlooking the river. 'Are you coming, Dad?'

He stared down into the water, watching it bubble and flow over some rocks, moving on no matter what was thrown in its way.

'Bye, Poll,' he whispered, before turning back to join his daughter and walk up the hill, together.

Do you love crime fiction and are always on the lookout for brilliant authors?

Canelo Crime is home to some of the most exciting novels around. Thousands of readers are already enjoying our compulsive stories. Are you ready to find your new favourite writer?

Find out more and sign up to our newsletter at canelocrime.com